The Paris Inheritance

The Paris Inheritance

Merryn Corcoran

Cork Publishing

ISBN 9798754814219

www.merryncorcoran.com
Find Merryn Corcoran on Facebook at www.facebook.com/merryncorcoranauthor

Dedicated to:

Catherine Mary O'Connell-Simperingham,
my dearest friend who left us far too soon.

Not gone, just out of focus and always in my heart.

"What a woman can conceive and believe,
she can achieve."

Acknowledgments

My heartfelt thanks to all my friends who read for me along the way: Michelle Amass, Mary Ciurlionis, Marilyn Morse, Cecilia Brown, Sally Coleman, Charlotte Everett, Felicity Price, Amelia and Tom Stafford, Dame Pieter Stewart, Alexis Parr and Graham Beattie.

To all those who contributed and supported me including Rose Lawson and Marc Bengué, Don Stewart, Joanna Murray and Pamela Lindsay.

To Malcom Lakin for his photography.

To Yealands Family Wines, Marlborough, New Zealand for sponsoring my book launches.

To Ann Neville for her editing skills and her patience.

I was so fortunate to have the 2014 Katherine Mansfield winning scholar, Mandy Hager, living nearby in Menton, France while I was writing this book. Mandy has been an invaluable mentor to me, imparting expert advice and direction.

Thank you all for your contributions and sharing your time.

With much love in my heart I salute and thank my patient, loving husband Tim and my beautiful daughter Emily. Without their continued encouragement, ideas and support I could not write.

1

1973

A high country sheep station in the North Island of

New Zealand

Mary Hampton wore gumboots no matter what the season though, unlike previous pairs, she hadn't as yet attacked the gumboots with her decorative pink paint pot. On the first morning of the school holidays, her favourite time of the year, she rushed from the house brimming with the joy of meeting her best friend, Jamie. She skipped down the steep, isolated driveway and skilfully mastered the shingle under her loose rubber gumboots.

Pungent perfume from the overhanging eucalyptus trees offered a fragrant welcome to the new day as two Tuis scrapped over the bursting flax flowers. Jamie had explained the importance of the flax which grew in clumps between the evenly spaced trees. His grandma would strip the long green leaves from the central bush and, once they dried, use them to weave baskets. Not only that, she and the other women wove

9

the flax into the wall panels of the Māori meeting house down the road.

Where the driveway flattened out, a mass of purple-flowering Agapanthus grew. Mary fluttered her hand along the star-burst blooms and plucked one to weave into the tangled curls behind her ear. She unhooked the chain latch on the large metal gate that led through the cow paddock and wrinkled her nose at the stench of a freshly deposited cow pat. She took the flower from her hair and pressed it to her face to block the smell as she poked the toes of her gumboots into the metal mesh of the gate and hitched a ride when it swung open. As she jumped off and swung the gate back to latch it she heard Jamie whistling the same tune as always.

"Kiss me honey, honey, kiss me." It was the most requested song of his father's weekend band. Jamie grabbed her hand. "Hurry, Dad's on the warpath 'cause I let the fowls out. We gotta move down to the creek real quick." He tugged her to speed up and they ran across the paddock, not stopping until they reached the shade of the Manuka trees beside the creek.

Jamie flopped down on the grassy bank laughing. He was twelve, two years older than Mary, though he only just topped her in height. But he was broad-shouldered, black-haired and strong, while she was bony with stick-like limbs and striking crinkly, russet-coloured hair.

Mary plonked down beside him. "How did the fowls get out?"

"Bloody silly things! I was practising my kicks 'cause they're choosing the new rugby team when we get back at school and the ball hit the chicken run. I shooed them all in but I must have forgotten to latch it. Dad was having his early morning cuppa with mum in the kitchen when that dam rooster wandered in. So I scuppered!" He laughed so freely she knew he wasn't really in too much trouble. "What we gonna do today?"

Mary smiled. "What about more tadpoles? I left everything in the hiding place last week."

"Come on then!" Jamie sprang to his feet and reached out his hand to pull Mary up. "What kind of hippy clothes are those?" he said. Mary glanced down at her tank-top striped with all the colours of the rainbow.

"So what! Hippies are very cool. I saw a top like this on telly and Mum helped me knit it," she replied.

"You knitted it?" He eyed the top more closely. "Not bad for a farm girl!" Mary slapped at him but he dodged her.

"Come on, let's go and check out those tadpoles. My frog was looking sad this morning. I reckon he needs some company." Jamie took the tatty net from under the dry log. The pond was located on the bank a few yards from the river which followed the road along to the neighbouring farms. After a couple of hours and a jar full of tadpoles they lost focus.

"I'm hungry, Mary. Guess we'd better head home. You don't want to be late and get your bloody dad all worked up again." Jamie gave her a wink as he walked off.

As she waved goodbye to her friend, Mary's joy dissipated. She slowly mooched up the driveway and a subtle darkened halo of malaise reappeared.

"Is that you, Mary Chantal?"

"Yes, Mum. What can I have to eat?"

Hazel Hampton kissed the top of Mary's head. As Mary

opened the fridge door she gently nudged her daughter aside. "Don't touch anything in there. It's nearly dinner time. I'll make you some Marmite on toast," she said.

"I'm starving. Can I have cheese as well, please?" Her mother brushed Mary's fringe out of her eyes.

"Only if you let me trim this. It's a wonder you can see!" "I like it long, Mum. Please don't cut it."

"Why the fuss? Don't you want people to see your beautiful big brown eyes?"

"No, I don't! They're just normal eyes, like everybody else's. Don't say that." As she stormed out the kitchen she heard her mother mutter, 'Puberty'.

Mary wanted to scream back it was puberty all right, but not in the way her mother meant. She escaped out to her new room, a converted shed at the rear of the house. She hated this room. In the last few weeks since she moved in, her father made a lot more of his 'secret visits'. His threats resonated in her head. She pushed the bad thoughts away as her mother hovered in the door-way with the plate of toast. Mary thought her mum was attractive, despite being a bit nervy. She had a near flawless complexion and hair the same dark russet colour as her own. But she looked tired and tense.

"I'm sorry, love. If it's that important to you then I guess we can leave your fringe for a bit," Hazel said as she entered Mary's bedroom. Mary shrugged. It was impossible for her not to respond to the worry in her mother's eyes. Mary couldn't conceive of adding to her worry by explaining to her mother that it wasn't really about the haircut at all.

"Come on, sit up, love. I thought you were starving?"

Mary wiped her eyes and sighed, then accepted the plate

from her mother rather than drag things out. "Thanks."

Her mother eyed the bare walls. "It's been nearly six weeks since dad moved you in. What happened to all the ideas you had about decorating the walls?" Hazel asked. To save answering, Mary crammed her mouth with toast.

"Would you like me to help you do one of your special collages? Or we could buy some new bright paints?" Her mother leant over and brushed a stray crumb off her daughter's cheek. Mary caught her mother's hand and held it tight.

"I liked being in the house near you. I promise I'll never wet the bed again. Can I move back to my old room please?" She laid her head on her mother's arm.

"Look, love, we've been through this a hundred times. Susan needs her own room and you and I now need a dedicated sewing room. Besides, we've nearly got the bed wetting sorted out. Dad went on about it for so long, and he's gone to so much trouble to make this nice for you."

How could her Mum be so blind?

"Then can I at least have Grandma's old books here in my room? The ones with the heavy covers?" Mary said.

"You mean The Women's Classics? You funny old thing. If my mother was still alive she'd be thrilled that you're keen to read those old stories." As her mother left the room Mary put her hands to her face. If only she could tell her mother the truth.

2

February 1974

Mary didn't really enjoy school. She endured it. Today was the first day back after the long summer break. Her new brown shoes and crisply ironed, blue gingham uniform boosted her confidence as she skipped hand-in-hand with her eight–year-old sister, Susan, down the drive to wait for the school bus.

The faded yellow bus trundled towards them. It was an old-fashioned square shape. Inside, the worn leather seats, once a rich maroon colour, smelt of old apples, though Mary had no idea why. In her mind she always associated the smell with Faith, the bus driver, and her ever present sweetness. The bus collected all the local farm children who named it 'The Butter Box'. Tiny Faith Price could barely see over the steering wheel despite the two embroidered cushions she wedged under her bottom. As she opened the door for Mary and Susan, they were greeted by her cheery smile.

"Morning girls, isn't it a grand day! All set for the new term?"

When Jamie sauntered on at the next stop, he winked at

Mary but sat at the back with his special group of friends, the 'Rugby Boys'. They were obsessed with the game. By the time the bus deposited them outside the school gates the air was buzzing with a mixture of anxiety and excitement. They were herded into the assembly hall to be allocated class rooms. Mary made straight for Gloria, who was the perfect friend. She didn't ask a lot of questions about Mary's home life, and she enjoyed art and sewing.

Mary was gutted to find herself stuck with the plump Miss Brown. The teacher was known for her temper and the way her nose flared when she barked an order, but at least Gloria was in the same class. They sat together on the step at play time and exchanged holiday stories.

"Quiet, children! I will tell you where you should be sitting so don't get attached to your seats. I won't tolerate talking in class and each week one of you will take a turn at being my monitor."

"Is that Jamie your boyfriend? 'Cause you always seem to talk about him," Gloria asked.

"No, he's just my friend. It's not love stuff, so don't say that."

"Don't get shitty with me. I was just asking."

∽

On the bus ride home, Susan fell asleep on Mary's lap. Mary laid her hand on the flat of her sister's back and wished she herself was still only six with the added bonus of soft blonde curls like Susan's. Her father still spoiled Susan. She vaguely remembered that he used to be like that with her until she was about eight. That's when his 'secret visits' and the games started.

When they reached their stop Mary gave her sister a gentle shove. "Wake up, sleepy girl, we are nearly home.

"Cheerio girls, see you tomorrow," Faith called out as they opened the gate.

"Can you give me a piggy back? My legs are so tired." Susan dragged her feet and her school bag through the dust.

"No, you're too heavy for me now." Susan pouted and began to whine. "Oh, for goodness' sake! Give me your bag and hold my hand. That'll help," Mary said. When they finally dropped their school bags in the hallway, their father walked out of the kitchen.

"Hello." John Hampton scooped his youngest daughter up into his arms. "How's my baby girl then? A big day at school?"

"Mary says I'm too big to piggy back up the drive. It's so steep, Daddy. Tomorrow, could you meet us?"

"If I'm not working darling, of course I'll piggy back you up the drive." As their father stroked Susan's hair, Mary noticed how alike they were, with their bright blue eyes and strong blonde curls. Their father then moved towards Mary but she quickly side-stepped him and busied herself by filling a glass from the tap.

"I have homework. Call me at teatime, please," she called and slipped out of the room before he could go on at her.

The kitchen featured an oblong eight-seat wooden table that had been scrubbed daily by three generations of Hampton wives. The chairs did not match the table having been made in the 1950s with tube steel. The plastic cushions had long since worn out. A large painted dresser was fixed on one wall and housed the 'special' family plates. The stainless steel sink was set into a green Formica bench stretching the entire length of the wall. The kitchen cupboards were painted a soft green to match the Formica. A large window had recently been added directly in front of the sink to give a view out to the piece of lawn where the children played.

John poured his first whisky before they started their evening meal. Just the smell of it made Mary's stomach churn. By the time he'd downed his second glass, his raised voice had altered the emotional landscape.

"You bloody kids should be seen and not heard," John snapped at Susan. Hazel's solution was to keep the children quiet and just agree with everything he said.

"May I leave the table, please?" Mary knew the rules.

"Start those dishes and don't you dare leave the kitchen till all the pots are done," John said. Then, when he'd finished eating, he abruptly left and sat in his armchair in the sitting room. He turned the television on and ranted on about 'no hopers' as he watched the news.

"Just stay quiet and I'll help you with the pots. It's just the whisky talking. He'll be back to himself in the morning." Hazel affectionately rubbed Mary's back as they finished the dishes together.

"Why does he drink it, Mum? Why can't he be 'himself' all the time?"

"Just keep your voice down and don't say anything to aggravate him. Go and finish your homework," her mother replied.

In its previous incarnation Mary's new bedroom had been a storage shed, originally built by her grandfather at the rear of the house for storing preserves like bottled fruit and home-made relishes. Her mother relinquished that tradition with the opening of a large local supermarket.

John lined the renovated bedroom with plaster board and painted it light grey to match the new marble-patterned lino on the floor. They moved in the furniture from Mary's old room, a chest of drawers, shelves for her books and a purpose-made cork board for her 'pin ups'. Mary propped herself up on her bed and leant against the wall reading 'Little Women' by Louisa May Alcott. The book was so heavy in its ornate cover that she had it resting on a cushion on her lap.

"Hello love, what's that you're reading? Dad's gone out night shooting for possums with Bill. Do you fancy doing a bit of work on that blouse I'm making?" Hazel asked as she sat on the bed beside her daughter.

Mary nodded. "I've done enough reading for now. I'd like to come inside with you." She enjoyed sewing with her mum. It made her feel 'normal'. She had full use of the old Singer treadle machine and sometimes was permitted to use her mum's new electric Bernina.

"I love it with just you and me, Mum. Dad always spoils Susan but I don't care. I'd rather just be with you anyway." Mary laid her head on her mother's shoulder and watched as her mother expertly threaded the sewing machine.

"I know you do, love. I am mum to both of you, but I've loved you the longest." Hazel lifted her long-legged daughter up on to her knee and stroked her hair.

Mary desperately wanted to tell her about the 'secret visits' but her father's threats rang loud in her ears. Guilt was all consuming. She could feel the words inside her throat and chest but she couldn't squeeze them out. She was terrified that what her father said might be true and she'd lose her mother's affection.

"Now, you sew those straight seams on that skirt and I'm going to see if I'm not too tired to make some bound button holes on this blouse," Hazel said as they busied themselves at the work table.

At nine o'clock Mary grudgingly left for her bedroom. Once inside, with the absence of a lock, she placed a pile of heavy books against the door before turning out the light. About an hour later she woke desperately needing the loo so she moved the books and slipped into the house unnoticed, just as John arrived home. She cringed as she heard her father's slurred words.

"Shut up, you bitch. I'll drink as much as I like. After all I've done for you! I'm not listening to any of your crap." His blonde wavy hair was dishevelled and his grubby shirt tail hung out of his trousers. When sober he was a quiet man, but drunk he was intolerable.

"Hush, John, you'll wake the children. I'm only trying to be supportive. I'm prepared to help with the accounts. I used to help my dad." Mary grimaced as she listened to her mother's placating tone.

"You and your fucking father and his fucking money. Once things come right I'll pay him all his dirty money back. My family have farmed here without loans for three generations. Since taking on you and your bastard daughter, I've had nothing but bad luck," he hissed.

Mary quickly peed and then scurried back to her room. She uttered a silent prayer that her father would fall asleep. When he first started playing his game with her, it just seemed like the 'tickling' game that they played when she was very little. But now he only did it when they were alone. Now he made her touch his 'thing'. Just the thought of it knotted her insides and she experienced a sharp pain in her head. She hurriedly piled the heavy books back against the door and pulled the blanket up over her head.

Breakfast brought light to a new day. Mary was chatting while braiding her sister's hair but, when their father walked in, the girls reverted to silence.

"Hurry up, you kids. The bus will be here soon," he said. It was as if the last night's performance never happened.

⁓

"Children, today you will all receive a brand new English dictionary. Treat these with respect. They are not to leave the classroom," Mary's teacher announced. "I want you to use at least one new word a day from now on in your essays. Find it in the dictionary and learn its meaning." Miss Brown then proudly handed out the pile of brand new dictionaries. It had taken her twelve months to convince The Education Ministry of the necessity for the purchase.

"Mary, see this. You can look up 'bum'," Gloria whispered to Mary at the back of the classroom.

"I don't think we are supposed to read rude words," Mary giggled.

"What did you just say?" Miss Brown roared. Mary stiffened in her seat.

"Nothing, Miss," Mary replied.

"Get out of the classroom." The teacher followed her out. When Mary turned around Miss Brown stood over her holding a piece of plastic-coated electrical wire.

"Abuse my dictionary, would you? You stupid girl, you've always had an over-active imagination. I'll not have you disrupt my class. Put out your hand."

Nose flaring, the fat teacher aimed towards Mary's hand but missed and whacked the wire across the soft part of her arm. The pain burned and tears filled Mary's eyes. She fought them back, determined not to show weakness. That seemed to enrage the wire-welding teacher even more. She whacked Mary again. This time Mary ducked and the wire caught her shoulder.

"Now get back inside," Miss Brown said but quietly added so only Mary could hear, "Look up the meaning of the word 'bastard' in your dictionary because that's what you are, Mary Hampton, a 'little bastard.'"

Mary forced herself to move on from her strapping. In the end, the humiliation was worse than the pain. And humiliation was a familiar visitor to Mary, so she was able to place it in the same compartment of her brain as other painful memories. She considered her dictionary discovery of the word 'bastard'. It referred her to another word she didn't know the meaning of - 'illegitimate' - but the bell rang before she could get to the correct page. 'Illegitimate' would have to wait till tomorrow.

"We're here, Mary Hampton. Wake up, day-dreamer, this is your stop," Faith called out as she stopped the bus.

"Mum, we're home," Susan called as soon as they were in sight of the door. There was no sign of Hazel, but Marmite on toast and Ovaltine were all laid neatly on the table. That was enough to satisfy Susan. Mary dropped her satchel and went in search of her mother. She could hear the slapping of the agitator washing machine. When she reached the window of the wash house, she peeped in. Her mother was in the process of opening a locked cupboard that Mary had never noticed before. She stayed put and watched as her mother took out a pile of what looked like letters. They were tied in a blue ribbon. Her mother gazed at them for a moment, then opened one and took out what Mary thought might be a photo. Her mother stroked her fingers over it for what seemed an age. Then she glanced at her watch, hastily placed the letters back in their hiding place and locked the cupboard door with a small key.

"Mum, it's me. We're home," Mary called.

"Hello, love. Your afternoon tea is on the table. I'll just get this washing through and then I'll be in," Hazel replied. Mary was slightly puzzled by the tears in her mother's eyes.

3

Five Years Later

The house was quiet with just the usual farm noises. A lost lamb bleated somewhere out in the paddock. Its little sharp baas seemed to continue for an age. Then the deeper sound of the mother's response rang out as they reunited. Mary felt reassured, knowing the mother had found her lamb. The constant croaking of the frogs evoked happy thoughts of Jamie. The joyful parts of her childhood had been played out between the river, the pond, the bush and, in the last couple of years, through the heroines of her grandmother's treasured novels.

Reading transported her to another place. She felt safe within her own imagination. Jane Eyre inspired her but she knew romance was something that only happened in Charlotte Bronte's books. She'd never witnessed any romance between her parents. In the unspoken part of her consciousness, she would have liked romance with Jamie, but he was just a friend and she wouldn't risk that friendship for anything. Besides, if he found out what her father did to her during his 'secret visits' she was sure Jamie would hate her.

Her father used to turn away after he forced her to touch him. Now he did the disgusting thing in front of her.

Mary had one eye on the bedside clock. Jamie had said 11pm. She figured it would only take about seven minutes to run down the drive. She'd hidden her eeling spear under the bed so she wouldn't disturb anyone when she sneaked out.

During that day, Mary and her mum had a great time sewing a new top. Her mum cut the pattern and then Mary trawled carefully through an old copy of an English Vogue magazine to get ideas. She styled her gumboots to complement the longer-look blouse she'd made. With the aid of a stapler and some glue, her basic, practical rubber gumboots were edged with pink chiffon net. In the British Vogue magazine they called them Wellington boots, which sounded a lot more posh. The Wellington boots in Vogue had been trimmed with tartan.

With ten minutes to go, Mary pulled on her newly styled gumboots. She held her spear with the knife end facing downwards and slipped out into the night. It was so dark she walked, rather than her usual run down the drive, aware there might be fresh pot holes. With only the moonlight to guide her, she needed to concentrate on where she stepped. Mary treasured her time with Jamie. He was her true friend. He listened without making comment and was always there for her. Even though he now seemed all grown up at 17 and away at boarding school, they still spent the school holidays doing the same stuff they always had... except for the frog catching that had been replaced by the more serious business of spearing river eels. Mary radiated pride when Jamie constructed a spear especially for her. It consisted of a sharpened blade from an old pocket knife. He'd wrapped the blade tightly onto a strong stick with flax-plaited rope and secured it with black, waterproof plumbers' tape. She heard his familiar whistle and replied with her own version.

"You know, Mary, you couldn't whistle if you tried for a year of Sundays. It's one thing you girls are useless at, so give it a rest!" Jamie called out. A large powerful torch was in one hand, his spear in the other, and he had slung an old canvas haversack across his shoulder.

He'd grown tall fast and was now six foot, the tallest boy in his class and on the rugby team. Mary had also sprouted up and at 15 years old she was 5 feet 10 inches, much taller than her petite mum. Her legs seemed to go on forever, over which the boys teased her mercilessly. Damp grass squelched under their rubber gumboots as they walked down towards the river with. Jamie flicked the torch around and the light caught Mary's gumboots.

"Jez, Mary, what ya done now!" He shone the torch full blast on the lower part of her body.

"In London, they call them 'Wellington boots'. I saw a Vogue photo shoot that showed how they styled them to complement each outfit. So that's what I've done." Mary had been very precise with the placing of the chiffon net. It was pleated neatly to ensure it matched on both gumboots.

"They just look like bloody chiffon-topped gumboots to me! Isn't that the material from the old top my mum gave you?" Jamie replied. Mary was delighted he noticed. "They better not scare the eels. Grandma's been on at me to get a few for her for the smokehouse."

They stood motionless with the torch turned to a very soft

light to attract the eels which encouraged them to slither up onto the bank. Once they were close enough, Jamie gave the signal and they went for an eel each with their spears, lunging as hard as they could. With their wet slimy bodies on the damp grass, the eels were fast. Mary often missed the mark. But this time she was in luck and she hit a big one.

"Bloody hell, I think yours is even bigger than mine. Grandma will be real chuffed when I tell her you caught it," Jamie said as they stood together with their spears stuck in the eels waiting for the final wiggling to cease, signalling death. "Make sure you tell her not to mention it to Dad. He goes ape-shit if he knows I am out with you in the dark." Mary dropped her gaze and shifted on her feet.

"He's an arsehole, your dad, no matter what you say. My dad says he's run that farm into the ground with his boozing and hang-ups." Mary didn't respond so Jamie changed the subject.

"Let's get their heads lopped off and clean them up. I won't be thanked for bringing the bad bits home." Jamie expertly cut off the eels' heads and gave their skin a scrape with his pocket knife. They buried the fish heads in some soft soil on the edge of the bank. He removed a plastic container of chocolate chip biscuits before placing the fat eels in the haversack.

"Mum made these fresh today so I nicked them. Well, not really nicked them. She bakes all my favourites when I come home. She knows the food at boarding school is real bad." Jamie offered Mary the container. Mary basked in Jamie's presence as they sat side by side on an old tree stump, scoffing the home-made biscuits.

"Are you around next Saturday? Mum says to ask you over

to ours for lunch. Gloria's coming, too. It's my sixteenth and, according to Mum, I'm well on my way to being a woman. But I think I'd rather stay a girl for a while." Mary swung her gumboots, gently knocking them against the log.

"Yep, I'll be there. Is ya bloody dad going to be?" Jamie asked.

Mary blushed and her body stiffened. "Hopefully not. He's due to go into town for shearing supplies and Mum hasn't said anything to him."

"Don't worry about him, Mary. Ya mum loves ya." Jamie reached over and gave her hand a pat.

"I know she does, but I don't understand why Dad is so horrible to me. It's even worse now," Mary muttered. Jamie jumped up and gave her a playful tug to get her moving.

"See ya Saturday," he said.

Mary stood and listened as the crunching of Jamie's feet on the gravel road and his familiar whistle which gave her hope faded away. Then she trudged up the drive, thoughts returning to her father's visits to her room, thoughts which invaded most of her waking moments. She tried every ruse possible to spend as much time as she could with her mother in the sewing room and even asked her mother in front of her father if she could have a lock on her door. Her father laughed and said, "We don't have burglars out here on the farm, silly girl."

She would squeeze her eyes tight when he touched her and then touched himself. But now he was doing it closer to her, his horrible grunting noises were louder. This would always be followed by his threats before he slunk back into the house.

4

"Come on, Susan, you need to work faster with that icing. Mary will be back soon and I really want it to be a surprise for her," Hazel said to her youngest daughter who was sitting at the kitchen table icing the chocolate birthday cake.

"She loves peppermint icing so I've mixed a little green in with it. I know she'll love it," Susan replied. Hazel grimaced.

"Anybody home?" Jamie called as he opened the kitchen door.

"My goodness, young man, you look nice. Mary will appreciate the effort you've made." Hazel smiled at Jamie who somehow overnight had morphed into a tall attractive man. His normally unruly hair was freshly trimmed, and he wore a clean blue shirt and jeans.

"Where's Mary then?" he asked as he clutched a rather inadequately wrapped present.

"What's in there, Jamie?" Susan cooed at him.

"Not telling you, squirt. It's for ya sister." He clasped the present tightly with both hands.

The table was set. Susan sat at the other end sulking at the rebuff, while their mum took the home-made sausage rolls out of the oven. Gloria sat quietly, discreetly studying Mary's princely friend whilst feigning absorption in a Women's Weekly magazine.

Mary smiled. She'd been standing in the hall listening as Jamie arrived. She wanted to wait to give her sister time to finish the icing. She'd spent the last two hours putting on and taking off different sets of clothes, before finally deciding on a gypsy blouse and maxi skirt. Her hair had been washed in her mum's apple shampoo and brushed out long then she wrapped a head-band, Indian style, around her head. Putting on new items of clothing that she'd made herself always made her feel better. They were like a mask of happiness that made her, for just a short time, feel clean.

"Happy Birthday to you, Happy Birthday to you." The group burst into song as Mary entered the kitchen.

"You look just like a hippie model from one of those magazines you read," Susan said.

"Hush, Susan, this is Mary's special day. Let's all sit down and let her talk." Hazel patted her youngest daughter's head.

The table was laden with all Mary's favourite food: hot sausage rolls, hot potato topped savouries, mini saveloys next to a small bowl of tomato sauce, Lamington cakes, and a large chocolate cake with 16 candles.

"Oh, Mum, this is fantastic. Thank you," Mary beamed. Once everyone was settled with food on their plate and a fizzy drink, Jamie turned to Mary.

"Ah, Mary, I got ya a present." He paused and fiddled nervously with the bedraggled gift in his hand. "Um, anyway, here you are." As he handed her the present, Mary blushed.

"Look, she's gone all red!" Susan blurted out.

"Thank you very much. What is it?" Mary whispered. Jamie arched his eyebrows and shrugged his shoulders,

"Open it, go on." Mary unwrapped the messy parcel to find a rather worn jewellery box inside. She slowly lifted the stiff lid. Sitting on a bed of black velvet was a beautiful, intricately carved, greenstone Tiki. It was small and delicate and hung on a fine gold chain.

"It's beautiful!" Mary held the Tiki up. With the light behind it she could see how translucent the stone was. It was a rich apple green.

"It's not just from me. It's been in our family for a while and Grandma says it's from all of us. She says it's good luck to give greenstone and we all wish you luck. I took the flax plaited string off and mum bought the posh chain 'cause I knew you would want it all proper." Jamie grinned as he delivered his 'family' speech. Hazel helped her do up the clasp, and then they chatted about Tikis, greenstone and Māori myths as they finished off the rest of the buffet lunch.

After a fun afternoon of playing rounders on the back lawn, Mary said a final goodbye to Gloria. As she walked Jamie to the door, Mary said, "It's been my best birthday ever. Thanks for the Tiki. I'll come over tomorrow and thank your family."

She was helping her mother clean up when they heard the vehicle pull up. Mary shuddered as she heard the car door bang shut. Her mother took a deep breath and quickly put the remnants of the birthday cake into the pantry.

"You shoot off to your room with your presents, darling." Hazel gave her daughter a soft shove. Mary used the loo on the way. She trembled behind the toilet door as her father stomped up the hall.

"Why isn't my dinner ready?" he demanded.

"It's Mary's birthday today and I've just finished clearing up. I'm about to do you something for your dinner now. Do you fancy a steak?" Mary flinched at the fear in her mother's voice.

"You know I hate her birthday! So don't even talk about it." He slurred his words.

"Shut up, John. The kids will hear you." Hazel hurried to close the door and Mary took the opportunity to bolt to her room.

Mary figured her father would eat his dinner and then crash in front of the television so she relaxed a little as she examined her birthday gifts. Mum gave her a second-hand electric Bernina sewing machine. Susan made her a special card, and Gloria gave her a sketch pad and a packet of pencils for her fashion designing. But best of all was the Tiki. It felt so romantic to wear such a treasure. Even if it had been made of plastic she would have loved it. She unfastened it from around her neck, carefully put it back in its box, and placed it in her top drawer, and fell into a deep sleep until something disturbed her.

He shoved the door open despite the pile of books up against it. Mary pulled the blankets over her head and curled into the tightest ball she could. But even under the bedclothes she knew from his stumbling movements how drunk he was, and even if he thought she was sound asleep, she was terrified that this time he would really hurt her.

"Mary, wake up. I've come to say happy birthday." John wrenched the covers back.

"So you're a woman now, are you? Come on, show me your big beautiful brown eyes and let's play our secret game," he said. His breath reeked of the familiar whisky smell. From somewhere deep inside her, she drew strength.

"You're meant to be my dad. It's wrong for you to touch me there," Mary said. He barely heard her, it was just a whisper.

"What's that you say? Surely you know by now I'm not your fucking father! You're a French man's bastard and I agreed to take you on. Now that you're a woman you can pay me back!" Mary opened her mouth and yelled, "Mum!" Her father grabbed her and clamped his hand over her mouth.

"Shut up, you bitch! I lined the walls of this room with sound-proof board so she can't hear you. Besides, if you tell your mother, I'll tell her you've been touching my cock for years. She'll never speak to you again. And what will your precious Jamie think? The stinking, thick Māori." He undid his belt.

He brutally pulled up her nightdress. She fought back, but he knocked her into submission. The whack to her face was so fast and such a shock she crumbled in a heap on the bed. He then threw his full weight on top of her as he pushed himself inside her, releasing grunts and moans as he pushed. Mary was convinced her most private place had been ripped in half as the pain seared through her fragile virginal body.

Once it was over, he pulled up his trousers and left without a word. Mary huddled back in a ball, full of confusion and shame. Then she smelt blood. She switched on the bedside lamp and could see blood trickling from between her legs.

Somehow she mustn't think about the revolting thing he'd done, then maybe it would be all okay in the morning.

She took a box of tissues and cleaned herself. Now she knew beyond all doubts that he was not her father. She had to push these thoughts beyond the pain and the shame. The truth about her real father had to be in the box of letters in the wash-house. She'd tried several times to open the cupboard but it was always locked and she couldn't find the key. It was several hours later before Mary fell into a fitful sleep.

"Wake up, sleepy head, breakfast is on the table." Hazel tapped respectfully on the door. When Mary didn't respond Hazel gently pushed the door open.

"Are you all right, darling?" she asked. "It's not like you to sleep in." Mary turned over in the bed, numb, and kept her eyes closed.

"Yes, Mum, I just feel a bit sleepy. I had a very bad nightmare. I'll get up now, have a shower and head over to Jamie's place."

Mary checked her bleeding. It hadn't lasted long, and she had wiped most of it with the tissues. But the bed was soaked with urine. She scooped up the sheets and shoved them in the wardrobe. She was in desperate need for a hot shower. Once in the shower she scrubbed herself until her skin felt raw.

"You've been in there for ages. Come on, get out, I need to clean my teeth." Susan banged on the locked bathroom door. Mary hastily threw on jeans despite it being a hot day. Her mum spotted her as she rushed out the door.

"Come on, love, have some breakfast, please." Mary could see her father sitting at the table with his head down in the paper.

"No, thanks, Mum, I'm not hungry. I'll have something later." As she spoke Mary's mind felt frozen, and her body seemed to belong to someone else. She did arrive at Jamie's house but she had no memory as to how she got there.

5

"Hi, birthday girl, come on in," Jamie's mother, Barbara, greeted her.

"I've come over to thank you all for my wonderful present," Mary mumbled mechanically, staring at her feet.

"Sit down and I'll make us a cuppa tea." Barbara ushered Mary to a seat at the kitchen table then yelled out the window, "Jamie, come on in, you've got a guest."

Jamie appeared in from the glass house in the backyard where he'd been helping his grandma.

"Hey, Mary, how ya going?" He'd caught his mum's discreet wink and shoulder shrug on the way through. He sat down beside Mary at the table.

"I'll just get some tomatoes for the sandwiches. Dad will be in soon for his morning tea," Barbara said then tactfully left the kitchen. She and Jamie's grandma were making the sandwiches when, on cue, Jamie's father, Huia, walked in.

"Think I'll have a piece of that cake as well, hun." The tall dark man patted his wife's bottom then noticed Mary at the table.

"Happy Birthday for yesterday." Huia's smile faded as he considered the girl's demeanour. Her shirt was all buttoned up wrong and she had on grubby jeans.

With the big crockery tea pot full, and the sandwiches piled up on the plate along with a large piece of cake, the three adults joined the two teenagers at the table.

"You look a little peaky, Mary. Are you feeling okay?" Grandma probed.

"I just came over to thank you all for the Tiki. I love it," Mary replied in a monotone as she toyed with her cup of tea.

"Maybe you're getting flu?" Huia attempted to draw her out. Realising this tactic wasn't working Barbara chatted to her husband about the shearing, while Jamie sat by Mary's side in silence.

As Mary stood up to take her untouched cup of tea to the sink, it slipped and fell out of her hand and broke on the floor. She yelped, slapped her hands over her eyes then burst into tears.

"It's just an old tea cup, child. It's no matter. Hush now." Barbara took Mary in both arms and held her close. Mary's body trembled as she sobbed onto Barbara's shoulder. Jamie looked on perplexed while Grandma quickly cleaned up the tea and the cup.

"I'm sorry, Mrs Allen, I just can't stop crying," Mary muttered between sobs.

"It's okay. A few tears never hurt anyone." Barbara handed Mary a paper towel.

"You don't have to tell us what's happened, Mary, if you don't want to. You just need to tell us what we can do to help you feel better." Huia was a man of few, but wise, words. Mary wiped her nose and eventually raised her head. Her expression was vacant - the light had been snuffed from her eyes.

After a stilted silence she finally spoke, "Well, if you can suggest where I can get a part-time job, somewhere to earn some money after school or on weekends, it would help as I really need to leave home as soon as I can."

"Mary, be assured, what you tell us here, stays here," Huia replied.

"Tell you what, Mary, with our boy away at school, why don't you come and work for me on Saturdays in the glass house and my flower garden. No-one else round here has much time for an old Toa like me. They're all too busy doing their own thing. What do you say?" said Grandma with a gummy smile.

"Okay, if you really need me, I'd love to." A seed of hope crept into Mary's voice.

"Come on, let's go and see Dad's new pups." Jamie nudged her and she followed him outside towards the kennels.

6

Six months had passed since Mary had first been raped. Her step-father's visits had become more frequent and she existed in perpetual fear. She withdrew from most of her usual activities. At school, she barely spoke to anyone and Gloria had practically given up on her. Mary discovered she could gain some respite if she went for a run each day. And she obsessively read her grandmother's books in the evening. The stories had the power to take her to another place. She fantasized about getting a job in fashion. But her immediatechallenge was to save enough money to escape.

Her mother questioned her at length about her weight loss and suggested they visit the doctor. However, in private, John convinced his wife she was worrying unnecessarily. He assured her it was just normal teenage hormonal behaviour.

Mary lived for Saturdays. Her new job was her saviour and she bonded with Jamie's grandma as if she was her own flesh and blood. Grandma's long-winded Māori stories and encouraging ways gave Mary some sense of worth.

"Kia ora, Mary, hope you are ready for some hard work today. We have to bring the fresh compost into the glass house to feed my tomatoes." Grandma peppered her conversation with Māori words.

"Don't you worry, Grandma, I can carry the bags myself. I'm pretty strong for a girl my age," Mary said.

"Let an old Toa tell you something, my girl. Strive to be strong in all things, especially in your thoughts. You have the power to take hold of all the good things that have happened to you and to discard the bad things. This part of your life is just a building block for what is to come. You are very talented. Be sure to concentrate on what is ahead, not dwell on what you've left behind." The old woman smiled warmly at her young friend, pleased that at least on the weekend visits, Mary would sit and eat with the family.

"For a slim girl, you manage to pack away a good lunch, Mary Hampton," Huia joked as the four of them sat around the kitchen table.

"She's a growing girl, Huia, so keep your comments to yourself." His wife gave him a kick under the table as she passed Mary the bowl of potatoes.

"Please may I leave the table while I'm waiting for Grandma? I'll just pop up to the kennels and pet the dogs." As she pulled on her gumboots at the back door she could hear the adult's conversation.

"Son, for God's sake, don't draw any attention to her eating. By the look of her weight loss, I think the only decent food she has is at our table on the weekends," Grandma said. "Jamie's home next weekend so no doubt that will give her a boost," Barbara added. Mary's heart always lifted a little at the mention of Jamie's visits home.

Hazel drove into town with the two girls. Mary opened a

Post Office savings account with her mother's knowledge and it was agreed that all the money she earned at her weekend job was hers to do with whatever she wanted.

"Mum, is it all right if I have a look in Brown's store on my own while you go to the supermarket?" Mary asked. Hazel nodded and took Susan with her as Mary headed off towards the small department store on her own. Once her mother was out of sight, she quickly back tracked and headed for Mr Kennedy's hardware shop and purchased a lock.

"Mary, phone for you, it's Jamie," Hazel called out the back door soon after they arrived home.

"Hey, Jamie, can you do me a favour? Can you please bring over a screwdriver and sneak around the back way out to my bedroom after dinner? Don't let the others see you," Mary whispered into the phone.

"Are you seeing Jamie today, love?" Her mother asked softly once Mary was off the phone and out of earshot of her husband.

"Only tomorrow when I go over for my work with Grandma Allen," Mary lied as she left the room.

"Jez, Mary. What's this all about? My heart is pounding inside my head thinking about what your old man will do if he catches me." They were in Mary's bedroom with the curtain drawn.

"Don't worry, he won't come out here, especially while the others are still up. I need you to help me screw this bolt lock on the door." Jamie recognised fear in her voice and decided against asking more questions.

"There we are, good and tight. It would take a wild bull to break in now," he said.

"Thanks, Jamie. Best you don't stay. I guess I'll see you tomorrow?"

"Sure thing. See ya." As Mary opened the door, the light lit up the darkness. For an instant she thought she saw a shadow at the kitchen window.

7

When Mary arrived at the Allen farm the next morning, Grandma announced a change of plan.

"You and Jamie are going to help Huia today with the mustering of the sheep in the top paddocks. Here, put this lunch into that back-pack. Jamie has already saddled three of the horses."

"But, Grandma, I'm not so great on a horse," Mary protested.

"Rubbish! I remember you riding last year. You're okay. Anyway, Dad only goes at Māori pace, so that means very slow. Besides, you'll be with me." Jamie smiled at her and gave her a wink.

As predicted, the trek up the hills was slow. Huia whistled and sang at the top of his voice, pausing only to call, "Get in behind," when the sheep dogs moved too far in front of the horses. After the first half hour Mary began to loosen up and by the time they had moved three hundred sheep into the lower paddock and stopped for lunch she felt confident on her horse and happier than she had been since her father's 'visits' began.

"That's actually your father's land just over there. He will no doubt be moving your sheep further down as well now it's getting colder." Huia pointed across the valley. It was clear to Mary where her father's land began as the ramshackle fence line was covered in untidy gorse and untreated moss, unlike the Allen fences which were neat and well maintained.

"Why don't you two go and have a bit of a look up at the caves. I'm going to have a sneaky smoke so the smell will be all blown off by the time I get back to your mother, Jamie." Huia took a crumpled packet of cigarettes out of his saddle bag, lay back on the crisp grass, and lit up.

Jamie led Mary up the hill in the direction of the caves. When they rounded the corner nearer the Hampton boundary fence, they heard the sound of a revving engine.

"Shit! It's Dad. Quick, let's keep out of sight." Panic rose in Mary's voice.

"We aren't doing anything wrong. What's his problem! Listen to him revving the crap out of that quad bike," Jamie replied.

"Believe me, Jamie, it's best he doesn't see you and me together up here." Mary sounded so frantic Jamie grabbed her hand and pulled her behind a large rock. When she appeared to have composed herself, Jamie decided to press her.

"Come on, Mary, what's going on? You've become a bit weird lately. I'm ya best friend. I can keep a secret." His undemanding words allayed her dread. She was desperate to share her fear.

"All I can tell you is that it is so horrible for me at home now that it makes me feel constantly sick." He put his arm around her shoulder.

"Mary, I promise, cross my heart and hope to die, I won't tell anyone," Jamie pulled her closer to him.

With her head snuggled into his chest and her eyes cast downward she whispered, "My dad isn't my dad." She spoke so softly he thought he'd misheard her.

"What! Then who is your dad?" He struggled not to over-react.

"Well, my Mum has a secret cupboard in the wash-house. It's locked so I'm going to have to find where she keeps the key because I'm pretty sure all that information is in a pile of letters I spied her going through. If I can get a look at them I may find some answers," Mary said in a tiny voice.

Jamie straightened and slowly dropped his arm. "So that's why he's such an arsehole to you then – not that that's any excuse."

Mary clammed up and after awhile Jamie glanced at his watch. "We better get back to Dad. He will have puffed away long enough now."

∾

It was later than usual when Mary finally arrived home. "There you are Mary. Where have you been? Supper is

nearly ready." Hazel busied herself at the stove.

"I went mustering with Mr Allen and Jamie on the horses. We had an enormous lunch so I'm sorry, Mum, but I'm just not hungry. I'll have a shower and then read in my room till I go to sleep," Mary replied.

Mary was sound asleep when she was woken by the sound of the door handle turning. She glanced at the clock

– 11pm. She shuddered realising who it would be. When

the door wouldn't open she felt, as well as heard, the bang as he kicked the door. She heard him say 'bitch' then it all went silent. Just as she breathed a sigh of relief, there was an almighty thud. The curtain flicked and he pushed himself through the bedroom window.

"You stupid, dirty, bitch. Thought you could lock me out, did you? I saw that black bastard leave last night and I saw you again with him today up in the rocks by the top paddock. You slut, give it to him, would you? Well, you can give it to me too!"

Her father grabbed at her but he was drunk and not as quick on his feet as her. Mary bolted. She flicked the lock across, pulled open the door and tore out of the room straight into the house. She grappled to contain her tears as she noisily turned on the bathroom light.

"Is that you Mary? Are you okay?" her mother groggily called out, clearly disturbed from her sleep.

"Yes, Mum, just me using the loo." She spoke loudly and then locked the bathroom door and waited, trembling as she sat on the closed toilet seat.

About ten minutes later she heard her father stomp into his bedroom. She waited until she heard him snoring, and then returned to her bedroom. The lock had been ripped off the door so she reverted to the pile of books even though she knew how ineffectual they were.

On Sundays her parents usually slept late. Mary hadn't slept at all so, as soon as the sun was up, she crept into the outside wash-house and took a closer look at the locked cupboard. It was a free-standing battered old dresser. She figured the key must be hidden somewhere close by. Mum usually hid the back-door key either under the big pot plant or above the door itself.

Mary lifted a few nearby old boxes and checked underneath, but to no avail. She pulled a stool over, climbed up and felt along the ledge above the cupboard door. Nothing. Then, from up on the stool, she noticed an old glass vase sitting on the top. It was only just within her reach but she could plainly see a small brass key in the bottom. Spreading her hand out as far as she could, she grabbed the vase and tipped the key out. Shaky from lack of sleep and fear of being caught, her hands shook furiously as she turned the small key in the lock.

The cupboard contained a couple of shoe boxes, one of which was full of old family photos. In the other box were some letters tied with a blue ribbon. She sat down on the stool, her hands sweaty as she wrestled with the ribbon. The dates of the post marks on the envelopes were clear. Mary opened the letter with the earliest post mark first. It was dated June 1964 and had been posted from Wellington.

My Dearest Chérie ,

I am so sorry to hurt you like this. I didn't mean to fall in love with you. It just seemed to happen as you are such a beautiful girl. I wasn't honest with you. I am not actually divorced. In fact, I have two children so I can't leave my wife to live with you. People here in New Zealand seem to be more accepting of unmarried mothers than they would be of my divorce and the scandal it would cause my wife and children in Paris. So I have made the brutal decision to return earlier than planned. Your parents, I am

sure will look after you as they seem like very kind people.
There is nothing else that I can say except sorry.
                                        André.

In a state of shock Mary re-read the letter, her tears tumbling onto the paper. Then she opened the next letter, which was in a large padded envelope, the type used to send small gifts. It had a Paris post mark but she could only decipher the numbers as the words were in French - 1965, the year of her birth.

Dearest Chérie,

Thank you for sending me the photo and letter. How clever of you to find me via the company. They quickly forwarded it to me. I have thought about you often but didn't dare to make contact as I didn't wish to give you any false hope. Our baby daughter looks beautiful, just like her mother.

My heart is very heavy that I'm not with you and I'm very jealous but I have no right to be. I still believe my obligation is here with my first family. Your marriage to the local man sounds suitable. It will give you a home and, if he is as kind as you say, he will adopt little Mary Chantal. I guess that's a good solution.

Should you ever need assistance, I am giving you a Post Office address where you could contact me by letter. I am leaving the wool-buying profession now to focus on my family estate.

My sincere admiration and thanks for your dignity in extreme adversity through this whole difficult affair.

I have enclosed one thousand Francs for you to put
towards something for the little one. My heartfelt
love to you.

André.

My contact details:
André de la Rouchefaucauld. Post Restant 45
06500 Paris
France

Mary took the envelope, with the letter and money still inside, and hid it in her pocket. She tied the ribbon back as it was, and placed it all back in the cupboard, locked the door and replaced the key. She listened to see if her parents were still in their bedroom, and then quietly phoned the Allen farm.

"Sorry to wake you, Grandma, but could you please get Jamie to the phone for me?" Mary asked.

"I was awake and up anyway. However he is not, but it will do him good to get out of his bed." Mary listened as the old woman shouted to Jamie to come to the phone.

"Please, Jamie, I need to be quick. Don't ask me any questions just now. I'll tell you everything later but can you please pick me up in the car tomorrow morning and take me to town?" Her voice was fractured and desperate.

"Sure thing. See you at nine at your gate," Jamie replied without hesitation.

∽

Mary didn't sleep for a second night. She discovered a small black and white photo of a man in the envelope and

48

assumed it was her real father. She studied it closely with a magnifying glass but couldn't identify anything familiar about him. Having missed her dinner and been awake all night, Mary felt light headed as she walked down the drive to meet Jamie.

"You look like crap, girl! Tell me what's up and where we are going?"

Sorry, but I feel like crap! I can't think straight but I need you to take me to the post office. I think that's where I'll be able to get a form to apply for a passport."

"Jez, I knew you would leave home, but going overseas! You're only 16." He pulled the car into the town public car park. "Look, you are the only person I can trust. You have to promise not to tell, not Grandma, not anybody." Mary looked directly into his face.

"Cross my heart and hope to die." Jamie spoke the words just as he had when he was ten years old. Mary had no reason to doubt him.

"I found the key and I read the letters. From what I can make out my real father was a French wool buyer. Mum loved him but didn't know he was married and when he got her pregnant, he left her and went back to France. Then Dad married her and they pretended he was my father."

Jamie thought about it for awhile before he responded. "So what are you gonna do? Go and find him? Jez, Mary, he didn't want you then. Why would he want you now?"

"Look Jamie, I can't tell you everything. You must believe me that my father, or rather that man my mother is married to, is evil. His words and actions are so belittling to me and they are all I can think about. I have to get away as quickly as

I can or he will destroy me. I can't tell Mum as she will hate me and I don't want to ruin her and Susan's lives. This André at least sent Mum some money for me, so he must care. Look, here's his photo." Mary handed him the snap shot.

Jamie peered at the faded little black-and-white photo showing a straight-postured, dark-haired man in what looked like old-fashioned clothes. Mary began to cry. He reached out and held her gently as her tears morphed into sobs.

"I do believe you, and I won't press you for any more information, but one day I swear I'll swing for that arsehole," Jamie said. He held her and wiped her wet cheeks with the cuff of his sweater.

"Come on, let's get a coffee and something to eat before we go to the post office." Mary experienced a new warm sensation as Jamie confidently held her hand when they walked into 'Nan's Koffe Shop.

"Hi Nan, we'll have two milk shakes and two meat pies, please." Jamie took five dollars from his wallet.

"Don't look at me like that, Mary Hampton. I know you love Nan's meat pies and I know you haven't eaten since yesterday. It's my treat, so say nothing and enjoy it." He smiled as Mary scoffed her pie.

"Thanks, you were right, I was starving! Now, let me tell you I'm not planning on going to Paris immediately. I'll have to work somewhere full-time for a while to earn enough for my airfare." Mary managed a smile as she spoke. Jamie looked at her thoughtfully.

"What about down in Christchurch? The Canterbury factory is there - that's where they make all the rugby jerseys so it must be a busy place. You are so good at sewing I'm sure they'd give you a job." He'd leant back in his seat and smiled at his clever suggestion.

"That's a good idea. I have enough in my savings account to catch a plane down there and to stay somewhere till I get a pay packet," Mary replied. They continued to formulate a plan as they walked towards the post office. I'd like an application form for a passport please. Mary felt uncomfortable as the woman who served her vaguely knew her mum.

"Are your parents going on a trip, dear?" the nosey woman enquired as she turned to find the appropriate form.

"It's a surprise trip her dad's planning for her mum so please don't say anything," Jamie quickly chipped in.

"Well, I hope he knows where she keeps her birth certificate," the woman replied as she handed Mary two forms.

"Shit, that was close, but what if she sees Dad and says something?"

"No-one makes light talk with your Dad, he's not the type, so don't worry," Jamie assured her. Once they were back in the car Mary turned to Jamie and took his hand.

"You've already done so much for me but can I ask you just a couple more favours?"

"Go ahead, what?" he raised an eyebrow.

"Well, you can go to the shops easily when you are back at boarding school. If I give you the money, can you go to a travel agent and buy me a ticket to fly to Christchurch? Make the date for when you're next home. It's easy for you to borrow your mum's car so then could you take me to the airport?" she asked.

"Course I will." He leaned closer and for the very first time, he gently kissed her cheek.

8

Having discovered the letters, Mary felt she understood her mother's unenviable situation a little better, and she also believed that Jamie loved her. Her constant fear of her so-called father was punctuated with pockets of strength. She was motivated by a belief that, if she could find him, her real father might love her. She smouldered with anger as she planned her next moves.

Mary was not going to let her father rape her again. He kept an air rifle in the wash house gun cupboard. It was one that the girls, under supervision, were allowed to use for target practise. After Mary loaded the rifle, she concealed it within reach under her bed. Then, although it felt dishonest going through her mother's drawer, it was necessary as she needed to find the old chocolate box she knew important family documents were kept in. When she found her birth certificate she saw that her mother must have married John while she was still pregnant, as the certificate named him as her father.

Jamie phoned her to say he would be home the following weekend and that her air ticket to Christchurch was booked for Sunday. He also said he'd booked her into an inexpensive hostel near the Christchurch city centre for seven days. They agreed she would go to work as normal on Saturday.

It was going to be difficult to sneak out from the house with a suitcase and overnight bag so she packed and squashed them into her wardrobe and just hoped her mother didn't open the door.

"Hi, it's me," Mary called out as she walked into the Allen's kitchen on Saturday morning.

"Kia ora, girl. You have relief from me today. I'm off into town with Barb and Huia but I expect you and Jamie to weed around all the tomato plants in the glasshouse. When you've finished there's cold cuts in the fridge for your lunch," Grandma informed her.

Jamie's parents and Grandma called out goodbye as they left the house in their best town clothes.

"What a stroke of luck! We have the place to ourselves." Jamie rummaged in the fridge.

"That's meant to be for our lunch, Jamie Allen," Mary jibed as they walked out to the glass house. After an hour of weeding Jamie was bored.

"Come on, let's get the lunch and picnic rug and have it on the lawn." He shook the well-worn tartan rug and spread it out under the walnut tree while Mary put the food onto their plates.

"Are you nervous about tomorrow?" Jamie asked once he finished eating.

"Yes, and scared, but nothing will stop me leaving." Jamie leant over and gently pushed her chin to bring her head up. He gazed into her eyes.

"Mary, you're my best friend, probably my girlfriend, which

I wouldn't tell you if you weren't taking off tomorrow. I don't want you to go, but I do want you to be happy." He softly stroked her cheek as he spoke.

"You're my best friend too Jamie. I'm sure we will meet up again one day." Mary wanted to kiss him.

"Before the others get back, let me get the tickets." He jumped up and went into the house. Mary was disappointed that the moment had passed. She cleaned up their plates and followed him into the house.

"How much extra do I owe you for the hostel or do I pay when I get there?" Mary questioned.

"No, it's all paid for by me. My treat - it's your Christmas present," Jamie grinned.

"Thank you so much. That'll give me a bit more to keep me going. I'm not quite sure how I'll find a room to rent. I guess I'll have to look in the paper." She felt an almighty knot twisting in her stomach.

Mary forced herself to be as cheerful as possible at dinner that night. It dawned on her that this would be the last time she'd clean up the dishes with her mother.

"Mum, thanks for all the stuff you do for me. I'll always love you, no matter what." Hazel threw the tea towel over her shoulder, placed the plate she was drying on the table and stared wide eyed at her daughter.

"What's brought this on?" She squeezed Mary's hand. "Nothing. I just wanted to tell you, that's all. I'm not all bad you know."

"Darling girl, I've never thought you bad at all." Hazel's eyes glistened.

"Don't cry on me, Mum! You may not think I'm bad but

your husband does." Hazel was lost for words.

"I'm off now, Mum. I'm going to read in my bedroom. Night night." Mary pecked her mother's cheek en route to the door. Hazel's arms dropped to her side and she hung her head as her daughter abruptly left the room.

Mary was still awake at one am when John slumped to her door. In the time it took him to drunkenly push open the door with the books piled behind it, Mary grabbed the gun from under her bed and sat upright. As soon as he'd fumbled his way in and stood about two feet from the bed, she flicked on the bedside lamp. The gun was pointed in his face. His belt and his fly were undone.

He'd stopped dead in his tracks. "Jesus, you fucking bitch, I hope that thing's not loaded!"

"Yes, it is, and I'll shoot your cock off if you move one step further." Mary stood up as she spoke, not faltering as she kept the gun firmly pointed at him.

"You wouldn't dare shoot me, you filthy bitch. You'd be done for murder," John said. A wave of defiant amusement swept over Mary as she witnessed her step-father's fear.

"I doubt an air gun could kill you but it could seriously damage one part of you. And how will you tell Mum and all the other interested people what you were doing in my room at one in the morning, drunk?" Mary exercised her new found confidence. John attempted to gather his thoughts.

"I'll just tell her you were gagging for it, you stupid girl. Who would believe a bastard like you?" Spittle sprayed from his mouth as he spoke. All the years of suppressed rage and shame imploded and Mary squeezed the trigger. John screamed as he hit the floor clutching his leg.

"You fucking bitch, you shot me! I swear once I get hold of you..." Mary stood over him still pointing the gun.

"You listen to me! You can flick that pellet out of your leg and wear long trousers and no-one will ever know. However, I'm still the one with the loaded gun, you arsehole. I may have shot you, but you raped me. I know you're not my father. I'm leaving tomorrow and you're not going to stop me. And you are going to make sure Mum doesn't call the police to search for me because, if I'm found, I'll tell them everything. Think about that when you're sober. Now get out of my room. I hope you rot in hell." He was silenced by the truth.

As Mary lay in her bed after he'd stumbled out, she made a pact with herself - she would never sleep in that bed in that room again. Amongst all her worry about what was ahead of her, she now found nuggets of hope.

The alarm jolted her awake at six o'clock. Jamie had said he'd be at the gate at seven. Before leaving her room for the last time, she placed a sealed envelope addressed to her mum in the top drawer of her bedside cabinet.

"Shit, Mary, I'm more nervous than you are. Dad saw me leaving. Thank goodness I was well out the door so he couldn't question me," Jamie said once Mary was in the car.

"I'm nervous, too."

They pulled into the airport car park and, as they walked hand-in-hand towards the terminal, Jamie noticed she was wearing the Tiki and affectionately stroked it with his forefinger. Mary checked in her bags and Jamie accompanied her as far as he was permitted.

"Make sure you write, and if you need anything, just ask."
He lent over, put both arms around her and kissed her full on
the lips.

"I love you, Mary Chantal Hampton, and I always will,"
Jamie whispered in her ear.

"Me too," Mary replied. Then she tearfully walked out to
the plane.

9

1978 - Christchurch, South Island, New Zealand

Christchurch seemed so big in comparison to the small country town Mary had left behind. During her first few days she just wandered around the central city. She observed couples who sat eating their lunch on the banks of the Avon River, and mothers watching over their toddlers as they threw bread to the cheeky ducks. She longed to be the little girl she was before her shame and pain began. She had vague recollections of her step-father playing with her innocently in a park on a swing. But mostly her memories of him were like a tight band threatening to squeeze the life out of her.

Mary followed a tourist sign saying 'Botanical Gardens' and discovered the lush gardens located on the fringe of the city centre. Vivid pockets of colour radiated from their neatly organised flower beds. The way the various flower varieties and colours were structured reminded her of fabric patterns on clothes she had sewn with her mother. She spent two afternoons just walking around or sitting alone on a park bench. The tranquillity of the fragrant gardens offered her some relief from the fear that was her constant companion.

There was a big knot in Mary's stomach as she approached the recruitment office at the Canterbury factory. The receptionist was friendly and gave her an appointment for the following day. She took some samples of her work but, after a preliminary chat with the recruitment woman, she was directed to a machine in what appeared to be a sample sewing room and was asked to sew up a pair of stretch men's underpants. This was a bit of a challenge as Mary hadn't worked with many stretch fabrics. However, she managed to adjust the sewing machine's tension and complete the task. Next she was given a plain cotton tee-shirt to sew. After readjusting the machine again she managed to complete the garment in no time at all.

The recruitment woman examined the pieces and then asked Mary to fill out a form with all the standard questions for employment. Mary mentally ticked off her first big achievement, securing a job! She was officially a seamstress. The Canterbury factory manufactured many brands. In addition to the famous rugby jersey, they made Jockey underwear and a small collection of ladies day wear.

Finding somewhere to live proved a little more difficult. Mary answered a couple of 'flatmate wanted' ads from the newspaper. When she turned up to view the first one, a rather rough looking chap answered the door and gave her a lingering look that brought up memories of her step-father. There was a girl in the flat as well but she showed Mary no warmth in her welcome.

The second place she visited was even worse. As the potential flat mate ushered her into the kitchen, Mary was struck by the rancid smell of stale food. The girl informed her she would be sharing with two men as well.

Mary realised she needed to find a better solution. The only person she had chatted with was the hostel receptionist so she pushed herself to strike up another conversation. Her hopes were initially dashed when the receptionist told her the owner didn't allow permanent tenants. However, she wrote down the phone number and address of another hostel for Mary to try.

When Mary went to view the establishment, the room they offered was basic with a single bed and a hand basin. She would have to share the toilet, bathroom and kitchen facilities with a few other girls. But it was a 'women only' hostel, very cheap, and within walking distance of the factory. So she handed over a month's rent in advance and moved in.

Within a few days of working in the sewing room doing the repetitive sewing of men's underpants, Mary was moved up to sewing rugby jerseys. The jerseys evoked thoughts of Jamie and she wrote him a short note telling him she had arrived safely and achieved her first two goals - a job and somewhere to live. She posted it to his boarding school and just hoped that he wouldn't show the letter to his parents.

Mary was using the loo in the shared bathroom at the hostel when three of the girls came in.

"That tall bird's a bit weird, isn't she?" one girl said.

"Yeah, looks like a stuck-up cow to me, too up herself to speak to us," added the second voice.

Mary cringed behind the door. How anyone could think she was stuck up? She was frightened of them more than anything else. They seemed a bit rough in her unworldly view. From then on she avoided the hostel girls and only exchanged pleasantries with them when forced to.

Although she felt ill with longing for her mum and Jamie, simple things, like being able to sleep all night without dread gave her the strength to keep going. After a month at the factory the boss, Bruce Lindsay, called her into the office. In trepidation she tapped at his office door.

"Mary, you have proved yourself as an exceptional seamstress but I sense you're destined for bigger and better things. How would you like to learn how to cut patterns?"

Mary beamed. "I'd love to."

"In that case, let's get you to do a couple of weeks sewing in the 'designer' room so you can fully convince me you can manage more intricate work. Then I'll give you a shot."

For the next two weeks, Mary focussed on every stitch. It was the same as putting a shirt together alongside her mother: how to sew the collar, complete the neat buttonholes, and pay attention to the front button panels. She felt their 'design collection' was very limited but it was a giant leap from sewing undies. She even allowed herself to fantasise about introducing some of her own design ideas.

Mary banked every cent she earned, only keeping enough out for her rent, food and small purchases on Saturdays when she rummaged through discount places for cheap but interesting fabric off-cuts. She spent at least three evenings a week in the library with head phones on listening to French lessons on cassettes, as well as studying her French phrase book every day. Her most expensive indulgence was to, once a month, purchase either a French or an English Vogue magazine. She figured if she was really careful she'd have enough money to buy her ticket to Paris in six months time.

Bruce Lindsay stuck to his word. She began training in the pattern cutting room exactly two weeks later. He even gave her a small pay rise, which would enable her dream trip to Paris to come a little sooner.

On her first morning, Julia, the cutting room supervisor took her through the basic techniques. Julia appeared so mechanical in the way she spoke, Mary got the distinct feeling she wasn't happy to have her there. There were two girls working in the adjoining room and the supervisor didn't even bother to introduce her to them.

After lunch Mary was directed to the other girls and, still without any introduction, instructed to follow their lead. Once the supervisor was out of ear-shot her new companions downed tools.

"Hi, I'm Lynne and this is Liz," the blonder of the two girls said. Mary was fascinated at the speed they were able to draw up the patterns by working with a triangle-type ruler and taking references from existing patterns. By the end of her first week, she was transferring their original patterns to heavy brown card and then hanging them with string on a pattern rail.

"Now, it's traditional in this department to go for a drink on a Friday after work. You're on the team now so you have to join us tonight, Mary," Lynne said as they ate together during the lunch break.

Mary faltered. She had never been in a pub before and was reluctant to tell the others she was only sixteen. All afternoon she tried to think of a plausible excuse not to go. At the end of the day she bit the bullet and bravely walked into the pub, acting as if it was a usual occurrence.

"What, only lemonade?" Liz said as Lynne returned with the tray of drinks.

"I don't drink," Mary said, deflecting the conversation by sipping on her lemonade through a straw.

Lynne laughed, "Leave her alone, Liz, we're not all pissheads like you!" Now she looked directly at Mary. So, what do you think of the factory so far?"

"Well, I'm not sure the supervisor likes me much. She's very abrupt with me." Mary fiddled with her straw.

Lynne laughed again. "Just ignore her. Firstly she's peeved off because Bruce promoted you rather than she having 'discovered' you and, secondly, she's always jealous of good looking girls." Mary blushed and pulled at her hair. Liz rolled her eyes.

"Come on, girl, you must know how good looking you are. Your legs go directly to your neck and underneath all that hair there's your large brown eyes. Not something us two have to worry about!" Both girls laughed at Liz's joke.

Mary felt uncomfortable. The compliment about her eyes provoked a 'step-father' memory, but she managed a smile, then accepted a glass of wine during the next 'drinks' round. By the time she left for the hostel a couple of hours later she felt she'd bonded with the girls and moved forward another notch.

The reply to her letter from Jamie was intense. He wrote that there were rumours flying around the farming community about Mary's departure but that, whatever Mary had written in the note to her mother worked, because her mother made it clear the subject wasn't up for comment or discussion. He also said he wanted to fly down to Christchurch and visit her. Mary panicked. She couldn't cope with any emotional distraction to her plan. She was flying out to Paris in around eight weeks and, once settled, would commence the search for her real father. As much as she yearned for Jamie, she was terrified that if she saw him it would be impossible not to reveal what her step-father had really done. It was the memory of the goodbye kiss at the airport that she wanted to carry in her heart.

She penned him a few lines telling him she had moved hostels so not to write again and that she would write to him when she got Paris.

～

By the end of the following month working with Liz and Lynne, Mary had acquired more skills.

"You're the best we've ever had through here," said Liz as they chatted in the bar during their ritual Friday night gathering. "What's your next move? You've not been sewing up all those new clothes after work just to wear to the pub with us, have you?"

"Actually, I'm off to Paris," Mary said. Her two companions' mouths dropped open. It was the first time Mary had seen them stuck for words. She took a sip of her wine. "I'm going to look for my real dad and, hopefully, get into the fashion scene there."

"You're adopted and really French?" Liz said. Mary didn't correct her or offer any more information and the girls didn't push it. They satisfied themselves with chatter and comment about Mary's French lessons and other people they knew who were adopted. Mary did, however, ask them not to tell their boss as she would prefer to do that formally herself.

On Monday morning Mary went to Bruce Lindsay's office and nervously knocked on the door.

"Come in," he called, "This is ominous. You've never requested a chat before."

"First," Mary said, "I want to thank you for giving me such a great opportunity and training me but I'm afraid I must give you two months' notice." He quickly stood up from his desk and walked around towards her.

"Look, if that Lee Holdings factory has poached you I'm prepared to give you a raise and I was going to offer you a design apprenticeship down the track. However, we could pull that forward if it will keep you here," he said, a flush rising in his face.

Mary struggled as she gave him an abridged version of her trip to Paris plans. He listened intently.

"Well, if there is anything I can do to change your mind, please tell me, but none-the-less I wish you well."

On her last day of work Mary was overwhelmed with a new sense of worth when the team surprised her with a special farewell lunch. They all dressed up in striped sweat-shirts and black berets attempting to set a French scene and served baguettes and Brie cheese along with a glass of red wine.

As she left the factory for the last time, she felt a pang of sadness at leaving her friends, but was spurred on by the anticipation of Paris and finding her father.

10

Paris, France 1979

Mary was sure her pack had gained an extra ten pounds as she hauled it up onto her back. Nothing could have prepared her for the crowds. She calculated, based on New Zealand's three million odd inhabitants that, from where she stood in Charles de Gaulle airport, there were that many people right there. They spoke an array of languages and all appeared to know where they were going. All except her. She breathed a sigh of relief when she saw a sign 'Gare'. Despite the haze of her jetlag some of the French words she'd studied began to transmit to her weary brain. The travel agent was right – the train station was practically within the airport.

Once on the train, which she discovered was called a Métro, she jammed her pack between her feet on the floor. With standing room only, she clung to the strap holds and anxiously scanned the name of each station. She managed to change lines at Gare de l'Est without any drama then finally left the train at Strasbourg - St-Denis. The pulse in her temple pounded as she stood on the crowded upward escalator. Where was the exit? After a few moments in the dirty frantic station she noticed the sign, Sortie. Yes, she remembered that meant exit.

Afternoon sun illuminated her arrival to the street. All the apprehension of the 24 hour flight and the train journey floated away as she experienced the intoxicating array of new sounds and smells. Then the visual feast kicked in. She had definitely arrived in the city of her imaginings. Nothing disappointed. Stylishly dressed people were seated outside cafés on plastic wicker chairs around small marble-topped tables. She breathed in the fragrance of their aromatic cigarettes, coffee and wine. The cadence of their voices offered Mary a sense of pure melodic romance.

The key reference point to finding her hotel was the Porte Saint-Denis, a huge carved stone archway that straddled the roundabout. She navigated her way across as chic European cars and scooters whizzed about her. Every street corner produced its own fragrance - scented tobacco, a wonderful freshly-baked pastry bouquet and a whiff of aniseed which appeared to emanate from the clear liquid several men were drinking. For Mary it filled the air with promise. At that moment she truly believed she'd been immortalised in a page of a French Vogue magazine.

Map in hand she struggled with the cobbled pavement in her cork platforms before eventually finding her way to the Hotel Saint Marie. It stood three narrow stories high, wedged between two taller, wider buildings. Most of the windows were flanked by battered shutters. The reception desk was empty as she approached but Mary heard noises upstairs. She cautiously rang the brass bell that sat on the reception desk.

"Oui, oui," a raspy voice called down from the staircase. A chunky, elderly woman with dyed ink-black hair wobbled down the stairs. She fired something at Mary in French. Mary struggled to respond in her practised French.

"Ah, so you're the Anglais girl. I guess you haven't had time to learn our language yet. First day, is it?"

"Yes Madame, I'm Mary Hampton from New Zealand. Here's my pre-paid voucher for a month's accommodation in a shared room."

"Oui, oui, I received it. You are sharing with a girl from London who arrived yesterday. She's not in now but here's your key. The room is on the third floor."

As Mary wrestled up the three flights of stairs with her pack, her visions of grandeur slipped somewhat. She was taken aback at how small the room was - nearly as small as her room in the Christchurch hostel. There were two single beds with a four-drawer chest at the end of each bed. An ancient looking, free-standing wardrobe stood up against the far wall.

Twenty four hours travelling had taken its toll. Mary left the pack on the floor and lay down on the bed. The enormity of how far she'd come and what might happen next crept into her thoughts. But within minutes she fell into a deep jet-lagged sleep, only to be woken about half an hour later by a pretty blonde girl who sat on the opposite bed.

"Hello, I'm Annabel Fraser. Sorry to wake you. I've left you some hanger space in the armoire." Mary was momentarily confused.

"Parlez-vous anglais?" The girl leaned forward. She had golden-blonde hair tied back in a ponytail which accentuated her intense blue eyes.

"No, I only really speak English. Sorry, I'm a bit slow - jet-lag. It's night time where I come from. I was fast asleep. I'm Mary Hampton."

"Golly, are you an Australian? That's a long way to come. Whatever brought you here?" She spoke like the Queen of England in a clipped posh accent.

"Actually, I'm a Kiwi looking for some lost family and adventure. What about you?" Mary hoped she sounded light hearted as she rubbed her eyes and started to undo her pack.

"To escape from my dreadful family and have an Adventure," the English girl chuckled.

Mary hauled all her clothes from her pack onto the bed and proceeded to fold them into the drawers. "So you call this battered looking wardrobe an armoire?" Mary asked as she pulled at its door.

"Yes, that's the French word. It sounds much better than plain old wardrobe, don't you think? You need to give the door a good tug because it sticks." Annabel yanked the door open for Mary.

"Do you speak French?" Mary asked.

"Well, I thought I did, but I don't think the French would agree! I learnt it at school but my pronunciation must be bad as I'm having rather a tough time making myself understood." Annabel laughed again. It was infectious and Mary was enchanted by the posh way she delivered her words.

After they organised the bedroom and Annabel had shown Mary the shared bathroom along the hall, Annabel invited Mary to join her for supper. As they walked along it gave

Mary an opportunity to study her new friend a little more closely. She wore ill-fitting black trousers and a simple button-through floral shirt but, underneath, Mary could see she had a great figure.

Along the nearby streets they scrutinised several blackboard menus, primarily for the cheapest price, and finally settled on a table for two outside a busy brassiere with an all-inclusive menu.

"I have to be careful with what I spend till I get a job, but this menu seems cheap enough - although I don't have a clue what we're going to be eating," said Mary as she attempted to decipher the food descriptions while they waited for the entrée.

"Me, too. I am determined not to ask my parents for any money. What type of work do you do? Fashion is my guess from the varied array of colourful clothes you had squashed into your pack. You look like you just stepped off the Kings Road in London. I didn't realise Kiwis were so trendy!" Annabel smiled each time she spoke.

"Well, hopefully in fashion. I've just spent eight months working in a clothing factory back in New Zealand. My mum taught me all the basics of sewing when I was younger. The sewing in the factory was a real bore at first but well paid. Then my boss had me cutting patterns and helping organise production. I'm keen to design. The boss gave me a reference so, if I can master some French, I should have something to offer in a fashion workroom. And, yes, you're right - most Kiwis aren't this trendy, but I am!" Mary said.

The entrée arrived. It was chicken liver pate and the girls immediately ceased chatting and washed it down with a glass of cheap red wine.

"I feel better now," Annabel sighed and sat back on her chair.

"So what work do you do?" Mary asked.

"Well, I love to dance, but I'm pretty sure no-one's going to pay me to do that! So it will be typing, I guess. I'll have to approach English-based companies, or try and get a job in a shop that sells to English speaking tourists." They lapsed into silence again when the main course arrived.

"Wow, that was yummy. I've never eaten chicken that sweet before. Such tiny legs." Mary finished the last piece of baguette as Annabel looked closer at the menu.

"Well, from what I'm reading, we didn't eat chicken. They were frogs' legs!"

11

I'm shattered." Mary flopped down on her bed. "Me, too. Did you have any luck?" Annabel lay nose-to-nose across from her on the opposite bed.

"A woman in a fashion alteration place gave me the name of a workroom in Sentier so I'll try there tomorrow. I'll have to get something soon as I'm running out of money." Mary sighed and closed her eyes.

"Well, I've got an interview with the owner of a large boutique next week. Apparently, he's keen to have an English speaking assistant," Annabel replied. "Come on, don't nap, we need to go forage for our dinner. I saw a really cheap place down a back street on my way home. It's about a ten minute walk if you're up for it?"

The girls freshened up and then counted out 50 francs between them which they put in the 'family purse' that Mary then zipped into her shoulder bag.

The first two weeks in Paris were full of frustration at every turn for Mary. She had many of the correct French words but the French people just didn't seem able to understand her accent. Thank goodness she felt comfortable in her relationship with Annabel. The farm seemed a life time away and she'd always known her friends at the Christchurch factory were temporary.

It was as if she was destined to be Annabel's friend. Annabel was one year older than Mary and she didn't pry. Her dress sense was a bit old hat and Mary was doubtful that she'd secure the position in the boutique if she went to the interview in her usual clothes.

Mary traipsed all around the fashion area of Sentier. The wholesale shops stood resplendent on the front streets showing off their wares in colourful windows, whilst the manufacturing factories and workrooms lurked behind in the back streets. After a lot of confusion with dodgy street numbers, she finally located the address the woman had given her. The door was ajar and she could hear the whir of sewing machines. As she walked in, the machinists all stopped working and stared at her. A swarthy skinned man with heavy face-stubble shouted at them and they immediately returned to their sewing.

"Oui?" he barked at Mary. With hands on hips he flicked his eyes up and down the length of her body. A wide gold chain glinted at his neck, surrounded by thick black hairs that protruded out over his top shirt button.

"Bonjour, Monsieur. Excusez-moi, je ne parle pas bien français."

"Well, I speak English so you're in luck. What do you want?" His English was tainted with what Mary assumed was an Arab accent.

"I'm looking for work. I can pattern draft, cut and sew, and I have references." She handed him her folder though she thought he seemed a bit creepy.

"By the look of you, I don't think you'd last a day here.

These ladies work hard, eight hours a day with half an hour for lunch. Besides, I only need a machinist." He handed back her folder.

"I'm happy to just sew. Can I work for you for one day for no payment to prove I have the endurance?" Mary forced a smile. He gave her a quizzical look and Mary could see the prospect of a day's free labour was appealing.

"Okay, be here tomorrow at eight."

"Whoopee, you got a job! Let's celebrate." Annabel took the cork out of a half bottle of red wine they had on the bedside table.

"I'm not there yet. I have to keep up with the pace and prove myself tomorrow." They finished the wine, scraped together another 50 francs and headed off to their cheap café for dinner.

◞◠

Next morning Mary arrived at the factory early. A group of girls were smoking cigarettes near the entrance. They were over generous with their foundation and eye makeup, but mean with their skirt lengths. Another group of girls wore head scarves, long skirts and no makeup and stood respectfully clasping their handbags. Neither group offered her any acknowledgement.

The boss arrived on the dot of eight. He greeted the girls with head scarves in Arabic, ignored the others, then pointed to a machine at the back of the room and told Mary to thread up. Then an older, podgy woman approached Mary. The woman's grey hair was tied tight in a bun and she handed Mary a pile of blouses to be sewn.

"I Madame Blanche. You understand me?" She spoke with a strong accent.

"Yes, Madame, thank you. Excuse me, but what is the boss's name?" Mary asked.

"He Monsieur Doaud. He Algerian. That lot, they the same." She inclined her head at the women with the head scarves who sat together near the front. "You speak only to me. I your boss, you understand?"

Mary quickly got the hang of the place. She carefully watched the girl next to her and fell into the same rhythm and sequence of which seams to sew first. By lunch time she had completed four shirts to her colleagues five. Madame Blanche took the shirts to the office and Mary could see her huddled over them in discussion with Monsieur Doaud. Just before closing time Madame summoned Mary to Monsieur's office.

"You seem able to deliver what we need," he said. "I won't pay you for today but you can start tomorrow. The pay is 900 francs per week." Monsieur Doaud made her skin crawl but she couldn't afford not to take the job.

The following day Annabel was to have her interview.

"Now you know I'm quite into my fashion stuff?" Mary said as they sat on their beds flicking through discarded magazines. "Are you trying to tell me something, Mary?" Annabel said with a grin.

"Well... I thought maybe you would allow me to 'style' you up a bit for your interview tomorrow. What do you think?"

"Oh, dear friend, I'd loved to be 'styled' by you! But I'm broke so you'll have to work with what clothes I have."

An hour later, Annabel was transformed. She wore cargo pants, the previous embodiment of which had been Mary's own wide leg trousers. They sat flat on the waist and over the stomach which flattered her friend's silhouette. Mary teamed the pants with a lemon coloured shirt tucked in at the waist and cinched snug with a wide leather belt. Annabel wore Mary's espadrille canvas-heeled shoes with tissues stuffed in the toes due to Annabel's smaller foot size.

"My god, who am I?" Annabel exclaimed as they both stood, crammed in front of the small mirror.

"Well, I just feel it's a fashion company so you need to look the part and cargo pants and wide belts are in the latest Paris Vogue."

"I totally trust you in the fashion stakes. Thanks, I look so much better. However, you can put those crimping irons down. You suit that crinkle-hair look but it's definitely not for me!"

12

The initial enthusiasm for her job had worn off and Mary was ambivalent about the repetitive work. It lacked stimulation and stifled her creativity, but each time she received her pay packet she experienced a ripple of relief. Besides which, working with a group that only spoke French had vastly improved both her accent and her vocab.

Mary observed that Monsieur Douad's body language was very derogatory towards the rougher looking French machinists. She heard him use the English word 'slut' several times, probably assuming the girls spoke no English. Whilst they were coarse by Mary's standards they were friendly and, bearing in mind her own background, she viewed them more in the vein of 'tarnished virgins'.

She did however feel a little threatened by some of Monsieur Douad's friends who visited him in his office. A couple of times she caught them gesturing towards her through his glass partition. They made her skin crawl.

Mary's domestic life, although pressured, seemed more manageable by being shared with Annabel. Her re-styling had proved successful and Annabel had secured her job. It was a natural conclusion that they share a flat and so they commenced their search. Restricted by their budget it proved an arduous task compounded by their limited knowledge of how the system worked. They both worked long hours without access to a phone so they missed out on getting to view properties, as most cheap places were snapped up immediately.

"Hurry up, hurry up, we can't be late." Mary yanked Annabel's hand as they flew out of the Métro at Place Monge. "It's the first one at the right price we've been able to view. Let's just hope it's not too small and that he'll give it to us!"

The flat was located on the busy pedestrian street of Rue Mouffetard. As they'd been instructed they arrived outside the door on the dot of seven. Five minutes later a Vespa motor scooter pulled up ridden by a young man. He beamed when he saw the two girls.

"Hi, I'm Marc Bengué." He spoke English with an upper-class clipped accent. "Lots of stairs and no lift I'm afraid." They followed him up three flights of very steep stairs. The flat smelt musty and needed a good clean. There was one small bedroom and a living room with a basic cooking hob next to an antiquated porcelain sink in the corner.

"I'm not sure, Mary - the electrics look a bit dodgy," Annabel said.

"Yes, and look in here. There's no shower, just this hip bath. My legs would hang over the edge," Mary replied. They both sighed in unison.

"I know it's a bit tired, but it's cheap and you can do what you like to it. I have to go back to the UK soon and my grandma can't get up the stairs anymore," said Marc.

78

Annabel squared her shoulders and said, "Well, here's what we'll offer. It's empty anyway so if you give us a month's free rent in lieu of us doing it up, plus a three year lease you've got a deal." They both smiled as seductively as possible at him.

He hesitated a moment then replied, "Well, I guess so... if you bring me a bank cheque tomorrow."

"Deal," Annabel said and offered her hand. They all shook on it and agreed to meet the following evening to sign the lease and exchange the cheque for the keys. He started up his scooter, then halted and turned the engine off.

"I don't suppose you two would like to come down to La Huchette with me?"

"What's that?" Annabel asked.

"It's a jazz club. Its full name is Le Caveau de la Huchette but we just call it La Huchette. They have a Swing band tonight if you like to dance. And it's pretty cheap. If you come I'll treat you to the first drink." Mary frowned and stepped back a little but Annabel squeezed her hand.

"Yes we'd love to. How far away is it?"

"Close by in St Germain des Prés. I can show you which way to walk and meet you there in say twenty minutes." He then proceeded to give the girls directions.

"Why did you say we'd go?" Mary was angry.

"Oh, come on, don't be such a spoil sport. Are you scared or something? There's no need to be - we'll be together. Come on, we haven't met many other friends. Besides, Marc is quite cute!"

Mary shrugged. "I suppose you're right. Sorry, I'm not good around men so please don't leave me alone with any."

As promised, Marc waited for them at the door. They

followed him into an old stone, windowless building then down some concrete steps to a darkened cavern-type room. All the seats were terraced like a sports arena around a dance floor.

"Let's get the front row so we can see more action. You two sit down and I'll grab us all a glass of wine." Marc guided them to a red leather banquette seat on the edge of the dance floor. The band was tuning up and lots of people who appeared familiar to one other began to arrive.

"Oh, Mary, I love to dance. How exciting." Annabel jiggled around like a sixteen-year-old on her first date. Mary felt nervous, being totally out of her comfort zone, but was riveted as she observed what everyone was wearing.

"I really need to pee. Do you want to come too?" she asked Annabel.

"No, you silly Kiwi, it's just over there. You can go on your own. You'll be okay." Mary reluctantly walked across the room towards the pink neon sign marked 'Toilette' which was near the bar. As she came out of the loo she saw Marc in front of her chatting animatedly to two other young men. As she got closer she could hear them talking.

"The blonde is attractive, but that tall bird with the wacky clothes and amazing hair is a looker. What does she do? With legs like that she must be a model. Wow, you old dog, pulling a couple of classy ones like that."

"Yes, she's something in fashion. They seem like good sorts. They're going to rent Grandma's old flat and, hopefully, do it up a bit," Marc replied, but their chat abruptly stopped when they saw Mary. Marc scurried behind her with the drinks.

Eventually, Mary relaxed. She was fascinated by the live

band and, wow, could Annabel dance! After the first dance with one of Marc's friends, others lined up. Annabel could dance all versions of the Swing and the new Ceroc. Several young men approached Mary to dance too but she declined, much to their disappointment.

Happily exhausted, at midnight they said their goodbyes and promised to meet the group there at the same time next week.

13

The girls scraped together enough funds to have a plumber sort out the water cistern in their new apartment as well as attach a shower to the bath taps and secure the shower head to the tiled wall. They purchased a small grill and two hobs, and beguiled the young shop assistant into delivering and installing them as well as removing the old one, all for the initial purchase price. They giggled at what a seductive smile could achieve. Then they had the broken double bed removed and replaced with two single, second-hand ones. They scrubbed and cleaned the apartment for the entire Sunday before they felt it was ready to move in. By early evening both girls slumped, exhausted, on the sofa and had a light supper along with a glass of wine.

"Right, we've both got jobs and our accommodation is more or less sorted. Now, what about this family you said you were looking for?" Annabel asked.

"Well, I'm a bit worried as I'm not sure how it all works here and I can't afford a lawyer to help me." Mary's voice trailed off. "I don't like to pry because, just like me, I understand you came here to get away from something or someone but, if there's anything I can help you with, I will," Annabel said.

Mary was contemplative. "Sorry if I seem secretive. It's not that I don't trust you, or that I even mind you knowing. It's just that other than my best friend, Jamie, back home I've never spoken to anyone about it." She bit her lip. "You read French okay so perhaps you could help me find out where I should go to find the address of someone who lives in Paris and owns their own home. In New Zealand we call it 'paying rates' to the council. I figure that could be a good place to start."

"Yes, we call it council tax in the UK. In France that information is held at the Hôtel de Ville which is the council office for each town or city. But they're only open in working hours so it could be a bit tricky for you. Having a phone with an answering machine should help - at least we can be left messages."

"My mum fell in love with a French man who was temporarily in New Zealand. She didn't know he was married till she became pregnant with me. A local boy who always fancied her agreed to marry her so long as my maternal grandfather helped him out of a financial tight spot. Mum never told me anything about it and I only found out by accident when I was sixteen." Mary's face flushed. She was on the verge of tears and tried to swallow the lump in her throat. "My step-father was a terrible man. I felt so deceived I ran away and you know most of the rest."

"Oh, you poor thing. Don't you worry, I'll help you track down this elusive father of yours and I'm sure when he sees what a beautiful daughter he has he'll be well chuffed." Annabel's voice was full of compassion.

"What about you? Why don't you speak about your family?" Mary said.

"Well, let's just say my parents are control freaks, especially my mother. She even controls my father and she's a dreadful snob. I don't want what she wishes for me, so the only way I could cope was to leave." Annabel fidgeted with her glass. Mary moved across the sofa and hugged her.

"I think it's fate that a couple of misfits like us met. We were destined to be friends," she said.

They bought a cassette player and the next evening Annabel gave Mary her first ever dance lesson. They kept bursting into fits of giggles because, as Mary was about five inches taller, Annabel had to jump to get their clasped hands over Mary's head for the Swing. They kept repeating the routine until Mary had the basic steps off pat.

"You're a quick learner, but it's a bit tricky with your height. Those English guys down at the club are quite tall, but the frogs are pretty short."

Over the next few weeks Mary worked hard to prove herself in the workroom. One day the cutter phoned in to say she'd broken her arm. Monsieur Douad was furious as he had to meet orders from clients. Mary volunteered to step in. She lied and said she had done cutting in New Zealand but the truth was she had helped out the cutter with the supposed broken arm on several occasions when Monsieur was out. Mary doubted she'd broken her arm at all – she sensed there was some other reason the cutter didn't want to come in. And she was right - the cutter never returned.

Mary took over her job and also drafted new patterns when needed. She was fast but even so worked at least an extra hour each day to cover all the work and help improve the machinists output.

In lieu of the extra hours, Mary requested Monday mornings off. Sadly she discovered that the Taxe d'Habitation Department at the Hôtel de Ville in France was forbidden to furnish any information unless Mary had proof that she was related to Monsieur de la Rochefaucauld. That was impossible. So the following Monday she queued at the Births, Deaths and Marriages Department to request a search for any information on her birth father. The first morning it took till 11.30 before she got anywhere near the front of the queue, so she had to forfeit her position to rush back to work before midday.

Monsieur Douad had become more attentive towards her. He moved physically closer to her when he was giving her instructions. His proximity gave her flash-backs of her step-father. She decided she would endure it a while longer, either till she had a little more money or until she found her father. One day they were going over some new designs in his office while Madame Blanche was out making a coffee.

"Monsieur, now that I am taking on more responsibility I wonder if you would consider giving me a rise in pay, please?"

"Hmm, I'll have to consider it. I will look at the financials. Why don't you stay after work and we can talk it through?" Before he finished speaking, Madame arrived back in the cutting room. She scowled at Monsieur Douad.

After work, when all the other staff had left, two of Monsieur's friends arrived. Like him they were dark and swarthy. They sat in the small room adjoining his office and puffed away on brown-coloured, scented cigarettes. Monsieur closed the big front door and invited Mary into his office. Her body was running hot and cold - her instinct was to bolt. Inwardly she reasoned she was perhaps being over reactive and waited for him to open the discussion.

"So, do you have a man or, what do you say, a boyfriend?" He moved over beside her and rubbed his leg against her thigh. The smell of garlic mixed with sweat exuded from his body. Mary was panicky. She stood up and stepped back.

"That's none of your business, Monsieur. You told me I was here to discuss my pay rise." She quickly moved forward and pushed the office door open. The other two men walked in. One was loosening his belt. Suddenly all Mary's past terror flooded back into her being.

"I'll give you the pay rise but, from the way you display yourself, I'm sure you want more than that." He reached out to grab her arm. But Mary was faster and bolted through the office door where she found herself face-to-face with Madame Blanche.

"What are you doing here, you fat bitch?" Monsieur barked at the older woman.

"Oh, I forgot my purse," she replied in a controlled voice. "Come, Mary, I walk you home tonight."

She poked Mary in the back and they both hastily left the factory.

"You too good for this place. You must go. He will do what he always do. Bad man." The elder woman's eyes brimmed with concern as she grappled with her English.

"I never want to see him again but I don't know what to do!" Mary trembled as the flood gates opened.

"Here," Madame handed her a handkerchief, "I give you

phone number. You say Madame Blanche sent you. This new boss man a poof so he won't try sex on you. He difficult but I know you deal with that okay." Mary took the piece of paper.

"Thank you, Madame, but what about you? And what about my pay?"

"Well, it only four days' pay, so my advice you forget it. Best you not come back. Douad a bad man. I old now. Nobody else want me and I need work." The old lady shook her head and walked off.

Mary ran for about ten minutes trying to evict the image of the man unbuckling his belt. It brought the memories of the rapes and abuse squarely back to her. When she arrived back at the apartment one foot was bleeding and both her designer sandals were broken.

"Mary, my god! Has the devil chased you?" Mary fell into Annabel's arms. Mary told her everything about Douad, the men and Madame Blanche's gift of the address.

"You'll find something else. Call the chap Madame recommended in the morning. Come on now Mary, Kiwi's don't cry," Annabel said as she gently placed Mary's battered feet in a large bowl of warm water.

"What is it with me and men? I just seem to bring out the worst in them." Mary noisily blew her nose.

"Did that Jamie you talk about try something sinister on you?" Annabel asked.

"No, no, he was perfect. It was someone else... someone I thought loved me. But I never want to talk or think about him again."

14

Mary woke the following morning at her usual early hour... then remembered she didn't have a job.

"Goodbye. I'm late for work." Annabel hurtled out of the door in her usual fashion. Mary had rarely ever been alone in the flat and found the silence disconcerting. The close shave of yesterday coupled with the lack of distractions allowed visions of her step-father to assault her. She struggled but finally managed to direct her thoughts to her beautiful mother. She yearned to talk to her and to hug her little sister. And, oh what bliss it would be to sit with Jamie and his family at their big family table and listen to his grandmother's precious Māori stories.

Eventually, as she boiled up the coffee pot and heated a slightly stale croissant, her thoughts morphed to her recurring fantasy about her real father, André De Rochefaucauld. Surely he would love her once he met her, even if they had to keep it a secret from his wife? The hot handle of the coffee pot jarred her back from her fantasy and she resolved to focus her attention on securing a new job.

Mary kept repeating out loud what she'd say in French till she felt she had it off pat before tentatively dialling the number Madame had given her. She made no headway with the receptionist who answered the phone until she mentioned Madame Blanche's name. Then the receptionist said something to a man who must have been close by and continued, "Monsieur Dubois will see you tomorrow for an interview at 10am." Mary scribbled down the address and hoped she'd captured all of the rapidly spoken instructions correctly.

As it was still early she decided to go to the Hôtel de Ville and see if she could queue and make it to the front desk of Births, Deaths and Marriages before they closed for lunch. She took her 'print out' number from the machine. Her heart sank - the queue was even longer than last time. Her feet ached in her high platforms which she's worn to flatter her wide legged jeans. With nowhere to sit she slipped off her shoes. At twenty-five past twelve she was at last next in line. The man in front of her promptly instigated an argument with the harassed clerk. So on the dot of twelve thirty the clerk tapped her watch, snapped her file box shut, stood up, and walked off.

"Shit!" Mary exclaimed as she stepped forward, trying to quickly move to the next aisle. Her foot caught in the hem of her wide-bottom jeans and, as she tumbled over head first, the contents of her handbag spilled out on the floor in front of her. "Shit!" she repeated as she scrambled to gather all the bits from her bag. A few stray tears of frustration trickled down her cheek.

"Now then, it's not worth crying about." A tall middle-aged man arrived beside her and handed her the lipstick that had rolled some distance away.

"Er, thanks. How did you know I was English?" Mary

swiftly slipped back into her platforms.

"You swore in English, and no French girl I know wears an Indian head-band, has crinkled hair and is six feet tall!" he said. He smiled and ushered her to a seat by an empty desk. When she noticed he was wearing a name tag, it dawned on Mary that he worked there.

"Now, I'm in no rush for my lunch. I'd much rather assist a beautiful, distressed woman. How can I help?" said the man, flirting with her in English. Mary took her father's tatty letter from her bag and fingered it as she spelt out loud the difficult surname. She gave an abridged explanation of why she needed to find him.

"Well now, de la Rochefaucauld, that sounds very aristocratic and uncommon so it shouldn't be too difficult. I will need to search in all three departments here then cross reference the results. I'll phone you with an official appointment when I've found something. Then you won't have to line up again." He wrote his name on a card and handed it to Mary, then offered her his hand. She shook it gratefully.

"Thanks, Monsieur Yves, you've been so kind."

Next morning Mary woke brimming with anticipation. Travelling on the Métro wasn't conducive to wearing heels so she wore her plimsolls and crammed her platforms in her bag. She gave herself plenty of time to find Monsieur Dubois's studio and to change shoes before the interview. The studio was easily identified by a large, glossy brass plaque. The words 'Santos Dubois - Designer' were engraved in bold, black-enamel letters.

"Bonjour," the immaculate receptionist said giving Mary questioning look.

"Um, j'ai…"

The receptionist interrupted. "I speak English. You must be Mary 'Amptom." The receptionist ushered her through a beautiful wooden door with an ornate brass door handle fashioned in the shape of a dress-maker's dummy. They walked into a small hallway with large floor-to-ceiling windows through which Mary could see various men and women using sophisticated modern cutting tools and sewing machines. The receptionist lightly tapped on the door at the end of the hallway.

"Entrez," a high-pitched, effeminate voice called out. Mary saw the receptionist visibly stiffen as they entered the room.

"Bonjour, Mademoiselle Hampton. Please take a seat. I will be one minute," the man said. His beige suit was clearly too tight and the small amount of hair he had left on his head was greasy.

Mary hesitated, then sat down on a cream, heavily-buttoned brocade chair. The stark, cool ambience of the room overwhelmed her. Highly glossed white walls were adorned with rows of framed black and white photographs. Some featured models in couture gowns. Others were images of Dubois receiving some type of award or posing with, Mary assumed, celebrities. The desk was Art Deco style finished with a lacquered walnut effect. It sat majestically on a floor of gleaming white tiles. Dubois barked a few orders at the receptionist, Wendi, then turned his attention to Mary.

"So, if Madame Blanche recommended you, you must be

competent. She is such an old witch - a great couturier in her time but not forthright with the compliments." His delivery of English was astute and precise but in an unusually high voice. Mary winced as his icy blue eyes bore into her skin as he studied her. Those eyes had the intensity of a hawk, back home on the farm, about to pounce on its prey.

"Would you care to look at my folder?" Mary said, nervously removing it from her bag. As he stood up to take the folder she noticed how short he was. He studied the folder suspiciously.

"Well, this reference from the New Zealand factory reads very well. I will, of course, telex this company to verify it," he said. He walked around to her side of the desk and beckoned for her to follow him. In her heels she stood over six feet tall. Even in his platform shoes, his head only came up to her shoulder. His baldness ended with a small circle of hair at the back of his head. She shadowed him through to the workroom.

"We have state-of-the-art technology here. I have only the best in my workroom." His tone became almost a squawk as, oozing with pride, he described all his machinery to her. Mary was impressed with the technology, but unimpressed by the total lack of warmth she observed between the workers and their boss.

After he'd toured her through the entire workroom he turned and faced her. It was clear he wasn't interested in her opinion. However, Mary felt compelled to say something. "Monsieur Dubois, your operation is so impressive. I've never seen anything as modern before. How clever you are. It would be such a privilege if you would consider taking me on in some role." She attempted to sound humble and was rewarded with what she assumed constituted a smile, though it looked more like a sneer.

"Weell, for a person from an island at the end of the world with millions of sheep, I suppose you have some graces. I will think about it and make contact with the referee you have provided and telephone you soon." With that he minced off leaving Wendi, who had quietly reappeared, to walk Mary back to the entrance.

15

Mary wasn't at all confident about her chances with Santos Dubois so she kept trawling the newspaper 'Situations Vacant' pages for other suitable positions. There were plenty of factory sewing jobs available but she reasoned her money would hold out a bit longer. She wanted to wait and give herself a better chance of getting an assistant designer position. Waiting also allowed her to do some extra study on her French. Two days later, the phone rang... twice in one morning. The first call was from Monsieur Yves at the Hôtel de Ville requesting that she visit him that afternoon if possible. The second call was from Wendi at Santos Dubois' office.

"Bonjour, Mary. Monsieur Dubois has received confirmation from your former employer in New Zealand and he is prepared to offer you a position as a trainee assistant designer. Can you come in on Monday morning to discuss the terms?" Success!

As Mary walked from the Métro to the Hôtel de Ville her heart beat a hundred times to every footstep at the prospect that soon she might be closer to meeting her real father. She hoped that time had changed things and he would now be interested in having some kind of relationship with her.

"Mademoiselle Mary, please come into our visitors' room. It is more private here." Monsieur Yves' voice carried a worryingly soothing tone. He held a heavy ledger tied with a black satin ribbon. The visitors' room was a cramped space that smelt musty, a lot like the geriatric ward her grandfather was in for a while. Mary sat apprehensively on one side of the table facing Monsieur Yves.

"I'm very sorry. I have sad news for you." He paused. Mary's stomach lurched. "What?"

"Sadly, I have here what I think is your father's death certificate. It appears your father, Count André de la Rochefaucauld passed away one year ago from a heart attack. He was 60 years old and is survived by his wife, Countess Edith, and two sons, Pierre-Louis and Claude." Mary stared at him open-mouthed. After a long, stony pause she found some words.

"But… but how do you know it's him"?

"Well, as soon as I commenced my search, I could see there was only one de la Rochefaucauld family and, even more telling, only one André. It is a very historic family, you know?" Monsieur Yves reached out and gently covered her hand. Mary grappled to compose herself.

"No, I didn't know anything! I'm his illegitimate daughter and, as far as I know, he worked as a wool buyer in New Zealand for a short time," she blurted out.

"Yes, that sounds right. Since the revolution the former aristocracy has had to work for a living but it would seem he later took over the family wine business." His words 'former aristocracy' carried a sting in their tone. He then handed

Mary a folded page.

"I have taken the liberty of photocopying the death certificate. I hope it may afford you some comfort in a difficult situation." Monsieur Yves' voice was full of compassion.

Mary felt wretched. She accepted the page, mumbled a thank you and hurriedly left the building, desperate for air.

16

"Mary, Mary, what's wrong?" Annabel asked. Mary was curled in the foetal position and sobbing on her small bed. Her friend squashed in beside her and gently rubbed her back.

"Turn over and tell your best friend everything." Mary slowly turned over, her face swollen from prolonged tears.

"It's my real father. He's dead! He died a year ago. I am too late," she wailed.

"Oh, I'm so sorry," Annabel said as she put both arms around her friend and pulled her up to a sitting position so she could embrace Mary.

"I know it's not like I knew him. It's the idea that he might have shown me what it was like to have a proper father. I'm crying for myself really, not him." Mary blew her nose noisily on the hanky Annabel handed her. "Thanks, I can rely on a proper English girl to always have a clean handkerchief," Mary managed to respond.

"And to make a cup of tea when the chips are down. Come on, Kiwi, I might even find a biscuit as well."

Once they'd drunk their tea Annabel asked, "What about your late father's other children. Perhaps you could contact them. After all, they are technically your half-brothers."

"That passed through my mind but I don't want to turn their lives upside down. I'm sure they'd have no interest in a mistake like me." Mary put her cup on the table and rested her chin on her hands.

"Well, as one door closes another opens, so they say. Are you going to write and tell your mother about your father's passing?"

"I'll think about it for a while first," Mary said. She then got up to make it clear the discussion was over.

By Monday morning Mary had closed the compartment in her brain that stored the 'hope component'. She would never meet her real father and he would never be able to right the wrongs of her childhood. Now her career would be her sole focus.

She deliberated for quite some time on what in her wardrobe would impress Santos Dubois. She didn't want to appear too 'hippy' looking. Having carefully scrutinised French women for six months, her standard of personal grooming had risen. Her fingernails, although filed short to enable her to sew, were beautifully manicured and painted a natural pink. She'd discovered 'waxing', so her long slim legs were smooth and, with the aid of fake tan, a caramel colour. Even though her flat roman sandals encircled her ankles, her legs still looked exceptionally long and elegant as they met with the luxurious knee-length suede skirt that she'd picked up cheap in a flea market. She noticed a few appreciative stares as she took the steps down to the Métro.

"So, I will tell you about the vision for my new collection so you can let me see if you can sketch what I describe," Santos said once she was sitting opposite him at his elaborate desk. He elongated his 'e's when he spoke English but Mary was just relieved he spoke English at all. She could see he'd be far too impatient to listen to her laboured French. He handed Mary a sketch pad and a pencil. After he'd shown her pages from Vogue and described additions and changes to various garments, he directed her to a small desk in a corner of the workroom and she proceeded to sketch.

His ideas were a play on the already established maxi dress in various florals. Mary sketched a series of 'off-the-shoulder' peasant dresses, one with a layered skirt fully gathered at each layer and one with a straighter skirt. She colour-blocked the garment styles in a rich purple with a lighter lilac print. The second colour palate was a soft lemon with a richer yellow trim. Then she thought about a way to gain impact on the catwalk. She sketched, using the same colour-way and 'off-the-shoulder' tops, but added cheeky miniskirts in bold purple and bold yellow. She included fantasy boots to emphasise the long legs of the models.

By six o'clock Santos still hadn't been to scrutinise or comment on her work. So when she saw the workroom staff packing up she closed her sketch pad, placed it on her desk and left with the staff. The following morning the sketch pad was gone and, just as she was about to approach Wendi, she heard, "Meery, come to my office."

"These sketches are interesting. You have drawn up my ideas quite well. You do understand they are my ideas? I pay you so what you do here belongs to me." Santos emphasized the 'I' and the 'me'. Mary nodded. "Now, I want to test your pattern-cutting skills. You can work with Katrine in the pattern-making room. Make sure you have covered all the basic styles by the end of the day."

Mary was puzzled by the resentment in his voice. He turned away as if studying something much more important on his desk and Mary understood she'd been dismissed.

Katrine seemed nervous. She spoke a little English but Mary had enough French to find all the things she needed. The pattern-making paper was the same as she'd used back in the Canterbury factory. As her ruler and triangle slid smoothly over the paper Katrine looked on intrigued. Once Mary was confident she had all the elements correct she transferred the patterns to the heavy brown pattern cardboard.

"You are so quick. I have never seen anyone work like you before," Katrine said.

"Thank you. Where I used to work in New Zealand I had to be fast and versatile. I'm nervous though, because Santos is probably an expert at all this and I want to impress him," Mary replied.

Katrine eyes widened, her lower lip twitched a little then, after glancing around the room to ensure no-one could hear her, she leant close to Mary and whispered, "He can't even draw. Making a pattern would be impossible for him. He's a crazy man. Don't call him Santos - he gets very mad. We must call him Monsieur Dubois." Mary's inner alarm went off as her work-mate's words sunk in.

17

Having completed her first week with Santos Dubois, Mary was looking forward to her Friday night out with Annabel and the crowd who frequented La Huchette. The two girls were like ships in the night with their work schedules. Mary's dancing skills passed muster and she even began to enjoy the attention of both the French and English men who lined up to dance with her and Annabel. The girls chatted over a glass of iced water between sets as they snuggled up in the corner on a tatty banquette.

"Tell me all about your new boss, Kiwi?"

"Well, he's like a demented woman who constantly has her period. And yet he's a married man with a son, so I guess he's not gay. Apparently, his wife is really rich. I don't want to cross him - I've seen how he lashes out at his staff. He has a high turnover of employees - most people won't put up with him."

"How long will you put up with him"? Annabel asked as she sucked iced water through a straw.

"Just while I'm getting some experience. He's so lazy and I doubt he could actually design anything from the drawing board. This week, after I'd sketched a whole story-board of ideas and colours, I cut all the patterns and, with the help of the team, made up the samples in calico. He never thanked me or acknowledged that he liked them. I'm choosing the fabric samples on Monday and then will have the collection made up for live models. They're for the Women's Wear Daily editor to preview the week after next so, hopefully, that will give me some kudos."

The band started playing again and a very tall man, sporting a geometric haircut that was lavishly punctuated with purple streaks, appeared beside their table. He was reed thin and wore low-slung, black satin hipsters, cowboy boots and at least four rings on each hand.

"Bonjour, lovely Anglais ladies. You look so fabulous. Would you humble yourself and dance with a shy French man?" he said and looked at Mary with a full smile showing pure white, straight teeth. Both girls burst out laughing.

"If you're shy, then I'm the Prince of Wales!" Annabel quipped.

"I could like your Prince of Wales!" he said to Annabel. "Your friend is tall like me and she dances like a Doris Girl." He then turned to Mary.

"Please allow me just one dance?" He took her hand and kissed it flamboyantly. Mary repressed her initial negative reaction. She was so mesmerised by his totally 'over the top' appearance, she allowed herself to be lead to the dance floor.

He must have been at least six foot four because he towered over even Mary. She managed to keep up with the Swing and the Ceroc number. Thank goodness she'd had those lessons with Annabel. When they returned to the table Annabel was on the dance floor.

"Allow me to introduce myself. I'm known as Lou-Lou."
He offered Mary his hand across the table. It was surprisingly firm.

"I'm Mary." "Enchanté."

"What did you mean when you said a Doris girl?" Mary asked.

"Well, I work at the Moulin Rouge and the chorus line dancers are called Doris Girls. You are willowy and tall and the moment I saw you dancing, I put you in the Moulin Rouge." He fluttered his eyelids at Mary.

"Are you a dancer?" Mary asked.

"In my fantasies I am, but in reality I just make the dancers' costumes. Well, mostly repair them actually." Mary couldn't take her eyes off him. Although he was very camp in his stance and movements, he spoke with a beautiful deep voice and his generous smile radiated natural warmth.

"What's happening? You two falling in love?" Annabel kidded as she sat down with the two new friends.

"I love all beautiful women... and some beautiful men," Lou-Lou swiftly replied. He then left for the bar and returned with a bottle of champagne.

"To my two new best girlfriends who seem to be on a water budget!" he toasted.

"My goodness, what a fabulous taste! My first ever champagne," Mary exclaimed as bubbles went up her nose.

"In return for my generosity, I propose that you two meet me for a picnic tomorrow at 1pm in the grounds of Versailles. What do you think?" Lou-Lou asked.

"Yes," they answered in unison. After a lot more dancing and lots of laughter peppered with camp dialogue they said their protracted farewells and agreed on where to meet the next day.

"Oh Annabel, tonight I've had the best time ever! I do love Paris," Mary announced as they walked arm in arm, happily inebriated, across the Place Monge toward their apartment.

⌘

The next morning they caught the train to Château de Versailles. Mary was gobsmacked by the opulence of it. The palace appeared as if it had come directly from a fairy tale in one of her younger sister's story books. Lou-Lou was waiting out front, exactly where he'd said and held a basket with a chilly bag inside it. He stood out as if he was one of the attractions. Tourists slowed down to give him the once over. His purple cord bellbottoms matched the streaks in his hair. He teamed them with a fitted floral shirt and an ostentatious white neckerchief. A Japanese couple were taking his photo and he lapped it up.

"Coo coo, ladies, I'm over here." He waved wildly with his one free arm. They followed him past the queues of waiting tourists around to the rear of the magnificent building. Here they were blown away by the sight of the acres of stunningly manicured gardens laid out before them.

"Now we will find a cosy corner where we can set up our picnic and watch all the action," Lou-Lou announced. Mary had crimped her long unruly hair and wore cut off denim shorts with a red and white check shirt tied at the waist. Annabel was in a baggy maxi dress and both girls' wrists were adorned with multi-coloured Indian glass bangles. As the vibrant trio made their way along the shingle path edging the tranquil lake, children peddled past on small bikes and courting couples walked leisurely hand in hand. Fragrance from the jasmine hedges further enriched the romantic mood of the day. Once they'd laid out their rug, Lou-Lou placed their offering of quiche, tomatoes, cheese and a fresh baguette in what could only been termed a 'designer fashion'.

He tapped his large Cartier watch and said, "Now sit down and watch the lake. I have organised something very special for you both." Then he stood up and waved his arms as if conducting an orchestra. Enchanting melodic music enveloped them from all angles of the gardens. Simultaneously, the giant statues of men, nymphs and horses that sat within the lake began to gush water fountains in time to the music. The girls shrieked in delight.

"Isn't this wonderful? It happens every weekend in the summer. I'm always trying to find an excuse to be here," he said. From the chilly bag Lou-Lou produced another bottle of champagne.

Satisfied from their lunch and with happy hearts they lay on the grass and chatted about everything and nothing.

"I'm going off to find the loo," Annabel said and skipped off in the direction of the Palace. Mary felt more comfortable with Lou-Lou than she ever had with a man, other than Jamie of course. She knew Lou-Lou was gay but it was more than that – it was like they were 'kindred spirits'.

"So who do you work for in fashion, ma Kiwi?" Lou-Lou enquired in a more sober tone.

"A rather difficult man called Santos Dubois. Do you know him?"

Mary's new friend abruptly sat up. "That creature? You

can't call him a man. He's a maniac! What are you doing there with him?"

Mary gave Lou-Lou an abridged version of her job hunting, the need for French experience in the fashion world and how she felt good about the collection she was working on. He listened intently before he commented.

"I don't want to be negative, but that dreadful man will just use you and spit you out. Working for him will be of no benefit to you because he's a jealous twisted man and will never give you any credit. He's well known in fashion and gay circles and we all avoid him," he said.

Mary was astonished. "But he's married."

Lou-Lou patted her hand as he spoke. "Yes, to a rich ugly woman who paid for him to become a designer in return for him agreeing to be her husband and a father to her son. But he's a confused twisted devil. You know, Mary, if you ever decide to leave him I can organise you an audition as a dancer at the Moulin Rouge. They train you first and, with your figure, you'd be great." Mary offered a gracious smile.

"Thanks, but I need to at least try with Santos first. Besides, if I was going to audition, Annabel would have to as well. It's a life dream of hers to be a professional dancer."

"It's her height that might be a challenge. They want tall girls but, you never know, she could wear extra high heels. You just call me when you're ready."

18

As Mary munched her toast she sat and stared at the note paper. She wrestled with what words to write and in what order. Her mother would know she knew who André was because she would have discovered the letters and money were gone. Mary squirmed as it passed through her mind that her step-father may collect the post. He could then destroy or conceal the letter from her mother. After redrafting the letter for the fourth time, she neatly wrote out the final version and stuck the stamp perfectly in the corner.

"Penny for your thoughts, Kiwi," Annabel said as she joined her at their table.

"I've finally gathered enough courage to write to Mum but now I'm having second thoughts."

"Oh, I see. Well, why not look at it another way. What was it that finally gave you the confidence to write?" Annabel asked.

"After I left home I lived in a soulless hostel with a group of girls I couldn't really identify with. Here in Paris, dancing at the Huchette, meeting Lou-Lou, and living with you in our small but perfect apartment has helped me realise how happy

I can be. So I guess I just feel ready to reconnect with her," Mary replied.

"I like the part in that statement that refers to me! So I'll do you a favour and post it for you before you can change your mind!" Annabel grabbed the letter and was out the door before Mary could protest.

∽

Mary accompanied Santos to the wholesale fabric suppliers. She hinted at what colours and textures she liked and he then flagrantly made her choices his own. As soon as they'd left the warehouse he grabbed her by the arm. His face was so close she could smell his stale breath.

"Next time we visit the fabric company, IF there is a next time, I don't want you seeking all that attention from the imbeciles who work there. I am the boss! Is that clear?"

Mary was rooted to the spot. "I'm sorry," she muttered. This wasn't a battle she chose to fight. Get the collection finished first, then she could stand up for herself.

Back in the workroom, Mary effortlessly held the large shears at waist height on the cutting table. She sliced through the new silk as easily as if cutting into a wedge of butter. The staff clambered to vantage points to watch through the glass petition as she expertly cut each pattern then placed it with its cardboard copy ready for sewing.

Santos's massive insecurity invaded every corner of the workroom. He snapped unnecessary orders and slammed doors. But Mary's determination outweighed any fear. The staff were inspired and empowered by her stance and scurried to assist her at every turn. The next day she arrived early to commence sewing the samples.

"What do you think you are doing, you stupid betch?" Santos sprayed his tirade of verbal abuse. "I pay a sample sewer to do that. It's not your fucking job!" Mary stood up from the machine. She towered over him.

"Monsieur Dubois, if your desire is for this collection to be perfect then I must insist that I sew the initial two or three garments. That way the sample sewer will be able to see how I've cut the patterns. Then, and only then, can she take over." She feigned a smile and then added, "I was sure this was what you'd wish." He glared at her for a moment, and then slammed the door as he left the room.

Mary experienced a huge surge of satisfaction as she slipped the first lilac silk configuration on the dressmaker's dummy. Her colleagues wisely played it safe with their admiration. They all appeared to be busy elsewhere. After the second garment was complete Mary needed to pop to the loo. Within a minute she was joined by about six of the staff, including Wendi.

"We must speak quietly, but we have to tell you, Mary. Your work is amazing!" Wendi spoke for all of them.

"I don't know that Santos shares your enthusiasm," Mary replied as she dried her hands.

"He's a maniac. The better you make the collection, the more he will fume. Be careful, Mary," Wendi said before they returned to the workroom.

By the end of the day, five beautiful purple and lilac dresses were lined up in the sample room. Mary's original sketches were pinned behind them on the cork board. As she passed by Santos's office on her way out, and after a moment's consideration, Mary took a deep breath, tapped and opened his door before he could speak. She quickly thanked him for the privilege of assisting with the collection, then said good evening and closed his door.

As Mary walked past Wendi, she noticed her eyes were glued to the glass partition into Santos's office. No words came from his mouth... it was froth emanating from their boss's lips. He grabbed his sterling silver letter opener and, fuelled with rage, his spittle sprayed as he viciously gouged at his previously immaculate lacquered desk.

19

Over a five day period, and under extreme mental duress from a manic Santos Dubois, Mary completed sewing the collection. It consisted of eight dresses, four tops, two skirts, and two different styles of trousers. She photocopied and added four more colour-ways to her design drawings and presented the drawings alongside the garments on the dressmaker dummies in the boardroom.

The French editor of the prestigious American magazine 'Women's Wear Daily' was due to arrive at 10am. Santos made it very clear he wanted no interruptions during her visit. He glared specifically at Mary as he barked his orders. Wendi hurried into the glass panelled room under the pretext of putting mineral water and glasses on the table. Mary felt sick to her stomach, but not because she wasn't included. She'd already surmised that would be a fait accompli. But what if the woman didn't like the collection?

At 10.15 a thin, chic, middle-aged woman with a pointy nose and an angular black bob haircut swept into reception. Within seconds of Wendi's initial greeting, Santos appeared in the reception area and was all over the woman like a rampant rash. The experienced editor raised her hand with a 'stop' gesture of distaste as Santos attempted to manhandle her towards the boardroom. Wendi beckoned Mary over to her desk. Although they could see through the glass partitions into the boardroom, they were out of Santos's return sight line. Wendi pressed a forefinger to her lips. "Shush," she whispered as she turned on the intercom switch on her desk.

"You clever woman," Mary mouthed as they listened intently to the bullshit coming from Santos.

"I've spent weeks on this collection. I was inspired by the freshness of the colour purple. It's not been used, in my opinion, effectively over the last few seasons but works well with the 'peasant' look which I anticipate will be current this year," he spouted. Sweat beads formed on Mary's brow - she wanted to scream. Wendi steadied her.

"Stay calm and let's hear what the editor has to say."

From under her heavy black eyeliner the bony editor peered at each garment and even inspected the inside of a hem. She carefully studied the sketches before she uttered a word.

"Monsieur Dubois, surprised as I am, given some of your previous disasters, I have to say your fashion sketches are totally current and beautifully executed. You have been hiding your light. I'd like the right to use the sketches in our new season edition. The collection is most impressive. I'll be in touch when we're ready to do our next shoot and ask you to send over the samples to be photographed," she said.

Once it was patently clear Santos had usurped every ounce of credit, Mary couldn't bear it any more. Consumed with anger, she just managed to make it to the loo before she vomited. She felt just like she had the final time her step-father tried to rape her and she shot him. If she had a gun, she'd shoot Dubois right now. Revenge would feel sweet.

"Mary, open the door," Wendi called from outside the toilet cubicle. "Please come out. I've told Monsieur Dubois you are sick and that you are going home." Mary reluctantly opened the loo door.

"You are not the first he has done this to and you won't be the last. However, in the five years I've been here, you are definitely the best designer I have seen. He still needs you to oversee the production, so you still have a job. Have tomorrow off. You'll feel better in a day or two."

Mary stomped the three mile walk across Paris to the apartment. Walking helped to dilute her anger. By the time she arrived home her highly charged emotions had taken another turn. She felt dejected and very sorry for herself. Annabel had gone straight from work on a date and Mary couldn't bear the thought that she'd be on her own. She rummaged through her bag and found Lou-Lou's phone number.

"Hi, Lou-Lou, it's Mary."

"Yes, I know, ma chérie. You are my only friend with a Kiwi accent." Lou-Lou was delighted to be invited to cheer up his new friend. "I need to be back at the Moulin Rouge at 9pm in time for any costume disasters at the early show." They agreed to meet at an inexpensive brassiere in Rue Mouffetard.

After they'd ordered a smoked duck salad and a carafe of white wine, Lou-Lou gently stroked Mary's perfectly manicured hand.

"I know what this is about without you even speaking. That arsehole Dubois! Tell Lou-Lou everything in English so I don't miss any details." Mary felt a rush of relief, to have such an attentive sympathetic listener.

"Even though I knew he would take the credit, I thought I could handle it. But it was all my creation and work and he robbed it from me. It felt like a form of rape. I don't want to go back." Her eyes glistened with tears. Lou-Lou was momentarily quiet. Then he put down his fork and placed both hands on the table.

"I've an idea. Next week, there's an audition at the Moulin Rouge for potential new dancers and I know the exact routines they have to do. So if you are up for some hard work and prepared to let me coach you all weekend as well as Monday I'd have three days to get you into shape. Yes, before you speak, Annabel can audition as well," he said.

Mary ran her fingers through her hair and let out a little sigh. "OK, why not, but I am going back to the workroom one more time, regardless. Although he may be able to produce the collection, I'm bloody sure he's not having my sketches."

20

M ary was awake when Annabel arrived home from her date. She updated her friend on all the day's dramatic activities and told her about the Moulin Rouge audition. Annabel was rapt and agreed she'd throw a sicky from work and audition as well.

"Lou-Lou said you need to be at least five feet eight inches so we will tease your hair up a bit and you'll have to wear these shoes. I've seen you dance in very high heeled ones before so you'll be okay."

Annabel scowled. "I'm so pissed off my bloody parents didn't breed me just two inches taller! I want this so much," she managed to reply.

"Don't blame your parents. Some people have received worse things than a lack of height from their parents! Look, from what I've learnt through fashion and clothes, it's all an optical illusion. Wear those slim-line black jeans and the fitted black top. With the black high shoes you'll be fine," Mary said.

Lou-Lou's small studio flat was entered through a long, wide hallway and, fortunately, he had very broad minded, indulgent neighbours. The hall was the only space where they could rehearse. He had recorded the four main routines currently showing in Frenesie, which was the name of the current cabaret. The main routine was the can- can. Mary loved the way Lou-Lou said it - 'Carn-carn'. He had them kicking as high as possible and the first time they attempted doing a cartwheel in their high heels Mary hit the wall and bruised her hip. Annabel, however, spun neatly back upright onto her feet. At the end of the first day, Mary could hardly move and only just managed to get up the stairs to their apartment.

"Okay, you soak in the bath first and leave the water. I'll be straight in after you." Annabel turned the hot tap on full. Mary lay in the bath in agony. She doubted, given what she'd attempted to dance today, that she had any chance of getting through an audition. Annabel, with her background in classical ballet and lots of practice in modern dance, seemed to immediately grasp everything Lou-Lou showed them. He told them that, although he loved both art forms, he had to choose whether he pursued dance or fashion. Long term, he admitted, he would never be able to sustain the discipline needed for dancing.

The second day of rehearsing Mary managed the splits. Her companions roared with laughter when she first attempted to navigate her long legs to the floor. By the end of the third day Lou-Lou had to catch up with work so his input was over.

Mary phoned Wendi to say she had the flu and that she would need two more days off. Annabel told her boss the same. The girls pushed the sofa, table, and chairs into their bedroom to clear as much space as possible in their apartment and rehearsed there for eight hours straight. The following morning, both girls blow-dried their hair and painstakingly applied their makeup as per Lou-Lou's instructions. They agreed to treat themselves to a cab in a bid to preserve their grooming efforts.

As the cab entered the Pigalle area in the 9th arrondissement, Mary was surprised how seedy the streets looked. Grubby looking sex shops and sleazy bars advertising 'Peep Shows' lined the rubbish-strewn footpaths. The vision of the distinct red windmill overhead, coupled with Annabel's squeals of nervous delight, diverted her attention from the squalor as the cab pulled up outside the Moulin Rouge.

Lou-Lou sauntered out a side door to greet them. "Excellent, you're on time. You both look amazing - such a stunning contrast to each other. Follow me. We have 30 minutes for you to have a sneaky practice."

The girls followed Lou-Lou to a sewing room. It was lined with lavish, sequinned costumes and colourful head-dresses. He pushed his work table back against the wall leaving a workable space in the centre of the room.

"Now, we can't have any music in case someone hears but let's do a warm up." He slid into position and gracefully paced out the routine to a 1, 2, 3 count. Annabel struggled in her high heels so Mary knelt down and tightened the ankle straps.

"Don't worry about the pain! The main thing is that the shoes stay on, you stay upright, and they think you are tall!" Mary said.

Just before 11 Mary and Annabel, now wearing leotards and footless tights, followed Lou-Lou along the dark narrow corridor to the audition room. The established Moulin Rouge dancers were easy to identify - all willowy with their long black lycra-clad legs punctuated by colourful leg warmers. They ignored the line-up of the anxious looking girls waiting to audition.

"Attention please," an austere reed-thin woman of a certain age shouted. "I am Madame Pamela the choreographer. Our Doris Girls are going to show you a simple routine. They will execute it twice. Then I would ask all the dancers auditioning to take positions in the front row facing the mirror and we will see how you perform alongside them on their third run through."

Mary saw the Doris Girls wore ankle strapped high heels of subtle varying heights – that boded well for Annabel. Their faces oozed a sense of confidence and superiority and their kicks appeared to go on forever. She squeezed Annabel's hand and whispered, "Shit, I'm never going to be able to do this!"

A couple of smartly dressed older men slipped into the back of the room along with Lou-Lou. On cue, Mary and Annabel moved into the front line with the other eight nervous dancers. Annabel moved and kicked with ease, but Mary's nerves got the better of her. Once the routine was finished, Madame Pamela shouted, "On the count of three, please repeat the routine twice. Relax girls, it's a dance, not a torture!"

When Mary caught Lou-Lou's smile in the mirror she relaxed. This time it seemed to flow better as she gave it her all. By the second time through the routine, she had finally found her confidence.

"Thank you, girls. Now, we'd like you all to wait in the green room while we discuss your performance," said the choreographer as she dismissed them. While the other eight girls made uneasy small talk, Lou-Lou joined Mary and Annabel. They hovered together in a corner of the airless room.

"The grey haired man is Monsieur Jacki Clerico. He's the big boss here. They judge new girls not just on dancing ability but on how they look and the potential they think you have," Lou-Lou whispered. "It's the Moulin Rouge's 90th anniversary this year so they need to have more dancers for all the extra shows."

The two friends were the last to be called in to face the judges. Mary went first. She stood uncomfortably facing the thin choreographer and the two men. It was Monsieur Clerico who spoke.

"Mary, we all agree your 'look' is perfect. You fulfil all our criteria visually, but your dancing requires more skill." He paused and Mary bit her lip. Then he continued, "However, if you can pledge to attend extra rehearsal sessions, we are happy to offer you a contract beginning next month." She thanked them and was still in a state of shock when she joined the other two. She didn't speak till Annabel walked through to the judges and closed the door.

"That's fantastic, ma chérie. We will be working together!" Mary breathed in Lou-Lou's excessive Chanel No. 5 fragrance as he enthusiastically hugged her. The minutes seemed like hours as they waited for Annabel. She walked out with a dead pan face.

"Well?" Lou-Lou said.

"You go first, Mary," Annabel said.

"Well, I'm not taking the position if you haven't been

chosen as well, and that's all there is to it." Mary shoved her hands on her hips. There was a moment's silence.

"Well, Kiwi, if that's all there is to it, we are both going to be dancing at the Moulin Rouge," Annabel announced as she hugged her two friends.

21

Mary walked into Santos Dubois's studio early the following morning with a larger than usual tote bag across her shoulder. The audition the previous day had restored her pride and confidence. She decided she needed to achieve two more things before closing the door on the second most dreadful man she had ever met. Just as she left the board room where her photocopied sketches were still pinned to the wall, Wendi approached her.

"Hi, Wendi. I'm handing in my resignation today so please could you have my cheque ready for when I leave," she said. "That's not going to happen. Monsieur will never approve it. No-one ever resigns here - they only get sacked. Be sensible, Mary," Wendi replied. She scurried after Mary as she walked swiftly to the drawing desk in the workroom. Mary pulled open the drawer, scooped up her original sketches and quickly rolled them up before concealing them in her bag. As the two women walked back into the hall Santos arrived in reception.

"So, you are 'weell' now," he sneered.

"Yes, thank you for asking. I'd like to have a private chat if

I may?" Mary followed him into his office.

"No, get out! I don't want to chat with you. Go and get on with the production. All that silk needs to be cut," he shouted as he moved towards her to shut his door. Mary was inwardly trembling and she felt sick again. She wanted to run but stood her ground. Santos couldn't pass without having to look up at her.

"Monsieur Dubois, I won't be doing your production - I'm sure you can guess why. Here is my resignation. Please give me a cheque for what you owe me," she managed to say with only a slight falter. Santos Dubois stamped his foot like a small child.

"You betch. I took you on - a nobody from the other end of the earth. Pay you? Get fucked!" Mary thought he was going to hit her. But she didn't move and focussed on freezing her facial expression.

"If you don't pay me, I will walk straight over to the offices of Women's Wear Daily and do a sketch for them so they know who really did the designs," she said. At that moment Wendi walked into the office, which momentarily deflected Santos's attention.

"Monsieur Dubois, in anticipation of you letting Mary go, I have her pay cheque here for you to sign," she said. White froth gathered at the corners of Santos's mouth. He hesitated, then scrawled on the cheque and slapped it on the desk. Mary swiftly scooped it up and, without a word, left the room. Wendi followed her out.

"See her off the premises. Don't let the oversized betch take a thing," Santos yelled. Once they were outside the building, Mary squeezed Wendi's hand.

"Why do you stay with that awful man?" she asked.

"I've been trying to get another job but it's very difficult, and I have a daughter to support. What you did in there was brilliant. I've never seen anyone stand up to him before. Good luck."

Mary took a pen from her bag. "Good luck to you, too. By the way, here's your indelible ink pen back. I borrowed it from your desk to make a few adjustments to the art in the boardroom."

22

For an entire month, all Mary and Annabel seemed to do was rehearse. They were at the Moulin Rouge for at least seven hours every day. Mary's long legs became acquainted with muscles and tendons she never knew existed. They spent two evenings a week watching the entire show from spare seats within the theatre to get a feel for the reality of what it would be like once their preliminary rehearsals were complete.

Mary read all she could get her hands on about the history of the show. She found it was based on the grand tradition of the historic French Music Hall. The show brochure boasted that over 600,000 spectators a year flocked there to see the most beautiful girls in the world. She was astounded at the number and diversity of people prepared to pay 800 francs to visit the Moulin Rouge.

There were two sessions each evening. The first, at 9pm, offered dinner. The second at 11pm was for just the show. Champagne was always available. Hordes of tourists queued on sumptuous red carpet surrounded by walls decorated in Belle Epoque style to admire the murals. Morris columns were adorned with original posters of the artists who had performed on the mystical Moulin Rouge stage, including some that Mary recognised like Edith Piaf, Frank Sinatra and Liza Minnelli.

Since they had begun rehearsals, Annabel and Mary were usually too exhausted to go out in the evenings. However, Annabel still managed to date Marc, their landlord, when he was in town.

"He won't take 'no' for an answer and besides, until we are on full pay, a girl has to have a night out," Annabel quipped.

"That's a bit cut throat, don't you think? Sounds like you're just using him," Mary replied as they lay face to face and toes to toes on the sofa.

"What about you, Kiwi? You should be dating. Whatever happened to put you off men can't last forever. This is Paris - you should have a boyfriend!" Annabel tickled the balls of Mary's feet with her toes as she spoke.

"Well, I 'date' Lou-Lou. I enjoy his company and he loves fashion as much as I do. He's even slipped in some suggestions of mine for the new costumes," Mary said. Annabel was now familiar with Mary's practiced avoidance at conversations about her lack of a boyfriend.

"Well, for one thing, life is not only about fashion, and secondly, in case you hadn't noticed, your Lou-Lou is gay." The phone interrupted Annabel's flow and Mary rolled off the sofa to answer it.

"Speak of the devil! We were just chatting about you." There was a short silence while she listened to what Lou-Lou was saying. "Yes, come over, we'd love some food and wine. See you soon," Mary said before she hung up. Lou-Lou visited often and was always lavish with gifts of interesting French food that the girls would not otherwise have tried.

"Now, Lou-Lou, it's opportune you called when you did

as I need back-up," Annabel said as she opened the door.

"Oui? What back-up do you need?"

"Our dear Kiwi friend should be dating as I don't think you'll be marrying her anytime soon!" Mary giggled.

"Oh, I don't know. I think I'd look great in a bridal gown designed by moi!" Lou-Lou spun around on the spot. As they shared Lou-Lou's food they cracked a few more gay jokes and continued laughing.

"Now, on a more serious note but staying on the same subject, I overheard a conversation from one of Monsieur Clerico's friends yesterday," Lou-Lou said in a more sombre tone.

"I saw you hovering not so subtly by those men yesterday at rehearsal," Mary said.

"Yes, it's customary for some of the regulars who entertain at the Moulin Rouge on a corporate level to have a peek at the new girls during their first dress rehearsal. Monsieur Clerico says it's 'Good Public Relations'." Lou-Lou was always a fount of information.

"Go on! What did you hear?"

"Well, first let me ask you, Mary, do you remember the tallest of the three men, the one with greying hair?"

"Yes, he was handsome in a James Bond type of way. Why?" Mary bit her lip again. Annabel was intrigued.

"He said he thought you were devastatingly beautiful, Mary." Lou-Lou paused for effect, slapped his hands on his cheeks and raised his eyebrows at Mary.

"Rubbish! That's a Lou-Lou terminology, not a James Bond one!" Mary exclaimed. "What did he really say?"

"Something to that effect. He's invited to the drinks party

after the first dress rehearsal of the new intakes on Monday afternoon. So be prepared, Kiwi. He's a good catch."

By Monday, the girls were both anxious and excited. As Mary stared at herself in the mirror, she wondered what Jamie would think if he saw her now. Would he even recognise her? Her makeup had been dramatically applied with an emphasis on glossy red lips. Her unruly hair was pulled tight in a chignon at the back of her head which enabled her to balance the anchored feather and rhinestone head dress securely. Lou-Lou had, with great ceremony, assisted her to dress in the first costume of the performance.

"My god, my Kiwi girlfriend, you are so beautiful and your legs go on forever. You were born to wear fishnets!" Lou-Lou gently kissed her cheek as she waited apprehensively at the side of the stage.

"Thank you for everything," she whispered as she heard her music cue. Although Mary had mastered the dancing routines, after an hour of solid performing and five complex costume changes, she realised that dancing was only half of the skill required. Lou-Lou manipulated things so he could be her dresser on that particular occasion but, once it was real show time, she would be allotted a dresser who she'd share with three other dancers.

When the girls had removed their heavy make-up and were dressed back in their own clothes, they joined the party gathered for drinks in the larger green room. A collection of Moulin Rouge management, sponsors and other dancers awaited them.

23

It was a relief to be out of her costume. Mary had slipped on a pair of denim jeans and a pastel granny-print shirt she'd made. She pushed through the busy party room towards the bar searching for her two friends along the way. As she turned with glass in hand, he was waiting for her - his distinct salt and pepper grey hair giving his open face a warm glow. "Hello, I am Gabriel." He offered his hand to Mary. She quickly juggled her glass and hand bag to accept, and in the process spilt half of her wine on the floor.

"Oops, sorry, I'm such a klutz at times," she said with a grimace. He smiled directly at her.

"I shouldn't worry. Let's start again. I am Gabriel and you are?"

Mary placed her glass on the bar before extending her hand again. As their fingers met a delicious sensation passed through her.

"I'm Mary," was all she could manage. His formality coupled with his eloquent voice quite unhinged her.

"Mary, you dance beautifully and look like you belong on that stage," Gabriel said. He moved closer and she detected a delicate but masculine fragrance.

"Thank you, and thank you for speaking in English to me. Where are you from?" Mary asked.

"I am French but with my work I deal with English speaking clients all the time so I guess I've become quite fluent. But this word 'klutz' must be from your country as I haven't heard it before. Where exactly are you from?" He smiled and handed her a fresh glass of wine.

"I'm a New Zealander and my friends here usually refer to me as 'Kiwi.'" At that moment Lou-Lou appeared beside her.

"There you are, ma chérie, we've been looking for you everywhere," he said in his loudest voice.

"Lou-Lou, this is Gabriel." Gabriel immediately extended his hand to Mary's friend.

"I think we may have met here before?" Gabriel said in French.

"Oui, I hover in the background at these affairs. But I must steal my friend away now as we have arranged to go for dinner." Lou-Lou gave Mary's back a gentle push away from the bar and whispered, "Just go with the flow." Mary smiled at Gabriel, then took Lou-Lou's hand as he led her through the crowded room.

"I was enjoying that," she said once they were in the hallway. "Why did you pull me away?"

"You don't want to appear too available or keen," Lou-Lou replied.

"Wait for me," Annabel called out behind them. "Where are you two off to in such a rush?"

"Lou-Lou tells me we are going for dinner but I'm skint, not having had a pay cheque for a while, so it better be a cheapy," Mary said.

The three friends sat at a pizza place in Rue Mouffetard dissecting every minute of their performance before the conversation turned to Gabriel.

"So will you go out with him if he invites you?" Annabel asked.

"I have to say he is the most attractive man I've met since I've been here, but with Lou-Lou whisking me away like that I may not see him again. He didn't even get a chance to ask for my phone number." Mary shot Lou-Lou a reproachful look.

"Tut tut. A French man doesn't operate like your sissy Englishmen. If he wants you, he will make it his business to find you," he replied.

ↄᴑↄ

The girls performed in their first show to a paying audience the next evening and Mary, who had to share a dresser, found it absolutely frantic backstage. By the fifth performance evening in a row both girls were shattered.

Early Saturday morning the buzzer from downstairs broke into Mary's sleep. Their end of the intercom had been permanently broken since they arrived so she poked her head out the window and called in French, "Who is it?" She could see a man with a peaked cap holding a bouquet of flowers.

"My delivery is for Mary Kiwi," he shouted back. Mary threw a robe on and flew down the three flights of stairs. When she walked back into the apartment with the enormous, fragrant bouquet, Annabel was up and filling the coffee pot.

"Are those for me?" Annabel asked.

"There's no bloody way I would have done those stairs that

quickly if they were. They are all mine!" Mary tentatively took the white, gold-edged card out of the envelope which had Mary Kiwi written on the front.

"Come on, read it out loud. What does it say?" Annabel poured black coffee into two mugs while Mary gazed at the card for a moment and then glowed as she read out loud.

'It was delightful to meet you on Monday evening. I'd be honoured if you would agree to join me tomorrow evening (Sunday) for dinner at 7pm at the Hôtel des Grandes Écoles on Rue du Cardinal Lemoin. It is quite near your apartment. I was unable to find your phone number to confirm but will be waiting at the restaurant regardless. I do hope you will join me.
Gabriel Aris.'

So he must know Sunday is my night off. But how did he find my address?"

"I'd hazard a guess that one of his chums at head office got it for him. It's on our pay info," Annabel said.

"Oh my god, what shall I wear?"

Late afternoon on Sunday, Annabel watched while Mary changed clothes for the fifth time. She finally decided on a black suede midi length pencil skirt and one of the latest 'body shirts'. It looked fantastic as it clung to her torso like a bathing suit, showing off her exquisite figure. It fitted so well because it was secured by two domes at her crutch over the top of her sheer black tights.

"Bloody hell, this contraption may look good but these

metal domes are sticking into my what's it," Mary exclaimed. "Well, you now have only twenty minutes to arrive at

the restaurant so you don't have time for another change. Or, knowing you, to replace the domes. Grin and bear it." Annabel was losing patience.

"Okay, okay, I know I'm a pain. It's just that this is a first for me." Mary wiggled in discomfort as she spoke.

"Yes, I'm aware of that fact and I don't mean to sound short, but you've been trying on clothes for nearly three hours now! And I really do want you to have a boyfriend. I was becoming a little concerned about your sexual orientation!" Annabel threw her friend a wink.

Mary walked up the path of the Hôtel des Grandes Écoles ten minutes late. To her surprise there wasn't really anything particularly grand about it at all. The tall gates and small garden walk to the entrance were charming in an old fashioned way, but the building itself was just a large villa. Gabriel was seated on the only chair in the restricted foyer, leafing through a copy of Paris Match. When he saw Mary he immediately stood up, walked over and took her hand to kiss it.

"You look beautiful, Mary. I suggest we go directly through to the restaurant."

They were greeted by a bespectacled hostess who led them to a table in the far corner of the room. Gabriel steered Mary to the chair facing the room. He told the hostess he would prefer to sit with his back to the room so he could directly face his guest. As the hostess adjusted the place settings, Mary took in the slightly faded grandeur of the intimate dining room, with its smattering of assorted guests. At one table there were tourists, at another an older married couple, and then two women on their own.

"The food here is excellent in an older style French way, and I thought it would be easy for you to find, being near your apartment." Gabriel reached over and squeezed her hand. Mary's natural instinct was to pull it away but she reasoned she would have to become intimate with a man one day, so maybe this was the first step. He explained the menu and Mary was happy to be guided by him, except when it came to ordering snails for a starter.

"You are in Paris, Mary. You should try everything. And the snails are smothered in so much garlic I'm sure you will find them tasty," he said.

"I was brought up on a farm. We killed and ate our own meat, but I draw the line at eating the slimy snails my mother used to exterminate for eating our vegetable garden." She had nearly finished her pâté when Gabriel leant across holding out the weird looking instrument he used to manipulate the snails from their shells.

"Open wide, just taste one." He popped the little lump of slime in her mouth and waited for her reaction.

"Wow! That's really garlicy. I wouldn't want to breathe on anyone too closely after eating those." As Mary wiped her mouth with her napkin, Gabriel leaned over and gently kissed her lips.

"That is why we both need to eat them, so neither of us will be offended." He sat back and smiled. Mary felt confused. Other than Jamie's kiss good-bye this was new to her. She always held her face away from her step-father and he was never interested in kissing anyway. She needed to try a few more to see if she really liked it.

While they ate their medium rare Chateaubriand steak, Gabriel slipped his foot out of his Gucci loafer and, hidden by the floor-length table cloth, subtly rubbed her leg. Mary initially stiffened and her reflex was to kick him, but she reminded herself that she should at least try. Accompanied by easy chatter and laughter, by the end of the meal she had discovered a new enjoyable sensation as his foot touched her inner thigh. It was right up near the dome of her body suit.

As he charmed her with stories of his travels she studied him carefully. His salt and pepper hair was cut so it slightly covered his ears and his skin shone with the remainder of a summer tan. But it was his eyes that captivated her. He looked directly at her as he spoke. It made her feel that in that moment she was the centre of his world.

It was a dry, serene Paris evening as they walked arm in arm towards her apartment and Mary experienced a new sense of anticipation with the warmth of his presence at such close proximity.

"This is where I live, up there." She pointed up to the third floor where the apartment lights were still on.

"Mary, I know you have three days off from next Sunday with the public holiday being on Monday so I would like to invite you to come to Monte Carlo with me. I have a little business to attend to there." As he spoke he held her hands and looked directly into her eyes, then gently pressed his lips to hers. Mary allowed the kiss then stepped back.

"I've never been away with a boyfriend before."

"It will be wonderful. We can swim and I will show you the sights." He kissed her again.

"Oh, all right, why not," she said. He took out a silver fountain pen and asked for her phone number. Then he kissed her once more before she pulled away and hurried upstairs.

"Oh, Annabel, I'm in love!" Mary said as she kicked off her platforms and flopped onto the sofa.

"Wow, that happened quickly. You don't think he's a bit old for you?" Annabel said.

Mary looked a little puzzled.

"Too old? I didn't think about that. Maybe I'm attracted to older men. Anyway, he's only about twelve years older," she replied. Annabel sipped on a glass of white wine.

"Is there enough in that bottle for a small one for me?" Mary asked. Annabel handed her a glass. "I just agreed to go to Monte Carlo with a man on Sunday. I don't even know where Monte Carlo is." Mary's face radiated happiness.

"Well, it's on the French Riviera and, according to my mother, quite the place to be. However, I remember my father saying it had become a 'sunny place for shady people', whatever that means. If it were me I wouldn't object, I'd be there in a flash."

24

Concerned about what to wear in Monte Carlo Mary managed, in between shows, to buy an off-cut of beautiful black silk de chine from one of her favourite fabric shops at the base of Sacré Coeur. She cut the pattern in Lou-Lou's costume room at the Moulin Rouge and he kindly offered to sew it up for her. Annabel insisted that Mary invest in some new underwear for her weekend away and, as the girls were leaving the building, they heard a call from behind.

"Coo coo!" It was the 'third musketeer'. "Did you think you were going to sneak out to Galeries Lafayette without me?" Lou-Lou asked.

"Well, to be honest, we didn't think you'd be interested in my undies," Mary replied.

"I'm interested in everything a woman wears. Besides, I need an excuse to have a look around the lingerie department myself and they tend to give me funny looks when I go there on my own," he said.

The striking threesome drew a few lingering looks as they rode the escalator to the mezzanine floor. The magnificent dome that lorded over the famous department store should have prepared Mary for the exorbitant prices charged for the supposed privilege of shopping there.

"My god, I'm not paying that much for a bra!" Mary said as she wrestled Lou-Lou to see the accompanying price tag. All three squashed into a fitting room as Mary tried on the most delicate, beautiful white lace creation she had ever seen. "Oh, Mary, it's divine, especially with the matching knickers." Annabel held up the transparent bikini briefs edged in delicate lace with a shimmering crystal in the centre of a tiny silk bow at the centre front.

"There's nothing to them. If I buy the set it will be half my first week's wage. That's ridiculous!" Mary blushed from her neck to her forehead.

"Have you ever been with a man before?" Annabel whispered out of ear shot of Lou-Lou.

"Have you?" Mary snapped, as she feigned interest in the bin of reduced knickers.

"Don't get all prickly, Kiwi. Yes, I've had sex plenty of times, as well you know, and I enjoy it! So if you want to ask me anything I don't mind." The girls continued to scour through a reduced price bin but none of the merchandise was anywhere near as exquisite as the set Lou-Lou had first chosen.

"Where's he gone? I think we need to be getting back to work. I'll just take the underwear I have," Mary said.

Lou-Lou reappeared. He held two small Galeries Lafayette carrier bags. "Now, mes chéris, a white set for you, Mary, and a black set for you, Annabel - my birthday and Christmas present to you both." He handed them the bags and kissed them both.

"I can't accept this. It's too expensive, Lou-Lou." Before

Mary could continue he shushed her with his finger.

"If you are going to have an affair with a wealthy Frenchman the first thing you must learn is to accept gifts graciously. Do not protest. We men only give because it gives us pleasure." He basked in the glory as both the girls squealed and hugged him at the same time.

~

The plane tickets were delivered to Mary at the Moulin Rouge. There was a note inside from Gabriel to say a taxi would collect her on Sunday morning at 7am from outside her apartment to take her to the airport where he would meet her. Because she only arrived home at 2am after her Saturday performance, Mary barely had three hours sleep. She wanted to look perfect so she got up an hour earlier to dress and carefully apply her makeup ready to meet Gabriel at the airport.

Once she sank into the comfy leather seat of the taxi she hoped she would doze, but uninvited memories and the fear of her step-father invaded her thoughts. The shame was imbedded in her psyche. She started to tell the cabbie to turn around and take her home then stopped herself. Annabel's words came back to her. She'd plucked up the courage to tell her friend that she had experienced a bad situation with sex and moved on, but that she was very nervous about how to handle this new situation. It was almost the truth.

Annabel said, "Take deep breathes and relax, have a really big glass of wine or bubbles, and think sexy thoughts." Mary had never had a sexy thought in her life until the other night at dinner.

The taxi pulled up outside the main doors of the airport and Mary spotted Gabriel before he saw her. He stood very tall and handsome next to his black wheelie bag with a newspaper neatly tucked under his arm. He wore a well cut navy blazer and a pair of casual, rust coloured corduroy pants. Mary felt her heart race as his eyes finally registered on her across the departure hall. His entire face lit up and his smile sent a shiver of expectancy through her body. He greeted her in the polite French fashion with a peck on both cheeks.

"Mary, you look so fresh considering how little sleep you've probably had." As they both only had 'carry on' bags, he directed her straight to the departure gate. Mary enjoyed the way Gabriel held her hand, and they chatted for the entire hour's duration of the flight.

On arrival at Nice airport a chauffeur, complete with peaked cap, held up a sign with Gabriel's name on it. Gabriel instructed the driver to take them along the scenic route to Monaco. Mary was captivated with how aquamarine in colour the sea appeared by comparison with the duller shade at the beaches in New Zealand. Gabriel explained there was only a small tide and practically no waves in the Mediterranean, hence the water appeared a lot lighter in colour.

As the chauffeur skilfully negotiated the large Mercedes around the narrow cornered roads down into Monte Carlo, Gabriel gave Mary a tourist-type commentary.

"Prince Rainier had to do something to save his nearly bankrupt principality from reverting to France. So he converted it to a tax free haven and married a movie star which attracted the world's attention to the city, which is in fact treated as a separate country, named Monaco. That part of the city overlooking the port, where the casino is situated, is called Monte Carlo."

Mary was enchanted with the smaller, older buildings with their frescos, ornate cornicing and blue window shutters. Sadly, these pretty buildings struggled to maintain their views of the ocean amongst the newer, ugly sky-scrapers that dominated the sky line.

Their car drew up in front of the Hôtel de Paris which was located directly to one side of the casino which dominated the square. A uniformed doorman opened the car door and Mary, fascinated by the whole experience, followed Gabriel through the swing-door entrance.

"Wow, this is amazing," she commented. The reception area alone was about the same size as two New Zealand homes. Polished marble floors were a perfect canvas for the oversized vases of fragrant fresh flowers that adorned the antique tables sitting strategically around the foyer.

Once Gabriel had checked in, a white uniformed bell boy escorted them up to their room. Mary's nerves nearly gave way. The bed was as big as Texas with an antique chaise longue along its end. Bevelled glass doors with extravagant brocade drapes opened onto a small Juliette balcony that overlooked the casino square. As soon as the bellboy left the room Gabriel took Mary in his arms.

"I have wanted to do this since I first saw you." He pressed his lips to hers and she relaxed as he gently probed her mouth with his tongue. Then Mary pulled away slightly and blushed. "Um, I'm new to all this Gabriel, so can we take it slowly?"

"Of course, ma chérie, I will take 'it' as slowly as you

desire." Mary nodded and leant towards him. As he kissed her they fell onto the large bed. He moved to kiss her neck and stroke her hair.

"Let's get undressed, ma chérie." Gabriel stood up and placed his jacket on the chair, then removed his shoes and shirt. Mary stroked his bare muscular chest and tried to think sexy thoughts. She inhaled his aftershave and noticed how it melded with his manly body fragrance. He very slowly unbuttoned her blouse and a flash of her step-father invaded her thoughts. As she struggled to push the memory out of her mind, she shuddered.

"What is wrong, my little Kiwi, are you frightened? It is not my intention to hurt you."

"No, I'm not frightened of you. It's just all very new to me." Gabriel continued kissing her then gently helped her undress. She was down to her new bra and knickers.

"My god, your body is so beautiful," he said. Mary blushed and realised she was probably beetroot red from head to toe, but Gabriel didn't seem to notice. She took deep, quiet breathes as, in one action, he undid the bra and ever so gently rubbed her breasts. Her nipples stiffened as her desire heightened. It felt so good. Maybe she'd finally won the battle.

She relaxed and rejoiced in the newness of lust as she welcomed each new sensation. He kissed down her torso to her thighs and, once he had gently slid her knickers off, he discreetly reached to the side-table drawer and skilfully peeled a French letter on his erect penis. Mary's passion now matched his own as he slowly entered her. In the next few moments all Mary's damaged memories dissipated and she lost herself to her first amazing climax.

When they had finally exhausted their love making, Gabriel filled the oversized marble bath, added Guerlain bath salts and they snuggled together in the warm water eating room–service, smoked salmon sandwiches and sipping on champagne.

It was late afternoon by the time they left the hotel room. Mary floated on air as they walked down to the port. They strolled arm in arm, admiring all the magnificent yachts, then wandered on through the shopping arcade.

"Please choose something and let me buy it for you." Gabriel stood beside Mary as she stared transfixed at the Channel Boutique window.

"Thank you for your offer but I prefer to wear my own designs. I just love to look at what all the designers are doing each season."

"Really? So there's another side to you apart from dancing? I'm intrigued," he said as he hugged her close.

"Ah, yes, there's more to me than dancing." Mary playfully flicked her hair. The next shop was a jewellery store. Gabriel pressed the security buzzer and guided Mary inside.

"I'd like to have a closer look at that delicate looking heart in the window display please," he said to the shop assistant. The assistant seemed to study them intently. Mary caught a glimpse of them in the mirrored wall and was momentarily embarrassed. It did look a bit like she was with her father.

"If you won't allow me to buy you a dress then you must allow me to give you this heart." The heart was sterling silver and very delicate. A tiny diamond was set in the scoop at the top of the heart, which hung from silver box chain. The assistant placed it in a black velvet box and handed it to Mary in a small lacquered carrier bag.

In the early evening Gabriel excused himself. He told Mary he had a quick meeting with his business contact in the bar. After he left, Mary searched everywhere for the hair dryer but had no luck. Desperate to wash her hair, she popped down to reception to ask for one. Across the lobby she spotted Gabriel engrossed in conversation on the public telephone. He didn't see her and she was keen to get herself looking good before dinner so discreetly returned to their room.

She took her time as she washed and blow-dried her hair, and then applied her make-up, a little heavier for evening as advised by Lou-Lou. She slipped into her new dress just before Gabriel appeared back in the room.

"That dress is so chic. Did you make it?" Gabriel asked.

Mary beamed. "I was influenced by one from Yves St Laurent's current collection."

The dress was a copy of a man's smoking jacket complete with a black satin revere collar and a double-breasted line of jet black buttons. The shoulder line was made to appear stronger by the addition of slightly oversized shoulder pads. It featured a self-fabric half-belt at the back waistline anchored by two more of the shimmering jet buttons. Mary wore sheer black tights and the dress length sat a good five inches above her knees. The retro, black patent-leather stilettos she'd found in a box in Lou-Lou's workroom showcased her long slim legs.

Gabriel dressed in a black suit, white shirt and a red tie. He placed the silver heart around her neck and lovingly kissed her décolletage as he secured the clasp. They stepped out of the lift at precisely the same time as Santos Dubois and his wife entered the restaurant.

"Oh shit! I think that's my ex-boss." By the time Gabriel and Mary had been shown to their seats Santos was already seated.

Mary was aware of the glances she received as she walked across the room. In her heels she stood as tall as Gabriel and, once the initial embarrassment passed, her heart swelled with pride at being at his side.

"Why 'shit'? And why is he your ex-boss, ma chérie?" Gabriel asked once they had chosen from the menu.

"He's a nasty piece of work. He owns a fashion house and I was his assistant designer. He treats his staff badly and took the credit himself for all my designs. So I resigned and Lou-Lou encouraged me to audition for the Moulin Rouge. The rest you know."

As Mary spoke she had a clear view of Santos's wife across the room. The wife had a faded kind of beauty and was wearing a dress she may have fitted into in a previous decade but now it was clearly too tight for her. Her blonde hair was just that fraction over-processed and this added to her aged appearance.

After the main course Mary needed to visit the bathroom. Gabriel directed her across the room near to where the Dubois's sat. Her preference would have been to return to the lobby but she was bursting after three glasses of champagne. As she returned to her seat, Santos stood up and moved towards her. He reeked of stale wine and intercepted her just before she managed to sit down.

"So it is you, betch! Are you working as a whore now? Wearing Yves Saint Laurent and staying in a hotel with a married man! Or has he told you you're his mistress? That old line! You have come down in the world."

His spittle sprayed Mary as he spoke. She couldn't quite register what she had just heard. Married? Gabriel was married? Santos's wife appeared at his side.

"Come Santy, don't upset yourself with this creature!" The sullen woman took his arm and guided him back to the table. Mary felt the entire restaurant focus on her. Very quietly and deliberately she sat down then leant forward and asked, "Are you married?"

"Yes," he replied. Although all Mary wanted to do was run, she forced her tears back and in a composed manner carefully stood up, walked to the door and out of the hotel.

25

Outside the hotel, Mary kicked off her stilettos and broke into a run. She slowed down once she reached the most screened-off part of the gardens in the middle of the square. The feet of her tights were ripped to shreds so she pulled them off and, bare-footed, slumped down on a park bench. Shame and humiliation engulfed her. An uncontrolled howl, full of all the despair and hurt that had been buried inside her for the past years, escaped her. She pulled at her hair then beat her fists on the bench until she drew blood. Gabriel quietly arrived beside her.

"Fuck off!" she managed to say between sobs.

"No, I won't. I want to talk to you." He kept his distance at the other end of the bench. Mary quietened down. She was exhausted and, besides, she had nowhere to go.

"I'm sorry, ma chérie. I wrongly assumed you knew I was married. I didn't mean to hurt you." She clutched her bleeding knuckles and glared at him.

"Assumed I knew! Why would I assume that? Do you think I'm some slut that knowingly sleeps with married men?" Mary wiped her running nose on her sleeve. "Why would I want to be with a married man? I'm only 18 years old and I've never made love to anyone before," she snapped. "I feel degraded." Gabriel dropped his face into his hands. When he looked up, Mary saw there were tears in his eyes.

"You are right. I have made a big mistake. I am used to the company of a different type of woman. My relationship with my wife is very bad but I have two sons, so I can't walk away."

"What! You have children? You are a complete arsehole! In fact, this all sounds so close to home I now understand how my mother felt when this happened to her. What a fool I am!"

As Mary spoke she completely lost control. Her body wracked with sobs of despair. When Gabriel tried to place his hand on her shoulder she slapped it away. Eventually she calmed down and accepted his clean white handkerchief.

"If I had somewhere else to go I would, but I'm stuck here. You can book yourself into another hotel room and change my ticket. I want to go back to Paris tomorrow." She loudly blew her nose.

"I will do as you wish. Come, let's go back to the hotel and have a drink." Gabriel stood up.

"Don't you tell me what to do. I've been bullied and deceived by the best. That's what I came across the world to get away from and I'm not walking into another pile of shit," Mary retorted. He sat back down.

"Please, Mary, your bile is burning my heart."

"Fuck your heart. You have been screwing with mine!" The tears started again. Mary sat back down. Gabriel waited a few minutes then moved beside her.

"As long as we are having an honesty session, what did

you mean about your mother?" Gabriel asked. Mary shot him a questioning look and then took a breath before responding.

"My mother was seduced by a French man in New Zealand. Unbeknown to her he was married and I was the result. He deserted her when he found she was pregnant. So the best she could do was marry the man who is my step-father, a vile warped man," she said and blew her nose again. Gabriel remained silent for a few moments before he responded.

"It is I who am the fool. I have never met a woman like you before. You are so genuine. I watched my own mother 'manage' my father and turn a blind eye to his mistresses - not that it's any excuse for my behaviour. I also didn't realise how young you are... but it's only a twelve year gap," he said.

"As you say, 'if we're being honest', what is so terrible about your wife that you don't want to be with her?" Mary asked.

"I loved her faithfully in the beginning. She was beautiful and enchanting but by the time our second child was born, she had become a most demanding person. I suppose I wasn't equipped to cope. Then I found out she had been secretly drinking wine every day - the house-keeper showed me the stash of empty bottles she had to conceal every week. In a way, I was relieved as I could blame the alcohol for all our problems. I confronted her and she agreed to attend a rehabilitation centre. But when she came back home she couldn't sustain it and started drinking again. So I leave her to it and seek female comfort in other places." He fidgeted on the seat.

"That's no excuse. I'm going back to the hotel now." Mary started walking back in the direction of the hotel. The well-trained doorman didn't bat an eyelid as Mary, with her mascara-smeared face, walked bare-foot into the foyer carrying her stilettos and handbag. She grabbed the key off Gabriel, gave him back his sodden handkerchief and walked swiftly to the lift. Once in the room she stripped off her dress and lay in her undies on the bed.

She hesitantly picked up the phone and dialled her home number. After a few rings it went to answer phone. She heard the funny message Annabel and she had recorded and wondered if she'd ever feel that happy again. Although she was tempted to phone Lou-Lou, after a short deliberation, she thought better of it. Mary wrapped herself in the hotel's thick towelling robe, took a half bottle of champagne from the mini bar and wandered out onto the balcony.

As she sipped her drink she asked herself, "Why does it always go wrong for me? Only a few hours ago I was making love on that bed and now look at me. Maybe that's all I'm really worth!"

Once she'd finished the champagne she drifted off to sleep. In the morning she was woken by a gentle tap on her door. When she didn't respond a voice called out 'room service'. She pulled on the discarded robe and opened the door.

Gabriel stood there with a room-service tray of coffee and croissants. "Before you tell me to go away, please let me bring this in as I have something to tell you about your flight," he said.

She begrudgingly allowed him in. He placed the tray on the side table and poured her a coffee. She took it and sat down on the bed.

"I am sorry, Mary, but I've tried all the airlines and, because it is a public holiday today, they are fully booked until tomorrow. So I'm afraid you will have to stay one more night." Mary stood up and walked to the open French doors with her coffee.

"Well, I guess it won't kill me," she said.

"Do you mind if I share a coffee and a croissant with you?" he asked.

"If you must." She sat down on the armchair while he perched on the uncomfortable chaise longue. They ate the croissants in silence.

"Perhaps you would feel better if you went to the beach for the day. I'm happy to escort you. A day in the sun by the sea is always healing." Gabriel offered her a hesitant smile.

"I'll think about it," Mary said. After a little more cajoling Mary agreed to go to the beach. As much as her heart hurt, she didn't wish to sit in the hotel all day. On exiting the elevator, she saw Santos Dubois holding court with his wife and a couple of friends across the foyer. Gabriel immediately appeared at her side.

"That bastard!" Mary clenched her fists.

"Listen carefully, Mary. No matter what's gone between us, do not let him see that he has had any effect. Retain your dignity. We will walk past him as if nothing has transpired and if there's any talking to be done, I'll do it. Understand?" Gabriel said. Mary nodded.

They both pushed on their sun glasses and Gabriel took Mary's beach towel and hung it, with his, across his arm. They looked every inch the united couple as they headed towards the main hotel doors.

"Oh, so your tiff is over, is it? All his money calm you down, did it?" Then under his breath Santos Dubois added, "Oversized betch."

Gabriel thrust the beach towels into Mary's arms. He strode over and stood directly in front of Santos, dwarfing him by at least six inches. Santos's wife and friends automatically stepped back. Gabriel clutched the effeminate man's shoulder hard enough to hurt. He leaned close into his ear.

"You listen to me, you revolting little man, you are a phoney and a bully. Mary designed your entire current collection, for which you gave her no credit. You speak about all my money. Well, I now intend to use some of it to make sure you suffer. So beware!"

He then let go of Santos whose face glowed red as hell's door and whose shirt had come adrift, exposing his white, wobbly belly. Gabriel spun around, took Mary's arm and they walked out the door. Once they were across the square and out of sight of the hotel, Mary removed Gabriel's arm.

"He deserved that," she said, "Thank you."

"I feel a lot better for doing it. That man is evil." Gabriel replied. Mary giggled. It was a welcome release after all the angst. At least now everything was out in the open.

"I did enjoy seeing the little creep's face when you man-handled him!" When they reached the outdoor lift down to the beach, Gabriel carefully took the towels back from Mary. "I would punch his nose if I thought I could get another laugh out of you."

The beach was a short walk from where the hill side lift delivered them. Gabriel explained that, for a small fee, you could rent a beach lounger and sun umbrella for the day as well as have drinks and food delivered. He eyed Mary expectantly as the attendant approached them.

"Sun loungers and an umbrella for two, Monsieur?"

Mary nodded and Gabriel embraced his reprieve. They followed the attendant to two loungers in the row directly in front of the sea. Mary didn't speak to Gabriel for the next hour. She lay down on the lounger in the shade of the umbrella so exhausted from all the drama, she fell sound asleep. When she awoke Gabriel was sitting quietly reading a book.

"Is the sea as good as it looks for swimming?" she asked.

"It's safe, if that's what you mean. No rip and no sharks like they have 'down-under.'"

Mary looked amazing in her yellow bikini as she plunged into the sea and swam out. She looked up and contemplated Monaco looming above her. Many self-doubts returned but she reasoned she'd at least won one battle. She had thought that she would never be able to enjoy making love. But she had. Maybe if she kept pushing herself she could win a few more battles.

She dived beneath the surface. In the clear, blue water Mary consciously shed the despair of the previous day's drama. As she floated gracefully up towards the sun, she decided the first breath of air she inhaled would be the first breath of her rebirth. Gabriel was a few lengths behind. He eventually swam up beside her.

"Another skill. You swim well. No doubt you can ride and shoot as well?" he said. Mary ignored him, swam back to the shore and dried herself off. Gabriel caught her up.

"Are you not speaking to me now?" he asked.

"Actually, I can also ride a horse and I shoot well enough to protect myself, as my step-father found out the day I left home!" Mary said and put her sun glasses on.

"I don't wish to push my luck, Mary, but may I invite you to have lunch with me up there at one of those tables?" Gabriel was struggling to gauge her mood changes.

Mary shrugged her shoulders. "Well, I'm hungry, so why not." Once they were seated they ordered giant prawns and Gabriel selected a bottle of rosé wine.

"Did you really shoot your step-father?"

"I knew as soon as those words were out of my mouth I would regret them. I don't even like you anymore and it seems I've shared more about my past with you than even Lou-Lou or Annabel."

"Well, that's probably because you know my sin is far worse than any you may have. I can accept that you don't like me today, but yesterday you did, so if I can hang in there for a little longer maybe, just maybe, you will consider liking me again tomorrow." Gabriel's face was awash with contrition. The wine loosened Mary's tongue, so she decided to be blunt.

"So will you answer me three questions?" she said. Gabriel nodded affirmatively.

"Was that an idle threat you made to Santos? Do you have a lot of money? And how do you make your money?" She then sat back and waited.

"To answer the last question first. Initially, I inherited my wealth from my father. That is how Santos would know me. However, I have added to my inheritance with diverse, strategic investments. One of the things I enjoy about you is that you had no idea about my family profile and wealth." He paused before continuing, "To answer your first question, I never make idle threats. I mean everything I say. I hate men who bully and I will protect the ones I love at all costs."

Mary remained silent. Gabriel leant across and topped up

her wine glass. Finally she said, "Well, let me know when you are going to punish him, I'd like to have a bird's eye view!"

Their chat moved on a little more comfortably as they spent the following couple of hours under the softer afternoon sun on the loungers. Most of the other guests left and Mary floated around in the sea while Gabriel stood in his speedos on the beach edge. Despite her anger and his deception she found herself reflecting on how attractive he was and how easy he was to talk to. Around 6 o'clock they finally dressed and walked back in the direction of the hotel.

"I still don't want to push you but would you consider sharing a light supper with me?" Gabriel asked.

"I suppose so, but nowhere near the hotel. I don't wish to be anywhere near Santos or any of his cronies."

"I think I know just the place. Let's meet in the foyer at 8pm." As Mary showered and dressed, her thoughts kept swaying from the negatives about Gabriel and the obvious problem to the positives such as how much she enjoyed his love making. The positives were reinforced when she saw how handsome he looked in his casual jeans and blue shirt as they hurried out the entrance door into the sleek hotel BMW car. Within minutes they were travelling up the hill and in the direction of the Italian border. It was only a ten minute drive to the border town of Menton.

The car pulled up outside a small beachside restaurant called Cocody Sun. The restaurant was slightly raised above the beach and they sat above the sea watching the sun set with a rich orange glow out in the direction of Africa.

"Have you been here before?" Mary asked.

"No, this is my first time. But I questioned the concierge

at our hotel when we arrived and he recommended it as somewhere with different attributes from Monaco."

They were greeted by the owner, an attractive woman who was casually dressed in tight white jeans and a tee-shirt. The menu featured simple food and the wine was served in a glass carafe.

Mary toyed with her salad and gazed out across the lazy bay as the sun set.

"A penny for your thoughts, as the English say?" Gabriel smiled at her.

"I was thinking about my childhood home, high up in the hills in New Zealand and my mother," Mary said.

"May I ask you a personal question?" Gabriel asked. "Depends," she replied.

"You told me in the heat of the moment last night no-one had ever made love to you before."

"It is entirely possible for sex to take place without love. A man of the world like you should know that!" Mary snapped. Gabriel then directed the conversation in a lighter direction.

On the trip back, Mary felt sexually aroused as Gabriel intentionally sat close to her in the car. Once they checked Santos wasn't lurking anywhere, they slipped into the American Bar, adjacent to the reception area, to have a night cap.

"Is there any way you can bring it into your heart to forgive me so we can at least be friends? Or, even better, that you may consider being my lover, my only lover?" Gabriel asked in a humble tone as he gently stroked her hand. Mary fingered her hair as she deliberated.

"I'm sure we can be friends. I can't give you an answer on

the lover question because I don't know myself." He walked her back to her room and, as she opened the door, he followed her in. When she showed no apparent objection he sat on the chair.

"Please may I stay the night? I promise I won't do anything you don't wish. Just a cuddle?" Mary ignored him and went into the bathroom to undress. She returned in her robe.

"I don't care where you sleep," she said as she discarded her robe and got into bed with only her knickers on. She switched off the lamp on her side of the bed. Gabriel wasted no time. He threw off his clothes, jumped into the bed and switched his side lamp off.

"Stay on your side," Mary mumbled and, although her thoughts were working in overdrive, she feigned sleep. He was as good as his word and after a short time snuggled into her back. Mary drifted off to sleep content in his arms.

26

The following morning was a frantic rush. They needed to be downstairs and in the taxi by 6am to catch the 7.15 flight back to Paris. Mary was subdued during the flight and Gabriel thought better of initiating any advances. They embraced when the taxi pulled up outside Mary's apartment building and he said he would call her soon.

Annabel and Lou-Lou were sitting at the small dining table drinking coffee.

"Have you stolen my boyfriend now?" Mary kidded.

"Not at all, my best Kiwi. I just had to be here when you arrived to get all the details first hand," Lou-Lou replied.

"Here's a coffee. Catch your breath and tell us all." Annabel poured the last of the coffee from the battered metal coffee pot.

"Well, it didn't go as I expected. Lou-Lou," Mary glared at him and pointed her finger, "I suspect you should have told me more than you did about Monsieur Gabriel Aris."

Lou-Lou blushed. "You mean that he's been married?" he said with a nervous smile.

"No, that he IS married." Mary stated. Annabel gasped.

"What? Lou-Lou, why didn't you warn her?" Annabel snapped.

"Listen girls, don't attack me. I'll tell you what I know." He gulped then continued, "Gabriel is from a well-known, rich Paris family, but I knew that wouldn't influence you, Mary. If the tabloids are to be believed his wife was, or is, a drunk, has been in a rehab centre and they are separated." Lou-Lou paused.

"Go on, I know there's more to come," Mary said.

"From what I've observed, he's always been a proper gentleman with no whiff of scandal about him, only about his wife. So I assumed if he was keen on you, Mary, he would be divorced or separated and he would tell you all that himself. I didn't want to be the one to rain on your parade." Lou-Lou reached out to Mary. "Am I forgiven? I'd never do anything to hurt you."

"I guess so. My own past has its secrets and demons so who am I to judge?" Wide-eyed the other two waited for Mary to elaborate. "However, in future I'd rather you give me the quid's up. I'm not big on surprises."

"My English is lacking sometimes. What is this 'quid's up'?" Gabriel asked. Both girls laughed. Mary then gave them an abridged version of the weekend, omitting the sexual details. "So are you going to continue seeing him?" Annabel asked once Lou-Lou had extracted all the details of the fracas with Santos.

"I think so. Even though the formality of his conversation irks me a bit, I fancy him madly and he promises I'll be the only woman he has a relationship with. Maybe a part of the attraction is he's a bit how I imagined my French father would be," she said as she cradled the coffee cup in both hands.

"Oh, how romantic," Lou-Lou swooned. "However, it will be on my terms."

They all had to work that evening and after the last show Lou-Lou made them a cup of hot chocolate in his small workroom.

"How was your black dress received in Monte Carlo?" Lou-Lou asked.

"The funny thing is, looking back on the drama, Santos assumed it was Yves St Laurent. Gabriel loved it."

"I know you are committed to the Moulin Rouge at the moment, Mary, but I really think you should keep up your fashion designing. I'm happy to sew anything you cut, in my spare time. It'd be a real joy for me," Lou-Lou said.

On Friday morning the doorbell woke the girls at 9 o'clock. Annabel poked her head sleepily out the window.

"I can't hear what he is saying with the traffic noise, but it's a massive bunch of flowers so I'm sure it's for you!"

Mary staggered down the stairs in her pyjamas. The large bouquet contained only white flowers, the dominant fragrance being of Lily of the Valley. She put the coffee pot on to boil before sitting down at the table to read whatever was inside the stiff white envelope emblazoned with her name.

My dearest Mary, These white flowers are for peace and also for love. I so hope you have forgiven me and

*will agree to meet me on Sunday so we can talk. I will
call you later this morning.*

All my love, Gabriel.

True to his word the phone rang an hour later. "So tell me what's happening?" Annabel asked.

"I'm meeting him on Sunday afternoon as he has his children every day till then. He wants to show me something and then have dinner with me," Mary replied.

"I hope you know what you're doing, Mary. I would hate to see you hurt."

"Thanks for caring but I'm okay." Mary gave her friend a hug.

❧

Mary had arranged to meet Gabriel at an agreed spot at the Tuileries Gardens. As it was a clear, dry day she decided to walk. She took the route across the island under the shadow of the grand Notre Dame Cathedral, keeping to the side streets to avoid the crowds of tourists. Gabriel saw Mary first. He briskly walked towards her dressed in a brown plaid jacket, chocolate-coloured corduroys, and a beige cashmere scarf around his neck. As he embraced her she was immediately stirred by his touch and the lustful memories that his fragrance evoked. They sat down in a café and ordered espresso coffee.

"First, I must state that I am not assuming you are willing to keep seeing me but, if you are considering it, I want to offer you a situation that may make you feel more comfortable," he said as he sipped his coffee.

"Go on," Mary replied.

"Well, with the vast difference in our working hours, and the fact that you share a flat, I have somewhere to show you. Come with me." He paid for the coffees and she followed him across the Rue de Rivoli.

They stopped in front of a book store. Gabriel took out a key and moved towards an adjacent door which was large and elaborately carved. Once inside the door, they stood in a cobbled courtyard that was dotted with decorative trees sitting in extravagant terracotta pots and groomed within an inch of their evergreen lives. Gabriel stepped into a side door, gesturing for Mary to follow him.

After one flight of stairs he took out another key and opened the door to a large dark room. He moved quickly across the room and threw open the full length window shutters. Daylight flooded in and revealed a balcony which looked across the street to the Tuileries Gardens.

The worn wooden flooring was crafted in intricate parquet and a large brown leather sofa dominated the room. An art deco cocktail cabinet, with an elaborate mirror above it, adorned one wall. Other than that, the high ceilinged room was devoid of any decoration or paintings.

"This is beautiful," Mary said. "Is it yours?"

"It belongs to my family trust. We usually rent it out but it just became vacant so I decided to take it for us, if you agree." Mary stood wide-eyed. "Don't panic. I am not suggesting you move in, but I hope you will at least agree to meet me here a few times each week and we can have our own space," Gabriel added.

Mary opened the French doors and walked out onto the balcony which was edged in traditional latticed wrought-iron and offered a magnificent view. Then she wandered into the bedroom and discovered a small en suite bathroom. The only piece of furniture in the bedroom was a super king-size bed. It sat majestically in the centre of the room and was made up in opulent white damask. Off the living room was a tiny kitchenette with just two gas rings, a basin and a very small fridge.

"You can choose whatever else you desire to decorate it," Gabriel said.

"Actually, I like this minimal look, just as it is." She looked at him directly in the eye. "Does this mean I'll officially be your mistress?" Gabriel shuffled uncomfortably.

"Yes, however I prefer to use the word 'lover' because, in France, 'mistress' implies I provide for you financially and that is not the situation here. I am sure you would rather work for a living." He followed Mary out onto the balcony where she gazed across at the Tuileries.

"Yes, you're correct. I enjoy working and I do want to be independent. Okay, I accept," she said, "But I must be your only lover."

"Of course, ma chérie, the only one forever." He took her hand and led her back inside. Then he took a bottle of champagne from the tiny fridge. He opened the cocktail cabinet to reveal a full array of 1920s' glasses, and poured two glasses of champagne.

"To us," he toasted. They sipped their drinks and then Gabriel coaxed her through to the bedroom.

"I bought all the linen and bedclothes yesterday, so we are the first and only ones to use them," he said as he slowly unbuttoned Mary's blouse and gently kissed her neck. Their love making began leisurely but, as Mary's desire intensified, Gabriel followed and the pace and energy that cumulated in a mutual orgasm took Mary by surprise.

27

Mary's life fell into a rhythm. She met Gabriel at least twice a week around lunch time for a couple of hours in their pied-à-terre and again every Sunday afternoon till late. On the days she danced at the Moulin Rouge she arrived a good hour earlier than she was expected so she and Lou-Lou could work on her collection. In their free time, they fossicked around the fabric area at the base of Sacré Coeur to pick up discounted remnants and interesting buttons and trims. After six weeks Lou-Lou was unable to conceal the rail of designs they had made up.

"We will have to find somewhere else to keep these garments. My supervisor has turned a blind eye till now but it's all becoming a bit too obvious," he said.

"Both your apartment and ours are too tiny but I may be able to take them somewhere else," Mary replied. Lou-Lou's radar shot up.

"Really? Where?" He gave Mary a knowing grin. "Somewhere I know you are just dying to visit," she said.

The following day was a lunch time rendezvous with Gabriel. He arrived at the apartment before Mary. When she arrived, he was inspecting a cobalt blue, stretch satin evening gown from the free-standing rail.

"My, you have been a busy woman. I can only assume this is all your work?"

"Well, not entirely my own. I come up with the concept and Lou-Lou builds on it. I cut the patterns and, depending on who gets to work first, one of us cuts the fabric. Lou-Lou always sews up. He is the best," Mary smiled. "I hope you don't mind that he helped to bring the rail up here yesterday?"

"Not at all. It is not only my domain - it is ours. You are free to entertain whoever you please."

Mary talked him through each of the twenty garments as they sat eating the salads she'd brought. Gabriel listened patiently then, once he felt she'd exhausted the merits of satin-backed crepe, he guided her into the bedroom where they made frantic but satisfying love.

Saturday evening was always the busiest at the Moulin Rouge. From the stage Mary could clearly see guests' faces in the front three rows but any further back it all became a blur. She wasn't on stage until the second act.

"There's a bunch of loud-mouth drunks in the front row to the right. That's your end, Kiwi, so watch out," her dressing-room companion informed her during a rushed costume change. When it was Mary's turn on stage she glanced at the group of four men seated directly in front of her. She recognised him at the same time she heard his high pitched voice. It was Santos Dubois.

As Mary was 'fresh skirt' to the performance, a young man she assumed was Santos's son nudged him and pointed her out. At first Santos didn't pay much attention, but as the routine finished and Mary exited she thought she caught his flicker of recognition.

For the next routine Mary was placed in exactly the same position and now she was sure he recognised her. Even above the music she heard him say 'betch'. When the music softened he stood up and shouted, "Mary Hampton, the whore!"

Mary was rattled but wrestled to keep control. Somehow she managed to keep dancing as the Moulin Rouge security men went over and supervised the unceremonious exit of the four drunken guests from the premises. As soon as the evening's performance finished Annabel was at Mary's side.

"My god, Mary, what a revolting man. He's crazy." She hugged her shocked friend.

"I guess everyone heard that? I feel like shit!" Mary said. "You have no reason to. He's the one who was thrown out.

It will be all over the tabloids tomorrow," Annabel's attempt at consoling Mary only heightened her horror.

"Bloody hell, I hope not. I don't want my name mentioned, or to have Gabriel implicated!" Still wearing their final costumes they both bolted down the corridor to the safety of Lou-Lou's costume room.

"Well, to what do I owe the pleasure of you two arriving in my kingdom before you have changed?" As soon as the words were out of his mouth he realised something was very wrong.

"Mary was verbally abused on stage by that fucking

Santos Dubois," Annabel said. Lou-Lou and Mary gawped at Annabel. They had never heard her say 'fuck' in the entire time they had known her.

The next day Mary paced the parquet floor as she anxiously waited for Gabriel at their apartment.

"What's wrong, ma chérie, you look terrible." Gabriel listened carefully as Mary told him the full version of the Santos episode. Then he exploded in French, "That bastard, I would kill him if I could!" He quietened a little as he turned to Mary. "I have a good friend at the newspaper, and the CEO at Paris Match is a family friend. So I will phone them now and see if we can put a lid on this. No doubt the PR people at the Moulin Rouge will be doing the same," he said. They spent the rest of the day reasoning it all through.

Mary returned to her own place that evening. As she lay in bed listening to Annabel's reassuring delicate snore she felt relieved that she had Gabriel in her corner. When she arrived at the Moulin Rouge on Monday, the manager's PA intercepted her.

"The boss would like a word please, Mary." Mary followed as the PA clip-clopped in her awkward stilettos up to the management offices.

"Have a seat, Mary." Monsieur Clerico motioned for her to sit down. "Whilst it is not my business to comment on the private lives of my dancers, the Moulin Rouge is my business and when a dancer's private life has an effect on my business, then I have to act. I'm not going to ask you for any details or for your defence. We are all aware of what type of men Santos Dubois and his son are. However, I am cautioning you. You must somehow make sure this situation never happens again. Am I clear?"

Mary nodded, "0ui, Monsieur Clerico." Then she left his office without another word being spoken.

28

The following day, when they met at the apartment, Gabriel listened intently as Mary recalled all that had transpired in Monsieur Clerico's office.

"I have been dwelling on an idea since I saw your fashion collection and, with this latest revelation at the Moulin Rouge, I feel it may be a good time to chat about it," Gabriel said once Mary had finished talking.

"Sounds interesting. Tell me."

"In my opinion you are clearly talented and committed, and your Lou-Lou is like your third arm when it comes to the operational side. However, I must point out that in this situation I'm foremost a business man and a lover second. But knowing you as I do, I believe any investment I may make in you will, in the long term, be a good one."

"What do you mean 'an investment' in me?" Mary interjected.

"Don't be impatient!" Gabriel said. "Hear me out. I would invest enough money for you to take a lease on a small shop. It would also provide for the minimum amount of equipment and fabric you'd need to put together a collection and have stock in the shop. Essentially, your own business." Mary was transfixed.

He continued, "You would work for the first twelve months for the bare minimum, only enough to cover your living costs. You and Lou-Lou would own 49 percent between you and I would retain 51 percent until such time as the business could afford to repay my investment. Then you would have an option on my shares. I don't believe the family name 'Rock' Lou-Lou uses is entirely correct but that is his affair - we all have our secrets. I suspect he receives a living subsidy from a family trust. If he gives up the champagne and hairdressing bills he can probably live quite comfortably on that for the initial twelve months set-up period." Gabriel paused as he waited for Mary's reaction.

"Wow, that'd be amazing. Obviously, I'm very interested but I'd have to do some of my own figures and speak with Lou-Lou. May I bring him with me so all three of us can have a round–table discussion on this?" she asked.

"I would expect nothing less," he said then leant over and kissed her and they both knew the business side of the meeting had concluded.

By Sunday Mary and Lou-Lou had gone over their plan many times. They had prepared a written presentation as best they could and had it photocopied three times. Lou-Lou made no comment on Gabriel's aside about his family name other than agreeing that, if he applied himself, he could manage on his family trust allowance. Mary loved the name Lou-Lou

Rock and, along with Annabel, they had made an unspoken pact not to probe into any previous family history.

Mary and Lou-Lou arrived at Rue Rivoli at the same time as Gabriel. Lou-Lou was unusually silent. He sat on the sofa with Mary, and Gabriel pulled up a small stool and sat facing them. Mary handed out the copies of the presentation and then opened the discussion.

"Lou-Lou has agreed not to take a salary during the set-up time but we would like it to be a condition that, once the business has sufficient money coming in, we both take a small salary," she said. Gabriel nodded for her to continue. "As the investor, you will be putting in the money. However, we will both be putting in everything we have. So for this reason we would require 50 percent of the business between us."

She paused and, though Gabriel said nothing, Mary was sure she glimpsed a smidgen of a grin. She continued. "It makes sense to wholesale the collection from the beginning to retailers, in just a small way to start with. That's because we will have to buy bulk fabric and it wouldn't be practical to manufacture just our own shop stock."

Gabriel interrupted. "Where would you manufacture?"

"I was coming to that." Mary said. "We will try to find a shop that is a bit off the beaten track but has a basement or an upstairs room that we could use as a workroom. Lou-Lou and I will make up all the samples and do 'specials' for the shop floor. Between us we know a few work-shops around Paris that do 'small runs'. They should be able to meet our orders to begin with."

Gabriel scratched his head. "So how does the selling to the retailer's work?

"Maybe I could answer this?" Lou-Lou said hesitantly. Mary nodded for him to go on.

"In my former life I worked for a fashion agent who sold collections on behalf of designers in return for a commission. We would provide the agent with the sample collection." Lou-Lou pointed towards the rail of garments. "They sell a season ahead so we don't have to manufacture anything until we have an order."

"OK," Gabriel nodded, "But why would an agent take on an unknown designer?"

"For the same reason you have offered to invest in Mary. She's a great designer!"

After an hour of questions and answers Gabriel opened a bottle of wine and poured them all a glass. "I am very impressed. You two seem to know your stuff." He lovingly stroked Mary's hand. "The next thing you need to do is find premises," he said as a conclusion to the discussion.

29

Mary barely registered a faint ringing sound. It was dawn and she'd grown used to the early morning Paris street sounds as they rose up through the open bedroom window. Her eyes were still closed when Annabel's voice invaded her sleep.

"Wake up, Mary. There's a Kiwi woman on the phone for you." Mary jumped out of bed. "Who?"

"I don't know. I'm half asleep because it's only 6.30am but she has an accent like yours." Mary stumbled through to the sitting room and apprehensively picked up the phone.

"Hello, Mary speaking."

"Oh, darling, it's me, Mum!" There was a silence. "Are you there, Mary? It's me, I received your letter. From the post mark I could see it must have come by sea post. It took over two months to get here." Mary's heart welled with a charge of lost love.

"Mum, I'm here. I was asleep so I'm just trying to get my head around the fact that it's actually you. How did you get my phone number?" she asked.

"We don't live in the dark ages here. I called international directory and you are the only M Hampton listed in Paris," Hazel said. Mary laughed.

"Oh, Mum, it's so good to hear your voice." Mary asked her mother how she was, then enquired about Susan and Jamie. They chatted on but neither made any mention of Mary's step-father.

"My big news is that Susan and I will be arriving in Paris in one month's time. Now don't panic, I figured you'd only have a small place so Susan looked up on the map where you live and the travel agent has booked us into a hotel nearby," she said.

When Mary finally put down the phone, Annabel was boiling the coffee.

"Wow, your mother! Do you want to share?" Annabel poured out two cups as she spoke.

"Yes, I'm happy to. Mum only just received my letter and she and my sister Susan are coming over to Paris for a two weeks holiday next month," Mary said. She sipped on her coffee and then added, "I'm not sure how they can afford it and she said nothing about my step-father. I guess I'll just have to wait till they arrive to get all the details."

Mary and Lou-Lou spent all the time they weren't required at the Moulin Rouge viewing shops. It was very discouraging as all the premises were either far too overpriced or too small. They agreed not to tell anyone other than Annabel about their plan and also not to give in their notice at the Moulin Rouge until they had a signed lease. Lou-Lou resurrected some of his fashion contacts as he was aware getting his foot in the door with a successful sales agent would take some smooth talking.

"Mary, can you meet me at 10 tomorrow morning?" Lou-Lou whispered as Mary struggled with her head piece for the last routine of the evening.

"Sure, but why?"

"The real estate agent left a message on my answer machine about a shop. It sounds in the right price bracket."

The following morning they met up at the Rambuteau Métro exit and walked along Rue Vieille du Temple and then into a small back street called Rue Barbette.

"It's very quiet along here," Mary commented. A well suited chap arrived beside them.

"Bonjour, I am Monsieur Georges." He extended his hand. The shop had a relatively narrow front but a large window with glass from floor to ceiling, and a glass door. When they stepped inside Mary was surprised at how far back the shop went - right through to another glass door at the back which in turn opened into a small conservatory. The conservatory opened onto a shared courtyard.

They paced out how much space they felt they needed for the actual shop floor then paced out what space would be left over for a workroom. As they had previously agreed on a negotiation strategy, it was Lou-Lou who did the talking.

"Well, it's big enough, but this area is very quiet for retail. And the shop needs a lot of renovation as well as having security installed, so if we were to make an offer it would be a lot lower than what you're asking." Monsieur Georges tut-tutted a bit, then murmured his client would probably consider an offer.

"Okay, we will chat with our finance director and get back to you." Lou-Lou shook the agent's hand.

"What do you really think?" Mary asked once they were comfortably seated in a nearby brassiere.

"I know what your hesitation is, Mary. The location. But the Marais area is up and coming. There are quite a few small artisan businesses moving in around here, mainly due to the lower rents. And it will be famous in no time at all once we move in!" Lou-Lou flicked his hands in the air.

"Oh, Lou-Lou, it's like a dream come true. What will we offer him?" Mary said.

"Two-thirds of what he's asking. My grand-mère often told me you need to be the architect of your own fortune. That's where we are going now - towards our own fortunes."

When Mary met with Gabriel the following day she was bursting with all the details of the shop.

"From what you have shown me the costs appear to stack up with the predicted income so it looks like you can go ahead." He squeezed her hand. She gave a small clap then moved in close beside him on the sofa and brushed his lips with hers. He led her to the bedroom where Mary slowly removed her jeans and tee-shirt.

"Oh, Mary, you are such a sensual woman," Gabriel murmured as he buried his head in her breasts.

Once she had showered, she said a hurried goodbye. She and Annabel had organised to share a rare night in, just the two of them.

"I hope you don't feel we are abandoning you, Annabel. Once we are in a position to take on a sales person you will be our first port of call," Mary said as they ate their egg foo yong.

Annabel raised her glass of white wine in a toast to Mary. "Thank you, Mary, but you know I'm the happiest when I'm on that stage dancing. It's what I've wanted to do since I was a little girl. If I work hard enough I may even make dance leader. I love seeing you and Lou-Lou working together. It seems natural somehow."

Mary smiled. "Yes, sometimes I feel we are peas from the same pod. With the month's notice we're required to give at work and then my Mum's visit, we have agreed to start the fit-out of the shop and all the other activity once she's gone. I want to give her as much of my time as I can."

"Will you tell her about Gabriel?" "Mmm, not sure yet."

30

"My god, my god, Mary, that dreadful man is stalking me." Lou-Lou joined Mary at the bar.

"Calm down, Lou-Lou. What dreadful man? Where?"

Lou-Lou made an extravagant gesture with his arms and flopped into the chair next to her.

"Let me order a glass of wine first and, before you say it, I know 'we' don't drink at lunch time but as 'we' are between jobs, so to speak, and I'm traumatised I am going to make an exception. One glass will be my medicine!"

He summoned the waiter. Once he had his glass in hand and Mary's cappuccino had been served, Lou-Lou nervously scratched his chest and continued, "Well, you know I've been schmoozing a couple of the commission sales agents to whom we may want to take our collection? One of them represents Santos and must have mentioned it to him. Anyway, I was sitting in La Perle two hours ago having a late croissant and who should front up to me but that creep!" Lou-Lou paused and took a gulp from his glass.

"Go on," Mary said.

"He told me if I was going to be working with you then we

better watch out because he was so well connected in the Paris fashion world he'd make our name mud as soon as he could. He also said a few other heavy things about your relationship with Gabriel."

Mary's face reddened. "That bastard! What did I ever do to him except design him an amazing collection?" She reached over and gulped down the last of Lou-Lou's wine.

"In my opinion, he's unhinged and fixated on you. It's a bit of a worry with regard to the agent I'm trying to impress. I'll give it a day or two then visit him again and test the water."

"Look, I'm sorry there's not much I can do right now. I'm meeting Mum and Susan off the plane tomorrow," Mary replied. Lou-Lou reached over and examined his empty glass. "Yes, I know, my Kiwi, and I'm sorry to have burdened you

but, you know me, I had to let it all out. I'm sure there's nothing that dreadful Santos creature can do to really hold us back. I'd better order two glasses next time!" Mary laughed and pecked his cheek goodbye.

The following morning as Mary sat on the train out to Charles de Gaulle airport, she pushed Santos and the other new business challenges to the back of her mind. She was excited at the thought of seeing her mum and sister but also uneasy as she knew that conversation about her step-father would be inevitable. However, in a small part of her psyche, she felt a sense of pride that in the past three years she had somehow coped and moved forward. Secondary to her step-father's abuse was the inner debate as to whether she should reveal Gabriel's marital status to her mother. In the end she decided that maybe it was best not to even mention him.

Mary worked herself into quite a state during the one hour

wait at the arrival gate. Then she recognised her mother's warm familiar face across the arrival hall. A surge of love overwhelmed her. She waved frantically and ran into her mother's open arms. Both had tears streaming down their cheeks.

"Oh, Mum, I'm so sorry to cry. It's just been so long," Mary said. Then she noticed a teenager with long straight blonde hair standing with the luggage trolley beside them. She wasn't as tall as Mary but she was beautiful.

"Susan, is that you?" Mary asked.

"Yes, this is Susan, sixteen now and all grown up. And you, Mary, look so beautiful - just how we imagined, isn't she Susan?" Hazel extended her arms to include her other daughter in the group hug.

Mary blew her nose and wiped her eyes. "Now, enough of all this crying. Let's grab a taxi. It'll be too much hassle with your bags on the train." Mary navigated them out towards the row of taxis.

During the journey into Paris they chatted superficially about the long flight. Although her sister appeared happy to be in Paris, Mary was puzzled by her sad eyes. She left her mother and sister at their hotel, which was just five minutes' walk from her apartment, and assured them she'd return in a couple of hours to collect them for dinner.

Annabel and Mary prepared a light but typical French supper and the four women happily squashed around the small table. Hazel and Susan were mesmerised as they listened to the flatmates' details of dancing at the famous Moulin Rouge. When Mary didn't add that she had resigned and set up a new business, Annabel took it as a cue to make her excuses and went out to meet a friend.

Susan and Mary had washed all the dishes then joined their mother on the sofa with cups of strong tea.

"Mum, I need to tell you something that will come as a shock, and Susan, I would rather you didn't hear it but I can't spend the next couple of weeks with you both without explaining why I left." Mary's eyes welled up. Before she could continue her mother reached across and pressed her arm.

"Love, we think we know why you left. It was because of your father, wasn't it?"

Mary froze. Her mother paused, the wetness in her eyes mirroring Mary's.

"It's all been my fault, an error of judgement." Hazel struggled to say the right words.

"He's an evil bastard!" Susan blurted out then dropped her face into her hands sobbing. Mary placed her arms around her sister.

"Susan, Susan don't cry. I'm through it now, truly I am. I've moved on," Mary said.

"You may have, Mary, but I haven't. I hope he rots in that prison!" Susan proclaimed.

Mary's jaw dropped. "You too? But you're his real daughter, aren't you?" She glanced expectantly at her mother.

Hazel found her voice. "It had nothing to do with you being his step daughter. I'm so so sorry I never saw it. I assumed he was a bit odd with you because you weren't his natural daughter. When you ran away I thought it was because you had found out that I lied to you. I had absolutely no idea about the abuse." She then added, "Yes, Susan is his natural child, Mary."

"How did you find out about what he did to me?" Mary was gripped.

"I spotted the bullet wound in his leg on the day you ran away. John was acting very strangely and I realised I'd put my head in the sand where your behaviour was concerned. I managed to get Jamie on his own and questioned him. Don't worry - he was totally loyal to you. He wouldn't tell me where you'd gone but I figured if he'd been party to it all you were safe and there must have been something bad going on in our home to push you away." Hazel wiped her eyes with the back of her hand and took a sip of her tea. Susan composed herself but kept clasping Mary's hand.

Hazel continued. "Then about two weeks after you left John suggested we move Susan out to your room. At first she was excited about it."

Susan interjected. "Then he started on me. At first I didn't understand but clearly I wasn't as great at keeping a secret as you were and I blurted out to Mum that I didn't like his sticky penis and that's when it all came out."

Hazel's face was ashen as her youngest daughter spoke. But she took up the conversation again. "To be honest, I was consumed with guilt. How could I have been so blind? I didn't know what to do so I went to Huia and Barbara. They said they suspected that's what had happened to you. I was in a state of shock, but by then I knew I had to go to the police. In the end John confessed everything about you and he's been in prison for two years now. He's very bitter. We've all had professional counselling and huge support with the farm from the neighbours."

The three women sat silently for a few moments digesting

the revelation. Then Mary spoke.

"I haven't had counselling but I've made some wonderful friends who have accepted some of my odd behaviour without asking questions. And I've finally managed to have a proper relationship with a man, something that was previously a big fear for me," she said.

Susan became animated. "Mary, do you have a boyfriend?"

"Well, sort of," Mary said. Susan smiled.

"You either do or you don't," her mother said, a twinkle returning to her face.

"All I will say on the matter is we are not engaged so it can't be that serious. I think we should now put this behind us. I want so much to enjoy this time with you in Paris, my new home," Mary replied attempting to lighten the mood.

Hazel opened her purse and took out an envelope filled with photos. "Here's Huia, Barbara and Toa with Jamie, and this one is of Jamie in his All Blacks kit." She handed Mary the photos'.

"My god, Jamie made it to the All Blacks!" Mary felt her heart soar.

"Yes, he made the junior All Blacks straight out of school and, being the brain box he is, managed to play and still do his law degree," Susan said.

"He often talks about you and specifically requested, when he knew we were coming to visit, that we send you his love. He will be in the UK later in the year on tour so, if it's okay with you, he'll phone."

"Yes, please," Mary replied.

"Oh, look, Mum, she still gets that dreamy look on her face when she talks about Jamie," Susan said.

After her mother and sister returned to their hotel, Mary sat alone on the sofa and reviewed her past three years. She shivered as if someone had just walked on her grave. She visualised her sister when she was small, blonde and vulnerable and the flood gates opened. She curled up and hugged her knees as she sobbed. Susan's devastating revelation, and the experience they now shared, gave her an odd sort of comfort. As she got up to grab some loo paper to blow her nose, she no longer harboured any doubts of fault on her part - it had all been her step-father's sin.

31

"Mum's looking quite thin. I guess it's been all this stress," Mary said to her sister as they waited outside a souvenir shop for their mother the following day.

"Yes, that as well as putting the farm up for sale. She's felt guilty about that." Susan glanced downwards as she spoke, and then added, "She's also been a bit unwell but seems to be on the mend now."

"You don't sound entirely convinced?" Mary searched her sister's face for confirmation.

"Look, Mum's coming. Best not mention it just now. She wants us all to be positive," Susan replied as their mother walked towards them.

"Okay, my two beautiful daughters, let's go and see this Eiffel tower they all talk about."

Over lunch Mary felt the time was right to tell them about her new venture.

"So there you have it. I have a business partner called Lou-Lou and a private financial investor. It's so exciting. We're going to move into our new shop once your visit is over," she said once she had given them all the creative details.

"Wow, Mary, you never cease to amaze me though I have

to say the dancing surprised me. But the fashion business doesn't. I'm sure it's somehow wired into your DNA," Hazel said.

"So, tomorrow we'll visit the shop and you can meet my special Lou-Lou." Mary smiled to herself as her sister and mother exchanged a knowing look.

The next day when they arrived at the shop, the door was unlocked.

"Lou-Lou must be around somewhere. Perhaps he's getting a coffee," Mary commented as she pushed the door open.

"It's a very quiet street, love. I hope you won't be dependent on passers-by," Hazel said.

"No, not entirely. To begin with we see ourselves as a 'destination shop'. It's all we could afford but it's an 'up and coming area' according to Lou-Lou." Susan interrupted her sister in a loud whisper.

"Mary, quick, there's a really weird guy looking in the window at me." As Lou-Lou opened the door Susan cautiously backed away.

"Oh, that's no weird man. That's my business partner Lou-Lou. Lou-Lou, meet my sister and my Mum." Lou-Lou replied to Mary's intro with a theatrical bow.

"Enchanté, Madame Hampton and Mademoiselle Susan, I have heard so many wonderful things about you both." Susan was spellbound.

"Please call me Hazel. We are very pleased to meet you and to hear what a great friend you've been to our Mary." Hazel offered her hand which Lou-Lou immediately lifted to his lips.

Mary walked her family through the planned lay-out for the shop and workroom while Lou-Lou embroidered her descriptions in his poetic way.

"Maintenant, Beautiful Women! As I now have three Hamptons together it is my pleasure to invite you all for lunch at my favourite brasserie," he said.

Hazel was about to protest when she caught Mary subtly pressing her forefinger to her pursed lips.

"Thank you, it would be our pleasure," replied Mary as she shot the others a knowing wink.

'Bofinger', Lou-Lou's beloved eating place, was only a five minute walk from the shop on Rue Barbette. As they walked he prattled on about how Bofinger was one of the oldest and most famous brasseries in Paris and that the literal translation for the word 'brasserie' was 'brewery'. Once seated, Lou-Lou excused himself under the pretence of using the bathroom.

"Wow, Mary, your Lou-Lou is so cool! Is he your boyfriend? He's very gay!" Susan's entire demeanour had done a big about change. She shone as she spoke.

"Well, yes, gay is the right word and, yes, he's a man and, yes, he's my friend but, no, we are not romantically involved," Mary replied. "I'm very comfortable in his company and we always joke we must have been connected in a previous life."

Lou-Lou returned with a stern-faced waiter who carried a bottle of Moët and Chandon Champagne in a glimmering ice bucket. Mary knew better than to protest. Lou-Lou was on a roll and there was no stopping him. She smiled as she watched her teenage sister experience her first sip of the famous nectar. Hazel made noises of protest but, like Mary, she became totally enchanted by Lou-Lou's charm and enthusiasm. Lou-Lou was in his element when the three women suggested he order for all of them. This was where he was at his best - in control of style, food and champagne.

"Chaud devant! Chaud devant!" the stern waiter called as he cleared the way to carry a giant silver platter of seafood to their table.

"My goodness, it looks amazing," was all Hazel managed to say as the waiter placed the platter on a raised rack in the centre of their table.

"Are these Bluff oysters?" Susan asked.

Mary laughed. "No, that's a bit too far to send oysters. These are France's finest - a little smaller than the New Zealand ones but just as tasty."

The lunch lasted till late afternoon when Susan declared the third course of crème brûlée was the best desert in the world. Mary shadowed Lou-Lou as he went up to the desk to pay.

"No, Mary, I know what you are going to say." He pushed his hand down on her bag. "I may never get this opportunity again and I so wanted to treat your Mama and sister. I know I'm on a budget now but today was very special." Mary's eyes glistened as she gently kissed his cheek.

They said thank you and all kissed good bye in a pronounced fashion and Mary accompanied her mother and sister up to their room in the hotel. Although her mother was clearly delighted to be with her daughters, Mary could see her eyes were quite blood-shot and that she was exhausted.

"Don't fuss, love, it's just the bubbly. Too much for an old girl in the middle of the day. I'll have an early night and be as right as rain in the morning," Hazel said.

The following day Annabel took Susan to the Louvre and Mary spent some restful time alone with her mother. Mary bought a couple of chocolate éclairs from the local patisserie and, once the other two had left, her mother lay on the sofa with her feet up. Mary pulled a chair up close and served the cakes with freshly brewed coffee.

"Now, love, given that we have cleared the air about the horrors of the past, you seem to me to be being somewhat evasive with details about your boyfriend." Hazel leant across and held her daughter's hand. Mary gave no immediate response so Hazel continued, "I can only surmise that there is something about him that you feel uncomfortable with?"

"It's not that I'm uncomfortable with it but I'm concerned that you might be," Mary said.

"Is he married, Mary?"

Mary nodded. "Yes, but it's not that straight forward. He doesn't sleep with his wife. She's an alcoholic and he stays for the sake of the children." Mary paused. Her mother took over.

"Does he tell you how much he loves you? Does he give you special things he knows you desire?" her mother asked.

"Yes, he encouraged me to leave the Moulin Rouge and start the business. He's our silent financial partner."

Hazel took a bite of her éclair and a sip of coffee. Mary remembered this technique from childhood as her mother's way of stalling for time while she carefully chose her words. "I think the only way I can respond is bluntly. I've heard it all before. You must remember your birth-father was a handsome charming Parisian man and I fell for him completely," she said.

Mary interrupted. "But Mum this is different!"

"No it's not, Mary. The bottom line is he's not available if he's not divorced. He's manipulating you into a situation where you'll be indebted to him. He'll never be free to marry you or to father your children," Hazel said then swung her legs around so that she was sitting upright on the sofa.

Mary stood up. "This is why I didn't want to tell you, Mum. I don't want to upset you and I don't want to argue." Mary sat down beside her mother.

"Love, I don't want to argue either. Perhaps I could offer you a part solution?" Hazel said.

"Yes? Go on," Mary replied.

"As you know, we are selling the farm to pay off the debts John has run up. However, the market's buoyant so it looks like we'll get a great price. Even after all the debt is settled there will be enough for me to invest in your business rather than this man, whoever he is." Hazel smiled reassuringly.

"I don't know what to say, Mum. First, his name is Gabriel and, second, we are already in the process of using his money. We've paid for the lease. Besides, you will need all that money to support yourself and Susan," Mary said.

Her mother reassured her that there would be plenty to go round, so they finished the conversation by agreeing that when the farm was sold and the money in the bank, Hazel would offer to replace Gabriel's investment. They also agreed it was best Hazel didn't meet Gabriel.

"While we're thrashing out this subject, can you tell me a little bit more about my birth father?" Mary asked.

"He was very aristocratic and very tall. In fact, if your Lou-Lou wasn't so 'camp', as you call it, he could remind me a bit of André. He totally bewitched me with his sensual French accent and his impeccable manners. He made me laugh, and brought me flowers. I'd never met anyone like him. New

Zealand men seemed so coarse in comparison. However, he didn't take me out anywhere in public or introduce me to his other French friends, something I should have picked up on. He knew I was a virgin and I believed we were both in love when he seduced me," Hazel quietly responded.

"Go on," Mary said.

"Not much else to say, really. Once I got pregnant, that was it. You've read the letters. John had always been keen on me and, knowing my father would put some much needed money into John's own family farm, and my father wanting to save face, they more or less brokered the deal between them. I was naïve and so ashamed I went along with it as the best solution for a bad situation. I now realise John had deep-seated problems. Apparently, he'd been abused himself, if we are to believe the psychiatrist," Hazel said. They both sat quietly for a few reflective minutes.

"Maybe you'd like to see the copy of André's death certificate. You can keep it if you wish." Mary took the shoe box in which she kept her important keepsakes from behind the large pot plant and handed the certificate to her mother. Hazel took the paper and slowly read the words she could decipher.

"I see André had two children. Have you considered looking for them?" Hazel asked as she handed the certificate back to Mary.

"I felt curious at first, but then decided I didn't want to cause any heart-break or disillusionment to any other children about their father. Remember what you used to say, Mum? Some things are better left unsaid." Mary placed the certificate back in the box.

By the time Annabel returned with Susan, Mary and her mother had gone as far as they could with the conversation about Gabriel. They both wanted their last few days in Paris together to be as joyful as possible.

"I'll get it," Annabel called as the phone rang. She was on her way out to the Moulin Rouge.

"It's for you Mary. See you later," she said as she placed the receiver next to the phone.

"Where were you, ma chérie?" Gabriel's pleading voice inquired as Mary said hello.

"Oh, just lying down in the bedroom. This tourist guide and reunited family stuff is exhausting, and we're all going to the late show at the Moulin Rouge this evening," she replied.

"Oh. And when am I going to see you, my little Kiwi? I miss you so much. Will I have the honour of meeting your mother?" Mary felt a surge of desire as she listened to Gabriel's familiar formal voice.

"Well, given your marital situation and the newness of my family reconciliation, I think it best to leave the introduction for this visit. They'll be gone in two days and then I'll be all yours." She could sense his hurt in the tone of his response. They continued their chat in a more reserved fashion, mostly about the new shop, and agreed to meet at their apartment after Mary had taken her mother and sister to the airport.

On Hazel and Susan's final day, once Lou-Lou and Annabel had said protracted goodbyes and the three Hampton women were jammed into the taxi en route to the airport, gloom descended on them all.

"Oh, Mary, I wish I could stay. I love Paris!" Susan said. She was squashed in the middle of her sister and mother on

192

the back seat with her head resting on Mary's shoulder.

"I promise you once the business is making money you can move over here and become our vendeuse."

Susan beamed, "I know what that means. Lou-Lou told me - 'head sales girl'. Yes please!"

Hazel said very little. She looked weary and Mary was pleased she was there to help lift the suitcases at the airport check in.

"Goodbye, my precious first born. Always know, no matter what, that you were wanted and loved." Hazel held back her tears.

"Mum, this isn't goodbye. It's more like see you later. When the farm is sold you'll be back in no time. Also, once our business is roaring I'm going to bring Lou-Lou to New Zealand. Now that will cause a sensation!" Mary tried desperately to follow her mother's example and not cry. She held tight to her mother's and sister's hands right up until they heard the final boarding call.

They both mouthed 'I love you' to her just before the doors closed to the boarding lounge.

32

Mary spent a longer time than usual preparing for her date with Gabriel. She gave herself a manicure and pedicure as well as setting her hair in the hated heated rollers to achieve the flicky style Gabriel seemed to favour. She wore her best white lace underwear and chose a new sample dress from her collection.

As she dressed, Mary pondered on her mother's comments about her relationship. Coupled with Lou-Lou's recent observations about Gabriel, she started looking into the future at what the consequences might be if she continued the relationship. In the two short weeks of absence from her lover, she had unwittingly moved forward with a fresh set of eyes in a different direction.

"Ma chérie, I was worried. It's so unlike you to be late." Gabriel was waiting close to the door when Mary arrived at the apartment. He pulled her to him and kissed her lips.

"You look stunning," he said.

"Well, I wanted to wear one of my own creations tonight. I'd love to go out somewhere equally stunning to show it off. Where do you suggest we go?" Mary asked. Gabriel was taken aback.

"I thought we would stay in. I haven't seen you for two whole weeks. It feels like a life time and I yearn for your body, ma chérie." He kissed her hand.

"My body and the bed will still be here after dinner. Let's make it last till morning." Mary provocatively stroked his cheek.

Gabriel suggested a couple of the secluded restaurants that they usually frequented but Mary showed little enthusiasm.

"This dress, I'm hoping, will become one of my signature designs and I would love to launch it somewhere appropriate. What about at Lasserre? Lou-Lou tells me that's where all the beautiful people go," Mary replied. Gabriel shifted on his feet and walked over to look out the window.

"You know I would deny you very little, but it will probably be impossible to get a reservation at this late time." He spoke without turning around.

"Oh, Gabriel, with your connections, I'm sure you can get us a tiny table for two in a discrete corner," Mary cajoled. He had no option.

While Gabriel reluctantly charmed the maitre d' at Lasserre on the phone Mary took two crystal champagne glasses out of the cocktail cabinet and poured chilled champagne from the fridge.

"Thank you, my darling. You have made me feel extra special." Mary clinked her glass with Gabriel's.

It was the first time since their sojourn in Monaco that she'd seen Gabriel so nervous. Mary didn't feel too concerned. The revelation from her mother and sister had mentally given her self-worth a big push upwards. As the cab drove along Avenue Franklin Roosevelt she revelled in the exhilaration a glamorous Friday evening in Paris could create.

She revelled in the moment as they pulled up outside Lasserre. The windows of the two-story building glistened with welcoming light from Titan chandeliers that hung from the ceilings on both floors. Luxurious drapes were pulled aside just enough to entice customers to enter.

Mary radiated confidence in her black stretch lurex dress. The fabric was shot with silver thread and clung to her body displaying her lithe figure. She wore it 'midi' length and it showcased her tanned bare legs and high, black patent heels. As Gabriel saw the shameless looks that the doorman and another male guest extended towards Mary, he subconsciously puffed out his chest and placed his hand possessively on her back.

They were ushered into a very small elevator with walls papered in rich red, flock wallpaper on which hung an opulent gilt framed mirror. Mary enthusiastically squeezed Gabriel's hand. Then as they entered the first floor restaurant Mary gave a small gasp. She had not expected such formality and glitz. Their appearance attracted some curious glances from the sophisticated diners.

"Monsieur Aris, please follow me." The mention of Gabriel's name from the maître'd attracted a low murmur from a nearby table. Mary noticed her lover's hand twitch slightly. She was ushered to the seat facing the room while the room had Gabriel's back. The formal, antique chairs were upholstered in heavy gold brocade which harmonised with the plush wallpaper.

Lou-Lou hadn't exaggerated about the décor. It was everything he had described. Tall white pillars divided the

196

restaurant into different levels giving the impression that each damask-draped table had its own special space, though still enabling the guests to discretely view each other.

"Oh, Gabriel, I love all the potted white orchids. How marvellous - what a great idea for our boutique," Mary said.

"I am a little reluctant to admit it but, at this moment, I am not seeing the ambience, just the potential gossip," Gabriel replied.

"I thought we were made of sterner stuff than that," Mary quietly jibed as the waiter appeared to take their order.

Gabriel listened while Mary chatted about her family's visit. Although he asked appropriate questions she could see his heart was not in it. He declined dessert and she reluctantly agreed they would forfeit coffee there to have it back at the apartment. As they waited at the entrance door for the taxi a large car drew up with a group of late-night diners. Mary instantly recognised the haggard face of Santos Dubois's wife as she stepped onto the pavement. The wife was followed by another couple and then by Santos. Mary tried to huddle in behind Gabriel so she wouldn't be seen. It was too late.

"My god, what a divine dress that tall woman is wearing! Is it one of your's, Santos? She must be a model," the Dubois' female companion commented.

Mary was certain she saw steam rise from Santos's head. His wife, sensing the drama that was about to unfold, swiftly took Santos's arm and steered him towards the door as Mary and Gabriel took off in the taxi.

"Bloody hell! That was close. It nearly happened all over again," Mary said.

"And that is precisely the situations I try and avoid."

Mary thought better of continuing the Santos conversation and they sat in silence during the rest of the ride back to the apartment. As they walked up the stairs, Mary gently caught Gabriel's hand.

"I want you," she whispered as he unlocked the door. She turned her back and asked Gabriel to unzip her. The satin-lined, lurex dress slid dramatically to the floor. Mary seductively stepped out of the fallen gown. She stood in the centre of the salon in her high, black, patent shoes and her pure white lacy underwear and gently played with her hair. In that moment all else was forgotten. Her lover's excitement was obvious as he lead her through to the bedroom. After the prolonged absence Mary's sexual excitement was heightened but, for the first time, she indulged in pure sensual pleasure, separating it from her emotions. The coupling was feverish and they climaxed in a mutual orgasm before falling into a satisfied sleep.

It was one of the rare occasions where Gabriel stayed through till morning. Mary was propped up in bed on a pile of cushions looking through her sketch pad when Gabriel joined her with fresh coffee.

"May I distract you for a little while from your work, ma chérie?" he asked. Mary placed her pad beside the bed and took the coffee.

"You seem to be a little upset with me in some way since your mother's visit. Normally you have been quite content to be with just me when we meet," Gabriel said.

"Yes, that's true. I was happy with that, but I'm not yet twenty years old and now I feel I want to break out a little. If I'm going to make my designs famous I need to at least see and hear first-hand what Parisian women do, say and wear at the popular restaurants and clubs."

"Now they sound like words Lou-Lou would say! He is putting ideas into your head." Gabriel's tone was sharper.

"Rubbish! I make my own decisions, Gabriel. I think this conversation is not about you wanting to be with me alone, but rather that you are married and don't want to be seen with me in public." Mary placed her coffee on the bedside table and folded her arms.

"Mary, I have been honest with you, ever since Monaco. You are the one I love," his voice rose even higher. Mary backed off. Confrontation was one thing but raised voices and yelling brought up other memories.

"Don't you yell at me," she said, "I'm going to have a shower."

When she returned, fully dressed and obviously ready to leave, Gabriel turned from where he had been staring blankly out the window.

"I am so sorry I raised my voice. Please, my Kiwi, let us not argue. We are embarking on an exciting new venture and I'm sure we can work out some compromise."

Mary offered no response. She just gave a token smile and said, "Come on, let's go and have breakfast somewhere discreet!" After breakfast Mary said goodbye and left for her own apartment.

As she walked in the door the fragrance of basil and tomatoes tickled her nostrils. Lou-Lou was installed on the sofa and Annabel stood at the cooker making her signature dish, Spaghetti Bolognese with pesto sauce.

"Bonjour Kiwi, ca va?" Lou-Lou cooed.

"You have timed it perfectly," Annabel said as she placed a

fresh salad alongside the bowl of steaming spaghetti.

"This is my favourite time of the week, when the 'three musketeers' have their ritual weekend lunch." Mary snuggled next to Lou-Lou. They chatted generally about the Moulin Rouge and the countdown for the shop opening. Then Annabel turned to Mary.

"So, how is it with Gabriel?"

"Umm, okay." Mary toyed with her food.

"Spit it out, Kiwi!" Lou-Lou prompted.

"Well, mum and I had some fairly frank discussion about the events that originally brought me to Paris. It's made me think about what may happen further down the track with Gabriel. So I've agreed with her that she will replace Gabriel's investment in our business once she's sold the farm." "Fine by me. In fact, I didn't like to commit previously as I'm never sure how the land lies at any one time with my mother. However, the family lawyer has informed me I'm due for a lump sum inheritance from my late father when I turn twenty-five."

"That's great news for both of you. So I guess, Mary, what you are telling us is your romantic future doesn't necessary lie with Gabriel?" Annabel asked.

The three friends chatted for some time about the pros and cons of being a mistress. Inadvertently, the frankness of their exchange revealed more about their family situations than ever before. Annabel said her father would be too scared to have a mistress as her mother's wrath would be a fate worse than death. Then Lou-Lou commented that his mother was sure his father had a mistress but when his father died no-one came out of the shadows.

33

Lou-Lou and Mary both arrived at the shop early on Monday morning to commence the shop fit-out in earnest. The shop fitter was due at 9am. Lou-Lou had wallpapered the partitions while Mary had cut and sewn stunning fitting room and window curtains. They fussed like a pair of expectant parents as the shop fitter patiently waited for their final decision on placement of the stained wood garment rails. Only once the rails were secured and the partition panels in place did they allow the harassed man to pop out for his lunch.

They gulped down a baguette and then hung the heavy beige, shot-taffeta curtains across the doorway to the newly partitioned back room and around the rails that were erected to make fitting room space.

"Dash! I should have got that chap to secure the curtain rail in the window before he went for lunch," Mary said with a sigh.

"Well, my Kiwi, I think between us we've pushed him to the limit this morning. This is France, you know. It's not usual for a Frenchman to miss a meal in favour of work."

"Do you mind if I go out and look for my orchids?" Mary asked.

"Please do. It will allow me to breathe and may provide some light relief if you're not here when our man returns." Lou-Lou placed his hands on his hips in an exaggerated gesture.

Mary spent an enjoyable hour in the fragrant flower and plant shop on Rue Mouffetard. She was on a mission. She pushed the shop owner's patience to the limit by insisting he check whether there were even better formed orchids in his store room. He was relieved when she finally requested he order her a taxi to take her and the 40 pots of orchids back to her shop.

As the taxi pulled up in Rue Barbette Mary's heart beat quickened. The shop sign had been erected and the expensive decision to not paint it but raise the lettering in a metallic silver finish was worth it - it looked magnificent. Lou-Lou had hung the curtains exactly how she had envisioned they should be - just skimming the edge of the large window and fastened with giant silver and beige tassels.

As Mary struggled from the taxi and placed the boxes of potted orchids on the foot path, Gabriel arrived beside her.

"Ma chérie you look so beautiful with your hair tied back, and surrounded by white flowers," he said.

Mary beamed. "What do you think of it so far?" She stood back to admire the shop front as Lou-Lou joined them on the pavement.

"Remind me again, how you arrived at 'Mousseline de Soie Chantal' for the name? Gabriel asked.

"Coincidently,   my   second   name   and   Lou-Lou's grandmother's name happened to be Chantal. Perhaps a little common but, apparently, it was the one thing my Parisian birth father requested, and we both love using silk chiffon. The wholesale collection will just be called 'Mousseline de Soie'," Mary replied.

They carried the pots of orchids inside and Gabriel inspected the almost completed space.

"Will you have all the garments ready for the opening?" he asked.

"I think we can relax now the fit-out is almost finished. The last lot of fabric will be delivered tomorrow so then we can focus on the opening collection," Lou-Lou replied.

Gabriel embraced Mary before he left and insisted that she agree to be at the apartment on Wednesday evening.

The following two days sped by with Mary cutting the fabric and Lou-Lou zealously, but precisely, sewing up each dress. They sent the trousers and shirts out to a small factory in Sentier but were minimising costs by, wherever possible, completing many tasks themselves.

Mary rushed via the Métro to meet Gabriel as arranged. She hadn't been home to change so she was relieved when he was late as it gave her time to wash and apply fresh make-up. At 7.30pm the phone rang.

"It is me, Mary. I have to make this quick. I'm at the hospital

'Necker-Enfants Malade'. My little boy, Jean-Claude, is very ill so I won't be able to make it. I'll call you as soon as I can." Then Gabriel hung up.

Mary felt empty. What could she offer? It dawned on her that maybe she'd been very selfish in not giving Gabriel much attention since her mother's visit. Thoughts of her little sister being sick as a baby, rushed through her mind. She flicked through the phone book till she found the address of the hospital then phoned, and in her struggling French, asked which Métro station was the closest.

She ran to the Métro and negotiated her way to Pasteur station as directed. The large hospital building was easy to find on Rue de Sèvres. Mary was directed to the relevant ward and slowed her pace when she recognised Gabriel's voice speaking French in a soft consoling tone.

As she approached the private side room, the occupants had their backs to her. A suddenwave of realism shot through her. Gabriel had his arm around a petite blonde woman, who was obviously his wife, and a small fair haired boy stood beside him. They were all focussed on the sick child in the hospital bed.

Mary then clearly heard Gabriel speak. She picked up most of the words especially 'ma chérie'. It hit her how stupid she'd been. She wasn't his exclusive 'my Darling' - she was just one in a line. Here were the people to whom he was committed. Mary backed away, turned and walked rapidly out of the hospital. A new type of shame seeped in as she thought of those innocent children and the wife who probably assumed they were Gabriel's only 'mes chéries' as well. By the time she reached home, Mary had a made a firm decision.

The following day, after Mary and Lou-Lou completed two hours of sewing, Lou-Lou broke the silence.

"Now, Kiwi, I may be reading it all wrong, but I strongly

sense something awful has happened since you were here yesterday."

Mary gave a sigh. "Yes, your sense is correct. I received a shock last night. Gabriel phoned to say his little boy was ill in hospital. Without thinking I rushed to the hospital to be with him and, of course, he was with his wife and other son. It was a technicolor moment. He's not mine and never will be. Those darling children have first claim and that woman is their mother." She rubbed her watery eyes. Lou-Lou took her hand.

"If it helps, I had a letter yesterday to inform me the trust money from my Papa has been paid into my bank account. So we can use that rather than any more of Gabriel's investment." Mary slipped her arm inside Lou-Lou's arm.

"I love you, Lou-Lou Rock, and it's the best kind of love - no sex, and no complications," she said. They then sat down and, without speaking, finished their coffees before returning to the sewing.

Mary didn't hear from Gabriel until the end of the next day. He sounded relieved when he phoned. His son had been struck with meningitis, but it was the less threatening strain. As they had him admitted to the hospital so promptly, it looked as though he would be okay. Mary listened then asked him if they could meet at the apartment the next morning.

It was with much trepidation that Mary walked the familiar route to Gabriel's apartment.

"Gabriel, first I have to tell you how much I appreciate all you have done for me..." Before she had finished he interrupted.

"If this is about the other day, please, my son was so sick."
"Hush Gabriel!" Mary said. "Let me speak. As I was saying,

I could never have started up the business if it hadn't been for your generous offer and your encouragement. But after seeing you at the hospital with your family, I know I can never be number one in your life. That slot is taken and, long term, I'm just not mistress material." She paused.

"What were you doing at the hospital? You must give me time, Mary. I will get a divorce. It will just take some time." He was desperate.

"I hadn't finished, Gabriel. You must hear me out." Mary raised her voice a notch. "Over the next 12 months, Lou-Lou and I will pay you out of your investment and, if you still wish to hold shares then, we will accept that. It's not that I wish you divorced. You have two children who must come first. I never came first with either of my fathers and I don't want to be involved in a situation where children are the ones to be hurt." Mary's tears mingled with her running nose. Gabriel reached out to her but she stood back and blew her nose.

"Please don't make it any harder than it is. I would love you to be at the shop opening as a business partner but, other than any professional dealings, for my own sake, we must finish this now"

She collected her coat. Gabriel sat with his head in hands. Mary resisted comforting him. She placed her keys on the table and left the apartment for the very last time.

34

There was only one week to go before all the garments needed to be completed for the shop opening. The invites for the opening night party had gone out and the response was tremendous. Nearly all the fashion media sent affirmative replies, as had Lou-Lou's huge diverse circle of friends and the Moulin Rouge crowd. Mary's concern was how they would all fit in the shop.

"It's such a quiet street they can spill out onto the pavement. The greater the crush of people, the more atmosphere," Lou-Lou announced. "Leave the party to me, Mary. That's one thing I'm good at." The two friends hopped off the Métro and grabbed Chinese takeaways to take back to share with Annabel in the apartment.

"It's amazing to think we are nearly there - almost shop owners with our own label. I have to pinch myself to believe it's real," Mary said as they tucked into their meal.

"So, are you missing Gabriel?" Annabel inquired. Lou-Lou gave her a grimacing glance.

"Don't worry, I'm okay. Yes, I'm missing him but, with you two and the love restored in my New Zealand family, I'll get over it," Mary replied. They had just settled into their second glass of wine when the phone rang.

"That will be one of your many admirers, Annabel, so I'm not getting it," Mary said, but she was wrong.

"It's your sister, Mary. She sounds upset." Annabel held out the phone receiver. Mary shuddered, a cold shiver coursing down her spine, as she took the phone. The other two were silent as Mary listened to her sister. They watched as the light extinguished from her eyes and her face turned a brutal shade of grey. After what seemed an age she managed a few words.

"Susan, oh Susan, how terrible. Yes, let me digest all this then I'll call you back soon." Mary dropped the phone.

"No, please god, no! Not my mother. Please let this be a nightmare," she wailed. Her entire body screamed in pain - raw, stinging, cold pain. Her limbs, her skin, her head, felt completely out of any control and she crumpled to the floor. Lou-Lou rushed to her while Annabel gently hung up the phone. Both friends sat down on the floor beside her, embracing her from either side. Mary shivered, she was frozen cold. Then she wept. After a prolonged period she gained enough composure to tell her friends what her sister had said.

"Mum had cancer. She didn't want me to know when she was here but she knew she was dying. Although Susan suspected it all, Mum made light of it until they arrived back in New Zealand. Then her health rapidly declined. She didn't want me to come back for the funeral. She wanted me to remember her as we all were, happy here in Paris," she said. Both Annabel and Lou-Lou began to cry.

"Oh, Mary, your beautiful mother, oh no," Lou-Lou sobbed. Annabel finally managed to put the kettle on and make tea.

"You and your tea! Thank goodness I have you two." Mary said. She phoned Susan back to talk through the details of the funeral. Lou-Lou offered to postpone the shop launch but Mary reiterated Susan's instructions.

"Mum was insistent that I didn't change any plans. She wanted to imagine the grand shop opening and it all going off well, so we must make it happen as planned."

That night Mary cried until she had no tears left. She lay in her bed engulfed in grief, memories flooding her body. They took her back to her childhood on the farm. She went chronologically through all the dress-making skills her mother had patiently taught her - the basic press and tack before you sew all your seams, bind any button holes that encase an obvious button, drape a garment on a body and don't let it cling.

She culled out any memories of her step-father. Jamie's presence in her thoughts seemed intertwined with her mother's. His teasing comments about her newly-made teenage designs, his wide smile and his amazing ability to catch a frog, spear an eel and kick a rugby ball. She finally drifted off with his last words of youthful love entangled in her dreams.

Mary was grateful that the following days leading up to the shop opening party were so busy. The activity helped distract her from her grief. Lou-Lou was stoic and managed all the details but still appeared at difficult moments when Mary had a wobble of panic and grief.

Annabel and Lou-Lou helped choose an appropriate dress for Mary to wear. She couldn't bear the thought of applying make-up and having her hair done when her mother was lying barely cold in the ground. But Susan's words rang in her ears with her mother's wish that Mary's business be launched as planned.

Annabel carefully put the finishing touches to Mary's hair and makeup in the workroom. Lou-Lou was out front greeting all the guests and ensuring that the very cute waiters correctly poured the champagne. He brought in a glamorous female assistant for the evening whose job it was to identify the media guests as they arrived and hand them a press release which included a bio on Mary and copies of her talented sketches of the garments that featured in Paris's latest boutique, 'Mousseline de Soie Chantal'.

As Mary stepped out to join the crowd, Lou-Lou rushed to greet her in a manner that would honour royalty.

"Gosh, the fashion show must be starting. Who is that stunning model?" the gentleman from Paris Match magazine exclaimed. Lou-Lou radiated excitement. He clapped his hands and asked for silence as he stood beside Mary with his arm around her waist.

"Mesdames and Messieurs, Counts and Countesses, Members of the Press, it is my absolute pleasure on behalf of my fellow directors to welcome you to 'Mousseline de Soie Chantal'. I am very pleased to introduce you to my partner and our designer, the exceptionally talented Mary Chantal Hampton. She is half French but born in the antipodes and now a resident of Paris." The guests burst into applause.

Mary struggled to believe it was actually her he was talking about. Beneath the grief she felt a sense of pride as she listened to Lou-Lou's words. This was a dream come true. But with her mother's death it was a dream wreathed in a nightmare.

210

She spotted Gabriel loitering uncomfortably at the back of the crowd. She could see his face was racked with concern. As she pushed through the crush of people to reach him, she saw Annabel intercept him. Mary was about to join them but, as she moved forward, Gabriel had his back to her and she could hear Annabel's words.

"Gabriel, please don't approach her just yet. Something terrible has happened."

"That is apparent," he snapped as he tried to move in Mary's direction.

"Her mother just died. Please believe me, I know better than you how to deal with this," Annabel said as she held his arm.

"Oh my god, my poor Mary." He clutched his cheek. "Gabriel, you have to accept she isn't your Mary any more. Lou-Lou and I are dealing with it. We are her family now."

Gabriel straightened up. In such close proximity to people, he had to lean close to speak clearly into Annabel's ear. "She may not be my lover anymore but you can't stop me caring for her! I will be back tomorrow when this rabble has gone." Then he pushed his way through the crowd to the street and walked off.

Mary managed to chat to most of the media that Lou-Lou and his assistant introduced her to. Her French was now passable and they seemed to find her accent endearing rather than offensive. Mary recognised the angular bob and distinct pointy nose of the woman from 'Women's Wear Daily'. The woman held a copy of the media release in her hands as she approached Mary.

"I recognise this style of sketches. Did you previously work for Santos Dubois?" She spoke forcefully in heavily accented English.

"Yes, I did work for Monsieur Dubois for about a month but, Madame, although he did pay me for my designs, they were my sketches," Mary replied, also in English. The journalist gave a rather strange mocking smirk.

"Do you not believe me, Madame?" Mary said.

"Oh yes, I do. That is why I have this look." She pointed to her mouth. "I always knew that dreadful man had no talent!" She then offered what Mary saw as a grimace, but realised it was meant to be a smile and, as Lou-Lou arrived beside them, the editor marched off clutching her media release.

" Kiwi, looks like you just won the dragon bitch over!" "Well, I don't know about that. I may have provoked Santos Dubois a little more though. She was on a mission to verify the validity of my sketches," Mary replied.

"Oh, merde!" Lou-Lou exclaimed and dramatically put his hand to his chest. "I didn't think of that consequence. It can't be helped. But we must be very careful of him."

The final guests left around midnight. Annabel and Mary treated themselves to a taxi home.

"I need to tell you, Mary, what I said to Gabriel. I hope I didn't do the wrong thing." Mary squeezed her hand.

"I saw and heard and I appreciate your concern but he is probably the least of my concerns just now." The two friends dropped exhausted into their twin beds and were asleep before their heads had even touched their pillows.

35

Lou-Lou arrived at the shop at exactly the same time as Mary. They held identical paper cups from the same coffee franchise in their hands.

"Touché!" Lou-Lou said as he tapped his coffee against Mary's.

"We have precisely one hour to get this all sorted before our first official opening time. Do you think we'll have any customers today?" Mary was suffering a moment of lost confidence.

"I am absolutely sure we will. It was the best thing not allowing them to try on the clothes last night. Some of those women were gagging to slip into your designs, my darling friend," Lou-Lou said.

By 10.10am no customer had appeared. Mary's confidence was really waning. She busied herself hanging the garments with precisely one and a half inches between each hanger and delicately watering her orchids.

"Parisian women are not early risers and won't be seen seriously shopping prior to 11am. Trust me, Mary, anytime now," Lou-Lou attempted to quell Mary's anxiety.

At 11.05 the first customer walked into the shop. She was a woman of about 30, immaculately groomed in a casual way, denim jeans, soft beige Gucci loafers and a pure silk, cream shirt with pearl buttons. They bid her 'good morning' and let her browse. After she completed a scrutiny of all the rails, she commenced a second lap and this time picked out garments. She cast an expectant glance in Lou-Lou's direction and passed him the pieces.

"Let me put these in the cabin for you, mademoiselle." Mary smiled at his inappropriate but flattering word and at the grand manner in which Lou-Lou held her designs as he minced across to the 'cabins'. She'd laughed the first time she heard this word as, in her mind, it evoked a picture of a small room on a boat.

At that moment two more women walked in. There was no first lap of looking with these two.

"May I try the outfit in the window, please?" the shorter of the two requested. Then the first customer also demanded Lou-Lou bring it in her size, emphasising the words 'size six!' The outfit on the mannequin in the window consisted of trousers, a chemise, and a jacket which happened to be the highest priced jacket in the shop. Lou-Lou moved at lightning speed to bring his customer's size from the stock cupboard, while Mary found her customer's size on the hanging rail.

By midday they had sold ten pieces and didn't stop selling till they finally closed the door at six o'clock. They were both on a high as they cashed up the receipts for the day.

"I feel guilty being so pleased about all this when Susan is out there in New Zealand without any parents," Mary said as she wrote up the brand new stock book.

"I can only imagine how you must feel. When my father died over three years ago I had been estranged from him for five years so it didn't impact me in the same way," Lou-Lou replied.

"Did you love him?" Mary asked.

"Yes, when I was a little boy I adored him. But it cut me to my core when he was embarrassed by who I had become. He said being gay was one thing but one should keep that fact quiet and in the closet where it belonged. Being as flamboyant as I am was not something he could accept, so he wiped me from that day on. My mother and brother took his side. So they are dead to me now, too."

Mary reached out and hugged her friend. "My mother and sister loved you. They were enchanted with you in every way. That was such a bonus for me. So we are your family now." Lou-Lou delicately dabbed his eyes to avoid his mascara running.

"Here, it should be you that's crying and look at me, a silly gay cry baby. Now, on that note, do you think we should fetch your sister back over here to work as our vendeuse? We are not going to be able to achieve our production schedule if we have to serve in the shop all day."

"No, she needs to finish her course at polytechnic and I think she may now have a boyfriend so best she stays in New Zealand for now. Also, she will need to learn French first so I think we will have to find someone French to begin with," Mary replied as they locked up the shop. "Let's make that Monday's challenge. I'm so looking forward to a day off."

Mary ambled down the Rue Mouffetard on Sunday morning with her wicker basket. Grief stole any hunger she normally had prior to the ritual weekend meal. Annabel shooed her out of the apartment stating she would do the housework and instructing Mary to go out and, in addition to having her coffee at her usual café, buy something delicious at the market for lunch.

Mary purchased a roasted chicken and fresh salad. She sat in the window of café Le Verre à Pied and gazed at her coffee, her grief taking her to a dark place. It hovered around her and she would burst into tears spontaneously as a memory of her mother fluttered through her thoughts. She was about to cry when she felt someone looking at her through the glass. She didn't look up but a few seconds later she sensed a warm presence at her back.

"Mary Chantal Hampton, is that you?" At the sound of his strong kiwi voice Mary felt her heart leap. She swung around. There stood Jamie. He had grown even taller. His deep brown, familiar eyes gazed at her. He wore his hair much longer and it sat in a wave around his ears. He was dressed in a navy sweater and Levi jeans. Mary stood up and he awkwardly hugged her.

"Jez, Mary, you are all grown up!" At the sound of his pronounced New Zealand accent she burst into tears.

"Yeah, I'm so sorry about your mum," he responded as he pulled up a chair. "I tried to get here straight away when Dad phoned me in England but we had one more match and it was impossible."

Mary scrutinised him - his smouldering brown eyes, his broad muscular shoulders, his familiar hands, and she inhaled his personal masculine aroma.

216

"Thanks, it's been so hard because I've just started up a new business. I would have preferred to go back to New Zealand to be with Susan but Mum was clear she wanted me stay here and open the new shop as planned." They chatted for a while then Mary realised the time.

"Shit! Annabel will be mad. I have the lunch here with me."

"Don't stress, she knows you're with me. That's how I found you." As he spoke his entire face lit up. Inside, Mary melted, but she kept walking and tried not to appear too smitten. When they arrived back at the flat Mary noticed how extraordinarily tidy it all was, with the small table set perfectly for three, complete with their very best cloth napkins. Jamie made himself comfy on the sofa as the two girls prepared the lunch.

"Jolly gosh! He is a serious hunk," Annabel whispered. "I guess so," Mary smiled.

"Don't you dare play this down, Kiwi. He is mad about you. I can see it all over his face when you speak," Annabel continued to whisper.

"Shut up, he'll hear you." Mary playfully bumped her friend's hip en route to the table with the chicken.

"That was a great lunch, girls. Do you mind if I crash on your sofa tonight? I'll find a cheap hotel tomorrow. I have to be back by Wednesday for Saturday's game. I managed 'compassionate leave' by saying my Aunty died," Jamie said.

"Yes," both girls replied simultaneously.

The three of them sat talking late into the evening. Annabel was enthralled by Jamie's childhood stories about Mary's adventures with an eeling spear, horse riding and gardening with his old Māori grandmother.

217

Mary couldn't get off to sleep that night. The thought of her first love being so close in the next room gave her goose bumps. He was even more handsome than Gabriel. She finally drifted off to sleep with imaginings of his love making. The next morning when the girls walked into the living room Jamie was already up and had neatly packed up the bedding.

"I have to be at the shop all day," Mary said. "How about you meet me at 6 o'clock and we'll go for a meal somewhere?" She wrote down the shop address and the name of the nearest Métro station.

"Oh, by the way," Annabel interjected, "If Mary's happy with you on our sofa, so am I. So don't go to a hotel on my account. Besides, I'm staying over at a chum's place tonight." She gave Mary a discreet wink.

"Thanks, girls. I'm happy on the sofa and I'll be at your shop by 6, Mary," Jamie said.

36

When Mary arrived at the shop, she up-dated Lou-Lou on Jamie's arrival - not that he could concentrate on what she was saying. He was ecstatic about the weekend newspapers' coverage of the shop opening.

"I cannot believe you weren't waiting at the newsagent door like I was on Sunday." He handed her a copy of Le Monde. "I was somewhat distracted by the blast from my past," Mary said as she read the article as best she could.

"Here, let me translate, Kiwi." Lou-Lou took the paper back from her.

"I practically know it off by heart. I so hope my mother and brother have seen it. That will show them!"

'Mousseline de Soie Chantal' –
the hottest bouliyue in the Marais.
New young designer Mary Chantal Hampton has
teamed up with flamboyant Lou-Lou Rock and created
what can only be described as one of Paris's most
desirable independent boutiques. This New Zealand
born designer has obvious French blood in her veins

as her soft feminine designs are precise and sexy.
With her russet coloured hair and long legs, many
guests at the launch of Mousseline de Soie Chantal
assumed the stunning Mary Chantal was a model.

He continued to read out the articles as they were written but with his own added dramatic touches. Mary laughed as she heard herself described in another article as a 'long-legged, chic antipodeans'.

At 10 o'clock Lou-Lou scooted out to the newsagent and returned with a copy of Paris Match just as the first client of the day walked in. While Mary devoted her attention to the middle-aged customer, Lou-Lou oozed over the magazine article and photo.

"Lou-Lou, that was rude! That woman just spent over 5000 francs while you were making all that noise at the desk. Why didn't you go out to the workroom?" Mary said.

"Get you! It was good for her to hear how famous we are! She will tell all her friends."

Mary grabbed the magazine and felt a surge of pride at the black and white photo of her in front of the shop window. She had just finished serving another customer when she glanced up from the desk to see Wendi standing in front of her.

"Wendi, it's so good to see you. What are you doing here?" She hugged her former colleague. "Do you still work for Santos?" she asked.

"Oui, and now he are worse than ever. He screams at me all the time and I cannot bear it. When I read the article in Le Mondi yesterday I thought maybe you could offer me a job," Wendi replied.

"You are manna from heaven. We desperately need a vendeuse. When can you start?" At that moment Lou-Lou appeared from the workroom.

"Lou-Lou, this is an old friend, Wendi. Wendi, my business partner, Lou-Lou Rock." Lou-Lou eyed the French woman up and down.

"So, where have you been working, Madame?" he said, rather too frostily for Mary's liking.

"I have been the PA for Santos Dubois but, previously, I worked in sales. I adore Mary's designs so it would be a pleasure for me to sell such beautiful garments," Wendi replied with an accompanying humble smile.

"Lou-Lou," Mary interjected, "It is my job to employ the vendeuse. So please allow me to continue my interview." She rolled her eyes at Wendi.

"Very well, carry on." Lou-Lou folded his arms and leant against the desk. Mary discussed the salary with Wendi which was less than what she currently earned but, based on their cash flow projections, Mary had built in a monthly commission once the targets had been reached. Wendi readily agreed and, after a couple of interruptions from customers, Lou-Lou and Mary shook hands with Wendi to seal the agreement. She would commence in one week's time.

"I don't think that attitude was called for," Mary said to Lou-Lou once the shop was empty.

"Well, you are too soft, Kiwi. However, once you were in flow, I could see you had it under control. I like the commission angle. I wouldn't have thought of that." He chatted as he dressed the shop window mannequin for the second time that day.

Later in the day Mary was hand-sewing some buttons on a jacket in the workroom when Lou-Lou popped his head around the door.

"Quick, Mary, there is the most handsome man looking in our window. Come and see!" As she walked out into the shop Jamie walked in through the door.

"Jez, Mary, you've really pulled it off. This is bloody wonderful. Just how I always knew you could be - in Paris with your own shop!" Jamie stretched his hand out to Lou-Lou.

"How's it going mate? You must be the famous Lew. I heard all about you last night from the girls." Lou-Lou practically swooned as he enthusiastically returned the handshake.

"Actually, it's Lou-Lou, not Lew," he said.

"Ah, well, you look like a Lew to me." Jamie gave Lou-Lou's hand another squeeze. Lou-Lou diplomatically declined when they invited him to join them for dinner.

"He nearly always tags along with Annabel and me," Mary said as they sat on the Métro.

Jamie cocked an eyebrow. "He may be poofy, Mary, but he knows when a man wants to be alone with a girl."

"So, you have two more days in Paris. Where would you like to go for dinner?" Mary asked.

"I've checked your fridge out and it looks pretty bare so if we're going to eat out I thought you might like to join me in doing the tourist thing." He gave a cheeky smile.

"I remember that look, Jamie, you are about to tease me!"

"Nope, no teasing. It's a fact! I've booked a table at that restaurant up the Eiffel tower. I wandered around today to check it out and figured you wouldn't have done that yet."

"Oh, I'm a bit afraid of heights but I'll give it a go. I need to change first though." They called at the apartment and Mary changed into a simple dress and heels then they found a taxi to take them the short trip to the base of the Eiffel Tower. Mary grasped Jamie's hand for the entire journey heavenward via the lift, followed by some stairs. Not once did she look outwards at the view.

"You can breathe now, Mary," Jamie said once they were seated in the Jules Verne restaurant.

"My god, it's so high. Just give me a moment to adjust." Jamie pulled his chair closer to Mary. "According to my

research, we are actually 125 metres up and, if you can stretch your gaze a bit further, you will see more of Paris than you ever have in one glance."

Mary's fear of heights dissolved as Jamie's humour and charismatic smile distracted her.

"Deux verre de champagne s'il vous plaît," he said in perfect French as the waiter approached. "I am impressed," Mary said.

"Yes. I've been practising that all day," he laughed.

They ordered what Mary termed 'safe' choices from the traditional French menu and after a second coupe de champagne she was quite tipsy.

"So tell me, Mary, I can see all the obvious things you love about this place but do you see yourself here forever?" Jamie asked.

"Paris has allowed me to create fashion and taught me how to dance. But more importantly Paris has shown me how to live and be loved. For me, Paris feels like a world that allows me a role," Mary said with a slight champagne slur in her speech.

"Very profound. Didn't you feel loved at all when you were

growing up in New Zealand?"

"Oh, I don't mean to be derogatory to my mum or you and your family. You were all so kind to me, but the bad stuff that happened overrode anything good that I felt." Mary's mood swiftly changed.

"Okay, let's change the subject. Tonight is about you and me from little old New Zealand having a great time out in Paris, France." Jamie squeezed her hand and gave her another one of his reassuring smiles.

Mary's mood swung back to the previous heady heights in the company of her first love and in one of the most beautiful settings in the world. The evening whirled by, fuelled by antidotes of childhood adventures, stories of All Black victories and Mary's hilarious recall of Lou-Lou's antics. Nothing was mentioned, or asked, by either party about any other romantic entanglements.

Once they arrived back at the apartment, Mary was making hot chocolate drinks when she saw that Jamie had started to take the bedding for the sofa out of the cupboard. She sat next to him holding the two cups of steaming liquid.

"Thanks." Jamie leant over and gently pecked her cheek.

"My pleasure," Mary replied and widened her eyes in a seductive manner. They sipped their drinks in relative silence and, when Mary had returned from her bathroom visit, she felt a wave of disappointment to see Jamie was already under the cover on the sofa.

"Thanks for a wonderful evening," she managed to say with a smile.

"Night night, see ya tomorrow," he replied in the exact same manner he had when they were children.

With Jamie on her sofa sleep didn't come easy for a second night. Mary kept imaging what he might look like naked. She worked herself into quite a sweat before sleep finally gave her some relief.

Jamie was already up when Mary appeared from the bedroom the next morning. He was studying a tourist brochure.

"Hi, I thought I'd see a few more sights today." They shared a hurried breakfast and Mary left for work after they agreed he would meet her at the shop around 6pm.

∽

"So tell me all - What happened last night?" Lou-Lou asked as they sat in the back room sewing on buttons before the shop opened.

"We had a divine evening up the Eiffel Tower. It was wonderful to hear all about his rugby career but, before you probe any further, nothing happened! He slept on the sofa," Mary said.

"What? Well, that's it, he's gay." Lou-Lou roared with laughter at his own joke.

"Hardly," Mary retorted. "Perhaps he's just a gentleman or maybe he just sees me as a friend," she said.

"You can't fool me, Kiwi. The look in his eyes was as obvious as Liberace's jacket. He clearly has a long term plan that includes you." As Lou-Lou spoke they heard a knock on the shop door.

"It's only 9.45. Surely it's not a Parisian woman with any class this early?" Mary quipped as she hurried to the door.

"Oh, are you opening late today?" a tall snooty woman

asked as Mary opened the door. Mary smiled and humbly stood back as the 'grande dame' sauntered around the rails making small appreciative noises. Lou-Lou poked his head around the door from the back room. His eyes widened and he quickly jerked his head back.

"Louis, I can see you peeping," the 'grande dame' called although she kept looking straight ahead and flicking through the garments on the rail. Slowly Lou-Lou walked into the shop.

"Cousin Françoise, how wonderful to see you," he cooed. The tall woman turned around and looked Lou-Lou up and down.

"Well, I can see you still haven't toned it down at all," she said.

"No, and I don't intend to. Please allow me to introduce my business partner, the designer Mary Chantal Hampton." He gestured towards Mary.

"Humph! I thought she was the vendeuse. She's far too pretty to be a designer," the tall woman replied.

"Je suis heureux de vous rencontrer, Madame Françoise," Mary said.

"Oh, so you speak a little French? How enchanting." Françoise continued looking through the garments. After a while she picked out four styles and requested that Lou-Lou bring them to her in her size. Mary was astonished by how quiet he appeared in the presence of this snooty cousin.

Cousin Françoise bought three of the four pieces she tried on. Mary delicately packed them into the large lacquered Mousseline de Soie Chantal carrier bag, then walked with her to the door.

"Thank you, Madame Françoise, for visiting us. I look forward to seeing you again," Mary said.

"Well, maybe you will be good for Louis. This certainly looks like his best effort at anything so far," she responded as she walked off.

"What was all that about, 'Louis'?"

"First of all, don't ever call me 'Louis'! He died a long time ago. I'm Lou-Lou and that's an end to it. Secondly, she is my father's niece and will stir my mother up by telling her the gossip first-hand about Mousseline de Soie Chantal." Lou-Lou was very clear that the conversation was over.

At 5.30 Mary refreshed her makeup and undid her hair which had been tied up in a chignon all day.

"Oh, so Jamie's meeting you again today, I see." Lou-Lou took the brush from her and affectionately gave her hair a few strokes. When they heard the door open they both stepped into the shop expectantly only to be surprised to see Gabriel standing there with a large bunch of white roses.

"Roses for the peace of your mother's soul, ma chérie," Gabriel said as he handed her the bouquet. "I am so sorry for your loss. I trust I have waited an appropriate length of time so as not to upset you any more in your grief."

"Thank you, they're beautiful roses," Mary responded just before the shop door opened again. It was Jamie. He held a small bunch of what looked like hand-picked sweet peas.

"Jamie, this is Gabriel. He has invested in our business as a silent business partner," Mary said. Gabriel stood rooted to the floor as he took in the size and physique of the tall Māori man. "Jamie is my neighbour from New Zealand. He's been in Europe playing for the All Blacks on their European tour."

"Pleased to meet you, mate. You've made a good investment here. Mary's always been good at the designing. Gee, your flowers look pretty posh! They must be for Lew. I got mine from a froggy's garden - they were about to drop anyway," Jamie quipped as he handed Mary the stolen but fragrant flowers. He managed a sneaky wink at Lou-Lou who had taken an observer's step back in the scene.

"My flowers are for Mary who has just lost her mother," Gabriel managed to get out.

"Yeah, that's why I'm here... close family friend. Thanks, mate, but we need to get moving. I'm leaving in the morning," Jamie said and then added, "Glad you glammed up for me, Mary. Grab your bag and let's go."

"I can see this is an inappropriate time, Mary. I will call you later in the week," Gabriel snapped then walked out of the shop.

"How wonderful! You did it all with such a straight face, Jamie," Lou-Lou said. "Gabriel really didn't know quite where to put himself."

"Hush, Lou-Lou. Gabriel is kind and was only being thoughtful. Don't gloat over his discomfort," Mary said as she suppressed her own smile and found a vase to put the roses in.

Jamie shook Lou-Lou's hand. "I won't see you again till I'm over next. Lew, I trust you to keep your eye out for Mary."

Lou-Lou gave him a mock salute as Mary gathered her hand bag and the modest bouquet of sweet peas.

"So what would you like to do tonight?" Mary asked as they walked towards the Métro station.

"Your Paris, your choice," Jamie replied.

"Well, if you're willing to risk it, I'll cook for you. It will be pretty simple and I'll have to pass by the market," Mary said.

When they arrived home they found a note from Annabel saying she had called in for a change of clothes but was staying over at a friend's again and would see Mary the next day.

"And here I've bought enough for three," Mary said, "Perhaps I should call Lou-Lou?"

"No, you see him every day. Let's just be happy with you and me, aye Mary?" Jamie opened a bottle of red wine. While the food was cooking Mary set the small table with the best napkins and cutlery. They had a couple of glasses of wine before she served up the chicken and the fresh salad.

"Not bad for a girl who was never that interested in food," Jamie commented as he ate every last scrap on his plate. Mary smiled. "Now that's the smile I remember," Jamie said.

"What do you mean?"

"Well, you used to always laugh at my jokes, smile at my antics and, as a kid, I never thought about it much. But once you were gone I never found anyone else whose smile and laughter made me feel the way yours did." Jamie's tone softened. "Why, did you only write the once? Didn't you feel the same way about me?"

Mary wasn't prepared for this. It was a long time before she finally spoke. "I'm sorry, Jamie. You were the only happiness in my life back then and I should have kept in touch. I still have your letters. But I was so confused and unhappy from other things that happened to me I believed the only way I could move forward was to wipe all my past and find my real father."

Jamie waited for her to continue, then after an even longer pause he spoke. "I'm pretty sure I now understand what that arsehole step-father was doing to you. But you have to believe none of it was your fault. You were an innocent child."

Tears streamed down Mary's cheeks. Jamie moved beside her. He put his arm around her shoulders and handed her a napkin to wipe her nose.

"I'm damaged goods," Mary blurted out between sobs.

"To quote you, 'you've moved on'. That arsehole's being punished, you're reunited with your family, and now I'm here. What more could you want?" Jamie gave her one of his special smiles.

Mary managed a laugh amongst the tears and gave him a friendly push. "You always were full of yourself, you big show off!"

They cleared away the dishes and shared the washing up before settling on the sofa with another glass of wine.

"So, now we have the scary stuff out of the way, tell me about this poncy Gabriel Frenchy?"

Mary took a gulp of wine. "Well, he's pretty impressive. I thought I was in love with him. However, I finished it and I'm not going back."

"I'm guessing he is married?" Jamie probed.

"In the beginning I believed what I wanted to. But yes, if someone is not divorced then they are married. Now I think, deep down, I believed it was all I deserved." She took another gulp of wine.

"Look, Mary, I've had more than a few relationships and, on reflection, I wasn't particularly honourable in any of them. My rugby status and the fact I've studied law seem to have the girls almost throwing themselves at me. So what was I to do?" He shrugged his shoulders.

"Still full of yourself," Mary said.

"Well, maybe I am. I've never confessed that to anyone but you. I wondered if I would still feel the same about you after all these years of not seeing you. Then, from the moment I looked at you through that café window, I knew that nothing had changed... except you looked even more beautiful."

Jamie leant forward and took Mary's face gently in his strong hands and lightly brushed her lips with his. Mary closed her eyes and, as she returned his kiss, shards of warmth ignited her being. They kissed for a long time. Jamie didn't move his hands any further.

"I so want to make love to you, Mary Hampton, but I want it all to be in the right way. So I think, if it's what you want as well, we should take it slowly?"

"I'm not sure what I want but that felt wonderful and 'normal' if that makes sense?" Mary replied. Jamie hugged her. After they'd horsed around, joking and laughing, Jamie began to make up the sofa bed.

"You can share with me if you want, but no funny business!" Mary said.

"I'd love to. I just hope I can control myself!"

Mary emerged from the bathroom with her neck to knee nightie on. Jamie raised a comical eyebrow before they fell exhausted and a little inebriated into her small bed and slept soundly till morning.

37

Mary said goodbye to Jamie at the Métro station. She offered to accompany him to the airport but he insisted she get back to the shop. Normally she would be inhaling the sights and sounds around her as she made the 20 minute walk through the Marais. But this day she was lost in thought as she pondered on the chaste night Jamie had spent in her bed. He just cuddled her with no hint of sexual overtones. Although grateful for his respect she didn't anticipate a repeat 'chaste' performance. His body was far too attractive.

"You look happy. You two obviously had a good time last night?" Lou-Lou commented as Mary handed him his coffee.

She smiled, "You wouldn't believe me if I told you, so I won't." At that point there was a tap on the shop door.

"Wendi, welcome to Mousseline de Soie Chantal," Mary said. Wendi was immaculately groomed, her hair tied tightly back in a chignon, wearing small pearl earrings and a simple black knee-length dress.

"I am so happy to be here. Monsieur Dubois went crazy when I told him I was leaving. I didn't tell him where I was going but, knowing his evil ways, he will have it out of one of the staff by lunch time," Wendi said.

"We must be very wary of that man. Believe me, he has a twisted mind. If you hear anything at all about him with reference to our shop you must tell us," Lou-Lou replied.

By mid-morning Mousseline de Soie Chantal was full of customers and by closing time Wendi had proved her worth. Most women took advantage of Mary's giving nature and encouraged Lou-Lou to be even more outrageous than usual. But Wendi handled the most difficult French women with an indifference that appeared to pacify them.

"What a great day," Mary exclaimed once they had locked the door and Lou-Lou had poured them each a small glass of white wine.

"I hope you are happy with me?" Wendi asked. Mary and Lou-Lou gave her a hug.

"I was a little concerned but you have totally won me over," Lou-Lou said as he replenished his own glass.

"May I suggest something?" Wendi asked. Mary nodded. "I think you should apply to show at Paris Fashion Week in September. I'm not sure of the exact requirements but I could phone tomorrow and get them to send us out the forms. I've done it all in the past for Monsieur Dubois and I'm quite friendly with the receptionist at the Paris Fashion Week office."

Lou-Lou clapped his hands. "Fantastic! That's something we were going to approach further along the track but, given all this positive publicity, my view would be there's no time like the present!"

"Do you really think we're ready?" Mary asked. "Absolument!" Wendi responded. Mary loved the way that word sounded in French... so much more affirming than in

English. Wendi continued, "If Monsieur Dubois can be in Fashion Week when he can't even sketch a dress, of course you deserve to be there."

The following week Mary received a letter from Jamie. It was full of humour but also peppered with endearments. She was impressed at how articulate he was with the written word. She found pleasure as she penned her response and felt confident he would enjoy hearing about all the shop goings on and about their application to Paris Fashion Week.

Annabel and Mary were a little like ships in the night with the different hours they worked, but that morning Annabel left a note on the table for Mary inviting both her and Lou-Lou for a meal that evening.

"I'm so glad to see you. I really do miss you both," Annabel said as she stood stirring her special pasta sauce.

"Sorry, we are a bit distracted, but we finally received the form from the Fashion Week people. It's a bit of a challenge to fulfil the criteria," Mary said.

Annabel stopped stirring and turned the element off. "But I thought Lou-Lou had several wholesale orders?"

"Yes, I do," Lou-Lou sighed, "But to establish ourselves as worthy of Fashion Week we need at least one international order and my contacts are all within France."

Annabel drained the pasta and poured herself a wine. "I may be able to help. I was saving my news for after dinner but this seems like an appropriate time to tell you."

"Tell us what?" Mary felt anxious.

"Well, after seeing your reconciliation with your family, Mary, I feel I should visit my family in London, especially as I've heard from my god-father than my father is unwell.

It's apparently not too serious but I'd never forgive myself if I didn't see him and something happened. I have two weeks holiday due to me so I may as well use it."

"I'm so happy for you." Mary gave her friend a hug.

"Me, as well," said Lou-Lou, "But how does this help us with Fashion Week?"

"Well, I won't tell you too much at this point but, trust me, I have a connection who may be able to help get your collection in front of an established London store. Give me a few days once I arrive over there to see what I can do."

"Sounds interesting," Mary said.

"I'm not sure of the mechanics of it but once I've done some investigating and asked a favour I'll phone you. Will you have sufficient money to fly over at short notice?" Annabel asked.

"Yes, for sure," Lou-Lou answered, "The sooner the better if we want to fulfil all the requirements within the time limit."

38

Mary was lonely in the apartment without Annabel coming and going. Gabriel phoned a couple of times attempting to lure her out for a meal but she resisted. She received three letters from Jamie and immediately replied to them all. With each correspondence they opened up a little more about their feelings for each other.

Mary spent at least twelve hours a day in the workroom designing and making all the sample garments, while Lou-Lou ran all over Paris sourcing the finishing trims and special pieces of fabric she needed to complete the look.

"I am so amazed how you show and tell Lou-Lou in your broken French and English which trim or buttons you fancy on a design and he manages to come back with the perfect piece! Your minds are so much in sync," Wendi commented as Mary joined her on the shop floor for a break.

"Yes, it always feels natural for me with him and we agree on most things," Mary replied. They were interrupted as Mary went to answer the phone.

"Oh, hello, Annabel, I was wondering if you would call." After a protracted conversation Mary had just put down the receiver when Lou-Lou walked in.

"Good news! Annabel has secured an appointment for us with the Harrods' Ladies Fashion buyer next Monday, god only knows how. She said she would tell me all when I arrive. She'll meet me at the airport on Sunday. I'm to take ten examples of the collection and all the sketches," Mary said.

"Merde! We will have to rush. Perhaps Wendi could phone the travel agents to do the flight bookings. Then I can sort out suitable baggage for you and the samples, and you can focus on which samples you will take and get them finished," Lou-Lou gabbled, sounding more than a little panicked.

That evening Mary phoned to inform Jamie of her trip. He made her promise she would spend at least two nights with him in London. The All Black test series had finished, with the Kiwis winning, and he'd chosen to stay on because he'd secured a temporary job assisting the coach of a London rugby team. Because of that, he had taken a short-term let on a studio flat in Chelsea.

Lou-Lou carefully encased each sample garment in tissue paper before packing them into two large, vintage Louis Vuitton cases that looked like they may have been his grandmother's. He packed Mary's own clothes in a small black leather bag. They caught a taxi together to the airport.

"Shit! The excess baggage was so expensive," Mary moaned.

"There was no way round it, Kiwi. We need to get the collection to London safely and those cases have served my family well for three generations," Lou-Lou reassured her. They both wore platform heels and bright coloured shirts. Their appearance drew glances from people going by as Lou-Lou gave Mary a protracted noisy hug before she disappeared to find her departure gate.

The flight was uneventful but Heathrow airport was daunting and it seemed an endless walk till Mary reached passport control. Then, when her cases didn't show up, she freaked. Finally, after a half hour wait, she was relieved to see the ancient Louis Vuitton cases tumbled out onto the luggage carousel.

"Kiwi, I'm so pleased to see you," Annabel said as she helped Mary push the wobbly trolley out the main airport doors. "I relented and borrowed Mummy's London car. I knew you would have a lot of luggage."

"I'm so grateful, and I'm so pleased to see you, Annabel. I've missed you like mad. Do you realise we've hardly been apart since we met over a year ago?" Mary said.

They just managed to fit the three cases into the two-door Jaguar.

"I've never thought of you as being able to drive. I guess that's because I never have." Mary belted up as they sped off onto the motorway.

"My parents have a town house and a country house so we all need to be able to drive. I've been with them in London since I arrived and, after my prolonged exit from their lives, they have agreed to accept my life style choice in Paris. They have gone back to the country tonight so we will have the place to ourselves," Annabel said.

"You don't mind about me staying with Jamie after tonight?"

"No, I would absolutely be doing the same if I was you. He's such a hunk!"

It was close to sunset as they left the motorway near Earls

Court but still light enough for Mary to see how different the architecture was from Paris. The buildings appeared more salubrious as they ventured into Knightsbridge. Annabel pulled the car up in front of a four story pillar-fronted white house with a wrought iron balcony on the first floor.

"Is your parents' apartment in here?" Mary asked. "Yes, but it's not an apartment, it's the whole house."

A chubby, smiley woman with messy grey hair and wearing some sort of uniform greeted them as Annabel unlocked the front door.

"Mary, this is Bonny. She has been with our family since before I was born." Bonny nodded at Mary and then made motions to carry one of the cases.

"No thanks, we will manage," Annabel said kindly as she lifted a case in each hand. Mary followed her with the other case towards the stairs. The stair case, with walls in navy blue embossed wallpaper, was lorded over by large paintings of stern looking men and women dressed in garb from what appeared to be various different centuries. Crystal chandeliers hung above the landing of each floor. Once they reached the second landing Annabel caught her breathe and opened a bedroom door.

"I thought you'd be more comfortable sharing with me, just like home," she said. The bedroom curtains and wallpaper were over-decorated with a matching chintz pattern. Two single beds were immaculately made up with extra little frilled cushions, and pictures of ponies and dogs decorating the walls. "Before you make a comment, Mary, my mother decorated this room for me when I was about eight years old. At least the beds are comfy and we have an ensuite." Annabel pointed to the door on the other side of the room. Mary opened the door to discover a large, equally floral decorated, bathroom.

"I love it all. I guess it's the London style."

Annabel gave Mary a tour of the house which included an impressive library, a dramatic dining room and a formal salon. They completed the expedition in the basement which housed a warm cosy kitchen. Bonny lifted a crisped potato-topped pie out of the large enamel Arga oven.

"I've made your favourite, Annabel," she said as she placed the pie, that smelt like fish to Mary, on a steel holder on the large scrubbed table.

"I'm pleased to have an evening here without my parents. They only eat upstairs in the dining room. This kitchen has always been my haven. It was usually just Bonny and I when they were away." Annabel squeezed the older woman's hand as she spoke.

Bonny went on to recall several stories of when Annabel was growing up. The girls listened in relative silence and Mary was reminded of Jamie's parents' large kitchen in New Zealand.

Once back up in the bedroom, Mary soaked in the large bath with the door open and they caught up on all the Paris news.

"Now, tell me the truth, Annabel. How did you get this appointment at Harrods?" Mary asked.

"Well, actually, my god-father is Sir Harold Fraser, the outgoing chairman of the Harrods' board. As I've been missing in action, so to speak, for a couple of years he was so pleased to hear from me that he pulled a few strings," Annabel replied with a smug grin.

The plan was for Annabel to accompany Mary to the presentation, but only speak if it seemed necessary for her to name drop. Both girls dressed 'to impress' as per Lou-Lou's instructions. Annabel wore a demure but sharply-cut trouser suit and Mary wore a bias-cut crepe de chine short dress in purple with low-heeled black pumps.

Mary's stomach was full of butterflies as the taxi pulled up outside Harrods. The exterior of the store was even more impressive than Galeries La Fayette. They were directed by an officious liveried doorman to the appropriate entrance and practically circumnavigated the entire store before locating the service entrance.

The doorman at the service entrance also wore a uniform but it was more of a smock and without the polished gold buttons. Once he phoned through, he placed the garment bags the girls were carrying on a trolley and motioned for them to follow him into a large elevator.

A well-groomed middle-aged woman dressed in a black suit greeted them as the lift doors opened on the fourth floor.

"Hello, welcome to Harrods. I'm Miss Higgins, the senior women's wear buyer." She extended her hand first to Mary and then to Annabel. Mary responded as formally as she could, introducing Annabel first.

Miss Higgins then guided them through to what Mary assumed was some sort of board room. In the centre was a large table surrounded by ten chairs. There were three long garment rails standing at one end of the table.

"I'll leave you ladies to prepare your collection and then return with the junior buyers," Miss Higgins said as she left the room.

"She doesn't look like what I imagined," Mary said as she shook the dress she was holding and then carefully hung it on the rail.

"The English are a very different breed to the French. 'Chic' doesn't often enter their vocabulary," Annabel quipped. Mary colour-blocked the garments on the rails as she'd rehearsed with Lou-Lou and, after moving the first two chairs away from either side of the table, she laid her sketches at its end.

Miss Higgins returned with five other women. Much to Mary's relief they were a lot younger and had a bit more style about them. The older woman introduced them individually and Mary caught a wink that passed from one of them to Annabel. Then they sat down whilst Mary took the floor. She outlined her concept for the collection, matched up the styles with other colour-ways from the sketches, and talked a little about the Paris boutique.

Miss Higgins asked about pricing and Mary handed out the price list for the buyers to peruse. At that point an old woman in a starched white apron opened the door and wheeled in a tea trolley. The group broke ranks from around the table. Some went straight for the tea and a biscuit but two moved over to look more intently at the garments. The girl who winked at Annabel spoke to Mary first.

"So how did you meet your assistant?" She pursed her lips and placed an emphasis on the word 'assistant'.

Before Mary could reply Annabel was at her side and whispered, "Hush Antonia, you always were a big mouth." The young buyer laughed and then cast a keen eye at each garment. Miss Higgins joined them at the rail.

"I have to say, Miss Hampton, you are your own best

advertisement. You look wonderful in the dress you are wearing. Don't you think so Antonia?" The senior buyer gave Mary an appraising look.

"Absolutely, Miss Higgins. With all the loose baggy styles we've seen this season it's refreshing to see something a little more feminine and sexy," Antonia replied. She spoke as if she had a large plum in her mouth.

"We usually just take your price list and a note of the styles, but could you leave the sketches with us for a day? Then you can collect them when we make the order the day after tomorrow." Mary's heart jolted as it dawned on her this was an actual order.

"I'll see Miss Hampton out, Miss Higgins," Antonia said and the older woman left the room with the others. Mary was carefully hanging the garments back in the bags when Antonia shut the door.

"What are you up to, Lady Annabel Louise Elisabeth Fraser? I heard a rumour you were dancing at the Moulin Rouge after you disappeared, but a design assistant? Whatever next?" Antonia exclaimed. Mary's eyes widened.

"Shut up, you silly cow. This is my best friend, Mary, who I'm helping and, yes, I am a dancer at the Moulin Rouge. All the rumours are true." Annabel put her arm around the girl.

"Mary, this is my second cousin, the Honourable Antonia Fraser, a snooty cow but an all-round good stick for pushing the order through."

Mary was momentarily lost for words. "Thank you very much," was all she managed.

"Oh, I do genuinely love the collection. It's what I do, you know, buy for the new designers' department. The old girl fancied you, I could tell. She's a raving lesbo," Antonio said.

Once they were out of the building and in the taxi, Mary gave her friend a prod. "So is that true? Are you a 'Lady'?"

"Only by virtue of my birth. I knew my title would have no effect on you and, as you know, many of our friends would dispute that term, given I dance in the Moulin Rouge for a living and hang out in La Huchette for my pleasure," Annabel replied.

When the garments were safely packed back in the cases, Mary gathered her own bag and gave her friend a hug. " I'll see you in two days' time when we're due to travel back to Paris together," she said.

39

Mary followed Annabel's instructions and easily navigated the tube system to Sloane Square. Jamie had given her instructions on how to find his flat - straight down Kings Road to Bywater Street on the right.

Although Mary was keen to see Jamie, the shops and the locals on the Kings Road were distracting. She was intent on absorbing as much of this new influence as she could. It seemed 'Punk' may have peaked and 'New Romantic' was the look on the street. Mary was fascinated by lots of butch-looking men wearing heavy, black eye makeup with their hair gelled up in spikes. Many of the shop window displays mirrored what was being worn on the street, which was a lot of colour punctuated with black. The dress code seemed a lot freer than that on Paris streets. Although there were several big-brand stores on the Kings Road, there were also many individual boutiques.

Mary was absolutely enchanted when she spotted a small shop on a corner called 'Moa', the name of an extinct New Zealand bird. The shop was fitted out entirely with Māori type decor. The clothes looked colourful and diverse but, just as she was about to look inside, she noticed the sign on the next side street - Bywater. She glanced at her watch. Moa would have to wait. Jamie would be wondering where she was.

Number six was a few houses along from the corner. Mary pressed the bell for flat two.

"Jez, Mary, where've you been?" Jamie called into the intercom as he buzzed her in. The flat was one big room with a sofa bed, a tiny kitchen and a shower room off a small hallway. Mary could see he had put in some effort. The place was immaculate and a vase of fresh roses sat in the middle of the small table.

"Did you steal these?" Mary asked as she sniffed the flowers.

"No, I bought them off that flower seller on the Kings Road, though I admit I waited till 7pm last night and he gave them to me at half price." Jamie raised his eyebrow.

Over coffee Mary filled him in on both the Harrods' visit and Annabel's family revelation. Jamie suggested a walk then an early supper at his favourite local eating place.

"Oh, damn. I wanted to look in the Moa shop," Mary said as they reached the corner.

"She shuts at 6pm. She's some Kiwi ex model and a bit snooty, if you ask me. The clothes aren't even from New Zealand," Jamie informed her.

They walked towards the World's End at the top of the Kings Road. Jamie pointed out the famous 'Pheasantry' building and Mary was captivated by the boutiques that only sold 'Punk' clothes. The window mannequins wore ripped fishnet tights and had all manner of piercings. After they'd paid homage to the famous Vivienne Westwood's weird boutique, they walked back to 'The Chelsea Kitchen', an old-fashioned diner with cosy booths for eating in. The menu was cheap and the food very English. Jamie informed Mary it had been there for twenty years. She figured they hadn't changed the menu in twenty years either but thought better of voicing that out loud.

When they arrived back at the flat Jamie lit a couple of candles that sat in a holder on the window sill, poured them each a glass of wine, and put on some music.

"I think I'm getting a bit tipsy. I'd better not have any more," Mary said as Jamie refilled her glass.

"Nonsense, you've done all that hard selling work today. Just relax. Anyway, I enjoy seeing you a bit out of control!" He put the wine bottle down, leant over, gently pulled Mary's head towards his own and softly kissed her lips. Mary placed her glass on the side table and put her arms around his body. He felt so strong. She sniffed in his unique body fragrance which evoked memories of their childhood together. Then he gently pulled her to her feet and, in a flash, had the sofa into its bed form.

To Mary, it seemed to play out in slow motion. They kissed and cuddled for awhile before he gently began to unbutton her shirt. Her nipples stood out rock hard through her white satin bra. She pulled her own jeans off as Jamie undressed. His body looked magnificent as his taut brown skin glistened in the flickering light of the candles. He gently kissed her lips, her cheeks, her eye lids and then moved downwards to her neck and ears before undoing her bra. His arousal was apparent as he slowly licked her nipples. Mary's excitement matched his as he slid her white lace panties down and

247

entered her most secret place. He rested on his elbows and looked directly into her eyes.

"You are so beautiful and you feel so amazing," he whispered before they both climaxed in an explosive mutual orgasm.

They dozed, they laughed and Mary cajoled him, till Jamie finally got out of the bed to get her a glass of water. She lay back on the fresh white sheets and basked in the afterglow of love making, a part of her wishing she could stay in this small flat with him forever.

"I only wanted water," she said as he returned with a bowl and two spoons.

"You've got to try this ice cream. It's amazing," he said popping a large spoonful of chocolate ice cream into her mouth.

In the following two days Jamie showed Mary his London which included Camden Market, Soho and, of course, the Twickenham rugby ground. They made love in the late afternoon, the evenings and the mornings.

"I'm so going to miss you. When do you think you'll get to Paris next?" Mary asked as they walked to Annabel's parents' house.

"I've committed to this coaching job and only have two consecutive days off every other week. I'll need to get the lie of the land with it all before I can confirm anything. Besides, you have a collection to prepare for Paris Fashion Week," Jamie replied.

"Well, it's not certain yet. We have the Harrods' order and several French orders, but we still have to be accepted by the panel but, yes, I'll have a lot to achieve."

Annabel was waiting in the hallway when they arrived at her house. Jamie helped the girls with their cases into the black cab.

"Gee, this is heavy, Annabel. What have you got inside - a gold bar?"

"My father bought me a video recorder for our television. I'm so excited because I can watch my own dancing now." She hopped into the cab.

Jamie took so long kissing Mary good bye that Annabel yelled, "Either get a room, you two, or get in the cab, Mary. I don't want to miss my plane!"

On the flight back Mary updated Annabel on her London adventures and Annabel shared a little more of her past with Mary. She spoke of her snobbish, middle class mother. From what she experienced growing up, Annabel thought her mother only married her father and gave birth to his children to gain the title and financial and social benefits that came with it. Annabel had never seen her mother show any sign of affection towards her father, and her mother never once told Annabel she loved her. As a teenager, she only ever criticised her daughter for the choices she made. Annabel's father was sympathetic towards his daughter and definitely not a snob, but he was spineless and would never stand up to his wife.

"We've reached a truce of sorts. Mother says as long as no-one in London hears about 'my carry on' in Paris, I'm welcome to visit them in England. However, until I prove I can get a 'proper' job or I land a decent husband, I won't receive my allowance as my brother and sister already do."

"Gosh, I find it so hard to understand that dancing can be seen as such a derogatory thing," Mary replied.

They went on to discuss the merits of the English class system and New Zealand colonial habits, and ended up agreeing that being a foreigner in Paris was the status they were both content with.

It was early evening when their plane touched down. Lou-Lou met them at the airport. They struggled to get all the luggage plus the three of them into a taxi. Lou-Lou was unusually quiet during the ride into Paris.

"Come on, boyfriend, what's wrong?" Mary asked once they were all seated in the girls' apartment with a glass of wine. "I don't like to say 'cause I think I might just be being paranoid," he replied.

"Well, what if you are? It's never held you back before," Annabel responded.

"Okay. Well, on three occasions I've seen the same flashy blue sports car cruise along our street, then slow down in front of the shop. Wendi says Santos Dubois has a car just like it. And he saw me in Café La Perle on Thursday evening and actually spat on the floor in front of me. It may be he's just pissed off that Wendi left him and is working for us but I'm afraid he is actually quite mad in the head." Lou-Lou let out an exaggerated sigh.

"Look, I don't doubt it was that evil man, but let's try and look at the situation logically. We are not going to sack Wendi just because Santos Dubois may be acting in a threatening manner. She's our friend and she is perfect for the job. Also, what can he actually do to us? Throw paint on the window?" Mary replied.

"I hope you're right but I just have a sick feeling in my stomach about him," Lou-Lou said.

40

Mary, Lou-Lou and Wendi spent all Monday carefully filling out the application for Paris Fashion Week. Lou-Lou had secured five orders from substantial French stores for Mary's first ready-to-wear collection and they were waiting for the one from Harrods to be confirmed. That meant they satisfied the first of the criteria - just. Wendi's receptionist friend at The Paris Fashion Week office slipped her a list of the ten committee names. They had the final say as to who was chosen and Wendi gave Mary and Lou-Lou as much information as she could about them.

"One of them is a closest queen who I know, so we should be able to get him on side," Lou-Lou commented as he scrutinised the list. "There are at least two here that Gabriel will know so, Mary, I think you should consider having a chat with him and see if he will put in a good word for us."

"Why? Don't you think my collection will stand on its own merit? Once we meet the first two parts of this application, it says five of the committee will come and have an informal look at our brand." Mary was of full of indignation.

"Get off your high horse, Kiwi. It goes without saying

the collection is up to it. However, unfortunately, in the real world it's fifty percent talent and fifty percent politics, and with manipulators like Santos Dubois in the arena, we have to play smart," Lou-Lou replied.

Mary took a big gulp of humble pie before she dialled Gabriel's work number. He needed little encouragement to meet her that evening for a drink.

"Let me say first off that this is a business meeting. As you are still a shareholder of Mousseline de Soire Chantal, I'm hoping you can help us," Mary said and took a sip of her wine. She explained about the approval committee and updated him on the wholesale orders they had secured.

"So you went to London? How very clever of you to even get in the door of Harrods," he said. "Yes, Lou-Lou's assumption is correct. I do know two of the committee members and, yes, I will have a word with them on behalf of the company... but only if you agree to meet me next week for dinner after I've spoken to them so I can update you in person."

Mary felt trapped. "Very well."

"I will phone you," Gabriel called as Mary hurriedly left the bar.

When Jamie phoned later that evening, Mary felt a pang of guilt as she opted not to mention her meeting or the forthcoming dinner with Gabriel.

Over the next few days she spent all the time she could sketching the final collection that would hopefully showcase in Fashion Week. Even if it didn't, they needed to get the spring/summer collection ready for the stores.

Lou-Lou put together a great presentation of all the publicity they had received to date, as well as a biography on

Mary and himself along with photos of the shop. The entire opening page of the presentation was their logo etched in silver paint on black card. To the best of their knowledge they had completed what they needed to for the first part of the vetting process. All they had left to do was deliver the application form, proof of the orders, sketches of the collection and the brand presentation folder to the Paris Fashion Week Office.

As Mary and Lou-Lou walked out of their shop, a low-slung, blue sports car crawled along the curb. Mary felt her skin creep as, despite his sun glasses, she clearly saw the face of the driver - Santos Dubois. They both ignored the car and hurried towards the Métro station with their precious application folder in one of the shop's glossy carry bags.

"Oh shit, I hope it's not a bad omen," Lou-Lou said once they were on the train.

"We have to try to ignore and forget about him. Goodness knows how he has time to drive around Paris in the early afternoon when he has a business to run," Mary replied.

The receptionist at the Fashion Week office was very friendly and assured them she would personally see the folder was put into the correct hands as soon as possible. She informed them they would receive confirmation by post within two weeks if they were accepted for the final stage, that being a shop visit by members of the committee.

Gabriel phoned but did not give anything away about his approach to the committee members. He told Mary that he had booked dinner at The Ritz and offered to send a car to collect her. She declined and said she would meet him at The Ritz bar. While Mary didn't want to appear provocative in her choice of clothes for the rendezvous, she was excited at the prospect of visiting such a prestigious hotel.

"Ooh la la, this man is really pulling out the stops to get you back, Kiwi," Lou-Lou said as they debated what Mary should wear. They were still working at 7pm so she was dressing there and leaving from the shop.

"Did you know Mademoiselle Chanel called The Ritz 'my home' in 1930? She moved in and stayed for 30 years. She even redesigned some of Monsieur César's Ritz rooms. Several of Chanel's rooms are still as she left them," Lou-Lou told her as she finally opted for bronze silk trousers and a cream silk chiffon shirt.

"Thanks for the history lesson but I'm late." Mary kissed him and sped out the door to find a taxi.

The cab pulled into the Place Vendôme and Mary wasn't disappointed. A line of archways that edged the square encompassed the hotel entrance where a white-gloved doorman opened the magnificent glass door for Mary. She reflected that Coco Chanel did this every evening after a day's work at her boutique. Her thoughts were interrupted as another uniformed man politely asked if he could direct her somewhere. He then accompanied her through the lavish foyer to the bar where she had agreed to meet Gabriel.

"Mary, you look amazing. The pearls are a wonderful touch. You are surely proof that one can improve on perfection," Gabriel said as a greeting.

"Lou-Lou encouraged me to wear the pearls. They are our tribute to Coco," Mary replied. She knew that in France, it was bad manners to bring up the main reason for a meeting too soon. So she did not push Gabriel immediately for answers. As they walked across the restaurant to their table he gently placed his hand on Mary's back in a subtle display of ownership. It really annoyed her but she bit her tongue.

Unlike when they first dated, Mary quite confidently, in excellent French, ordered her own choices from the extensive menu. They chatted easily about the business and the Harrods' visit. Gabriel feigned intrigue about Annabel's English social status. Mary could see an annoyance in him, as if he had been overtaken in the influence stakes in some way. However, she saw his reaction as a good opportunity to allow him back on top.

"So tell me, Gabriel, have you been able to influence the two committee members we talked about?" Mary smiled.

Gabriel cleared his throat and Mary was confident she had him back in his comfort zone. "Yes, actually, I'm 90 percent sure that after the conversations I had with them that they will approve Mousseline de Soie Chantal to show at Paris Fashion Week," he said.

Mary squeezed his hand across the table. "Thank you so much. We really appreciate your help," she replied.

"I hope you are aware that if you get accepted in the first stage, you have to cover all your own costs for the show. I may be able to assist if you need extra finance," he said.

Mary gave a forced smile and murmured a 'thank you'. They finished the meal with coffee. Mary was desperate to leave. Gabriel was making advances and she didn't want a scene. He insisted that he escort her home in the taxi. As they stood outside the Ritz in the glow of the street lights, he put his arm firmly around her waist.

"Gabriel, we were lovers but we are now just friends. I

appreciate your help but it's over."

"But, ma chérie, I miss you so badly. Please come back to me. I will give you anything," he said.

"I don't love you, Gabriel. You have a wife and a family and, besides, now I'm in love with someone else." Mary quickly pulled away from his grip.

That did it. He dropped his hands to his side. At that moment a taxi pulled up. Mary thanked Gabriel again and quickly jumped in the taxi alone.

41

Two weeks passed with no word from the Fashion Week committee. Both Lou-Lou and Mary were on tenterhooks.

"I can't stand this waiting. I'm going to call that old queen I know on the committee and take him for a drink tonight. See if I can find out anything." Lou-Lou sat beside Mary who was hand finishing a silk jacket.

"Shall I come as well?" Mary asked.

"No, I think this is a gay-on-gay situation. Besides, it would be a bit obvious if you stumped up."

The next morning Lou-Lou looked quite glum as Mary arrived early at the shop with the usual coffees.

"Tell me," she said.

"Well, after a few drinks and a lot of flirting on my part, he told me they had a hung jury. The final place was between us and two others. He did say that this would be the first year they were allowing 'foreign' designers to show, as they realised they were lagging behind London and New York Fashion Weeks. So he revealed that the two Japanese designers, Rei Kawakubo and Yojo Yamamoto, have been approved. I may have been grasping at straws but the only thing I could think of to say was that we would provide a contrast as your collection was fitted, feminine and sexy as opposed to the baggy look the Japanese and a few of the others were doing. I also emphasised you were half French," Gabriel replied.

"Lou-Lou! Mary! Quick! It's Santos in the blue car again," Wendi called through the curtain. They hurried out into the shop.

"He's been parked out there for about 20 minutes but I had a customer and didn't like to call you." Lou-Lou perched himself in the shop window and could see the blue sports car parked up the street from the shop.

"He must be spying from his rear vision mirrors, the stupid man."

"I think he followed that last customer here. She used to buy a lot of his clothes when I first worked for him," Wendi added.

"I'm going to go and confront the arsehole!" Mary strode towards the door.

Lou-Lou held his hand on the closed door. "No, that won't help."

"I won't be intimidated by him. We've done nothing wrong," Mary snapped.

"Trust me, Kiwi, I have a better understanding of his personality than you. Anything we do will rile him and make the situation worse. Best to pretend we haven't seen him." Lou-Lou guided Mary back to the workroom as a customer appeared at the door.

The confirmed order arrived from Harrods but Mary and Lou-Lou were still desperately waiting to hear if the committee would visit. The call finally came – yes, they would arrive the next morning.

They were up till midnight styling the sample garments on ten dress maker dummies in the workroom. Lou-Lou accessorised each garment from his amazing collection of costume jewellery and Mary went behind him taking half of it off.

"Sometimes, you are just too subtle, Kiwi!"

"You can go out in the shop and accessorise the current collection and the window pieces as much as you like. But I have the final say with the new collection until it's accepted." Mary gave him a gentle shove through the curtain into the shop.

All three were in at 8am the following morning. The committee wasn't due until 10. "I think you should close the shop while they are here. It will help make them feel more important," Wendi said. By 9.45 Mary's anxiety was matched by Lou-Lou's. It was a rare occurrence that they were both in such a state at the same time.

The committee was punctual to the minute and consisted of three men and two women. Without exception, they all wore the arrogance of their position on their faces. The women were dressed in current French fashion pieces and the men wore jackets in varying navy colours along with the predicable beige chino trousers and Gucci loafers.

Mary was sure one of the women actually sniffed as she walked through to the workroom, her nose was so far in the air. As they inspected the collection, one of the men took a keen interest in Mary's sketches that lay out on the cutting table.

The entire visit was over in 20 minutes and, as Mary walked them to the door, her heart dropped. Along the street she spotted the now familiar blue sports car.

"That was terrible," Lou-Lou said as he accepted the coffee Wendi brought in.

"They gave nothing away. Their facial expressions never changed the whole time they were here," Mary sighed. "They must have hated it.

Just before closing time Mary answered the phone. It was Wendi's friend at Fashion Week. After a quick conversation where Mary mainly listened she slammed the phone down.

"Bugger!"

"What's wrong, Kiwi?" Lou-Lou put his arm around her. "We haven't been accepted for Fashion Week. She said not to be discouraged and to try again next year."

Lou-Lou slipped out and bought a bottle of wine and, once Wendi left, they locked the door and proceeded to drown their sorrows.

"Well, at least we have a great collection that several stores, including Harrods, want to buy. And I don't have to crawl to Gabriel anymore," Mary said as she downed her second glass.

42

A week passed and Mary managed to guide her thoughts to a more positive place. She was sure Santos would know that they hadn't been accepted for Fashion Week and hoped that would stop his stalking.

She had all the patterns and colour-ways for her collection completed and had sourced the fabrics. But she wouldn't confirm the order till she had decided which small factory would manufacture the wholesale stock.

"So how did you get on?" Lou-Lou looked up from his desk where he was adding up the orders.

"Well, I've walked my feet off but Madame Blanche, who was very kind to me when I worked with her on my arrival in Paris, is now with a small factory called Allouette. I will feel confident if she oversees things, so we will go with them," Mary said

"Great. I'll order the fabric tomorrow. We can only afford limited stock, as it's being customised especially for us and, because we're new customers, we have to pay in advance." Mary was impressed with the way Lou-Lou was managing the finances of the business.

"Excuse me, there's a gentleman to see you." Wendi poked her head around the curtain.

"See who?" Lou-Lou looked up from his folders.

"Both of you, I think."

They exchanged a puzzled glance when they saw one of the men from the Fashion Week committee standing in the shop.

"Bonjour Mademoiselle Hampton, Monsieur Rock. Please forgive me for arriving unannounced, but would you be so kind as to allow me a private word with you both?"

"Please," Mary gestured with her hand towards the heavy curtain. Lou-Lou offered the man a seat and he and Mary pulled up two chairs opposite him.

"First, let me formally introduce myself. I am Monsieur Cohen. Before I retired I owned a fashion manufacturing business. So I pride myself on knowing great workmanship when I see it." He paused. Mary smiled willing him to go on.

"I was very impressed with your collection and the feminine touch you have with the silk and the chiffons. The Fashion Week selection committee has to be commercial as Paris is seen to be the leading city in the world for fashion and the general consensus was that you were still too new to deserve a place."

He took another pause. Mary could hardly bear it. Lou-Lou squeezed her hand. "Sadly, we've had one designer withdraw their collection due to a financial crisis. That leaves us with a gap. We feel if we approach any of the established designers on our list at this late stage, they would be insulted at being a second choice." He paused again.

"Yes?" Mary said. Lou-Lou squeezed her hand tighter.

"We wondered if you would accept being a replacement

designer in our Young Designers' section." He finally got it out.

Mary's heart ascended to a new place. But Lou-Lou got in first, still grasping her hand.

"We will have to have a chat about it. Can we let you know?" Mary couldn't believe her ears. What was he saying?

"Very well, but I need to know by seven tonight as we make the official announcement of all this season's designers to the media tomorrow. Here is my home number. Please call me either way."

Monsieur Cohen handed Lou-Lou his card, politely nodded to Mary, and walked to the door.

"Yippee! How bloody fantastic." Mary pulled Wendi and Lou-Lou into a hug.

"Yes, I agree, but I wasn't going to bow down immediately," Lou-Lou said.

Mary threw her arms in the air and squealed, "Oh, don't be so French. We don't have our noses in the air. I'm just grateful to be in Paris Fashion Week."

Lou-Lou convinced Wendi to sort a baby-sitter, Mary phoned Annabel who just happened to have the evening off, and they descended on her at the apartment with bottles of chilled champagne and Chinese take-aways.

"Here's to 'Mousseline de Soie Chantal.'"

"To Mary Chantal Hampton and Lou-Lou Rock," Annabel proposed as the second toast.

Once the others left and Annabel had gone to bed, Mary phoned Jamie in London and Susan in New Zealand to tell them the great news. Jamie said he always knew she'd make it. Susan sounded ecstatic for her and, in turn, up-dated Mary on her new flat and new boyfriend.

As Mary lay in bed that night a little tipsy she listened to Annabel's soft reassuring breathing beside her. She considered how far she had come - her friendships, her love life and this amazing opportunity for her designs. Then, as always, her mind wandered back to the farm, and memories of her mother flooded her. She thought about all the skills she had that she owed to her mother's patience in teaching her - all about patterns, fabrics and sewing. But as Mary drifted off a small fear, similar to the one she always had in childhood, nagged her. But now it involved a blue sports car.

The following morning Lou-Lou and Mary excitedly talked through the schedule and planned for what they had to achieve in the next four months.

"We need to allow enough fabric for the wholesale orders and for extra garments on top of the sample range for the catwalk show. If you can roughly work that out today, I can place the order. We need to be consistent with all the colours and we have left it a bit late," Lou-Lou said applying his practical side to his 'to do' list.

"I feel confident about the overall look for the collection but, from what I understand, we need to source our own models. And I haven't come up with one key 'hook' yet that will make an overall statement." Mary rearranged all the samples on the dressmaker dummies in a new colour order as she chatted.

"Well, we still need to get one big name model. God knows how we can achieve that with a limited budget and such a new brand," Lou-Lou said

"Get your arse out there and network, Lou-Lou Rock. It's what you do best." Mary gave him an affectionate squeeze.

43

There was a sharp knock on the shop door at 9 am. "Who the hell is that at this time?" Lou-Lou looked up from his order book.

"Maybe Wendi forgot her key. I'll go." Mary pulled back the curtain to walk through and open the door.

"You could have given me the courtesy of telling me you qualified for Fashion Week before I read this in the paper." Gabriel stormed in clutching a copy of the morning paper.

"I'm sorry. We only found out two days ago. It's all been a bit overwhelming," Mary said with a nervous smile.

Lou-Lou joined them on the shop floor. "I don't know why you are upset, Gabriel. It's a compliment to you, as you were the first person to have faith in our idea."

"That may be so, but the landscape has changed a bit since then. Even though you have transferred the funds back to me, my name hasn't yet been removed from the company as a director. So technically I'm still responsible for the company's actions and that is included in the article about 'Mousseline de Soie Chantal.'" Gabriel slapped the paper down on the counter.

"So will this upset your wife?" Mary asked.

"Do not be so bloody immature, Mary. I don't care about that. It's common knowledge I have a diverse range of investments. It is that bloody Santos Dubois. He seems obsessed and he obviously still thinks you are my lover. He's been stalking me and making trouble socially whenever he can." Gabriel straightened his tie.

Mary sighed. "He's been doing the same to us. He parks his blue car up the street most days. We try to ignore him," she said.

"My god, is that his sports car? I've noticed it outside the house some evenings," said Gabriel in a more sympathetic tone.

"Let me make us all a coffee and we can talk this through calmly." Lou-Lou went through to put the kettle on.

"My, you are economising. Making your own coffee?" Gabriel managed to smile.

"I don't get it. He's far more established than we are and he's shown for the last three years at Fashion Week. Why is he so bothered about me?" Mary took a cup from the tray Lou- Lou brought out.

"It's clear neither of you have looked at the designer list in the paper. Santos Dubois is not included." Gabriel handed the paper to Lou-Lou.

"But I heard only last week that he was definitely in," Lou-Lou said as he scanned the list.

"I had my accountant do a little digging around and, apparently, since that last collection, which we know Mary was actually responsible for, he has been in big trouble. His last two seasons have bombed," Gabriel said.

"Shit, he must have been the one that pulled out and we

replaced! Oh my god, what will he do now?" Mary held her face in her hands.

They continued talking till Wendi arrived and agreed they would keep each other informed of any Santos antics. Then Mary walked Gabriel out onto the street.

"Please, ma chérie, just give me another chance. I miss you so much."

"Gabriel, don't go there. I've told you, it's over." Mary pressed his arm and walked back into the shop.

She fretted over the Santos issue with Lou-Lou who couldn't do much to reassure her. He reiterated his belief the man had a major screw loose and that they would need to be vigilant.

Over the following days the constant demands of the business pushed Santos to the back of Mary's mind. She had little time for socialising and her special non-work pleasure was phone chats and letters from Jamie.

When Jamie managed a weekend break with Mary in Paris, Annabel moved out for those two days. She often spent weekends with Marc, their landlord, as he was now officially her boyfriend.

"You really have this sorted, Mary. I always knew you could do it," Jamie said as he admired the rows of garments in the workroom.

"It's been touch and go. I'm so fussy about the fabrics that we made an exclusive order so no-one else can show anything too similar. However, we've nearly used it all up so there is no room for mistakes." Mary snuggled in beside Jamie on the new sofa Lou-Lou had put in a corner of the squashed workroom. Jamie kissed her tenderly then began to unbutton her shirt.

"What if someone comes in?" Mary sat upright.

"It's seven o'clock on a Saturday night, the shop is locked and Lew's on a date. Who's going to come in? Besides I bet no-one's ever done 'it' in here before." Mary chuckled as they lay on the sofa entangled in each other's arms.

"What's so funny?" Jamie untangled himself and got up to get a glass of water.

"Oh, I was just imagining what Lou-Lou would say if he could see us now, both naked in the workroom." Mary stood up and stretched.

"Bloody hell, you are so beautiful, Mary Hampton." Jamie put down his glass and took Mary in his arms. There was a loud thud out in the direction of the shop.

"Shit, what was that?" Mary rushed towards the closed curtain doorway.

"Mary, you're naked!" They quickly pulled their clothes on and ran into the shop. It was dark and they heard a car roar past the window. Then they registered the glass window. Jamie unlocked the door and the smell hit them.

"It's poo! From an animal, I hope," he said as Mary joined him.

"Oh, it can only be one person! It's really worrying me now." Mary kicked the filthy plastic bucket that the excreta had been brought in into the gutter. They decided against calling Lou-Lou as there wasn't anything he could do, but Jamie persuaded Mary to report it to the police.

"If you don't and something worse happens, there should be a record of this episode."

When the police arrived, Mary managed, in limited French, to ask if the incident could be kept quiet as she didn't

268

want any adverse publicity. They assured her it would only be filed as a report at this stage. They took a photo of the bucket and the window and then left.

"Come on, it's all cleaned up now. Fretting won't help. I'm only here till tomorrow night so let's head down to La Huchette for a dance." Jamie threw the plastic bucket into the street rubbish bin and washed his hands.

"I guess you're right. Give me ten minutes to wash and change." Mary managed a smile.

The atmosphere was electric in La Huchette with the dance floor in full swing when Mary and Jamie arrived. They had a glass of wine each, sitting side by side on the edge of the dance floor. When the band had a break, several of Mary and Annabel's friends popped over to say hi and give Mary's boyfriend a closer look.

"These Frenchies are very polite!" Jamie commented after the third friend had shaken his hand.

"Yes, it's a cultural thing, but underneath they are just as nosey as they would be back home. You are the only straight man I've come down here with, and they all know you're an All Black."

Mary kissed his cheek. They enjoyed a lazy Sunday together sleeping late and sharing a casual lunch on Rue Mouffetard in Mary's favourite café.

Later that evening, after Mary said good-bye to Jamie, her thoughts kept lingering back to Santos Dubois and what he may do next.

"I just knew that creep hadn't finished with us," Lou-Lou said when Mary gave him the bad news in the morning.

"Well, there's nothing we can do. We have only eight weeks to complete everything and we don't have any models booked yet." Mary gave Lou-Lou an expectant glance.

"Ah well, on that note, I had a chat with a friend of mine who is a model agent. He doesn't think ours is a collection Jerry Hall would do but her chum, Marie Helvin, apparently loves the more feminine collections and has been known to work for a lower fee if she really likes the clothes."

"So how do we approach this?" Mary paused as Wendi unlocked.

Lou-Lou continued, "The agent suggested we send Marie an outfit in her size so she gets to know our name and style. Then we'll have to wait and see if she responds."

Wendi talked about an up-and-coming model agency that hired out newer models at a lower rate.

"I guess we can allow extra rehearsal time to get them into shape," Mary commented after they agreed Wendi should follow that up.

Mary scoured through the gossip pages of her English fashion mags studying photos of Marie Helvin. Usually she was snapped with her husband, the famous photographer, David Bailey. After an involved discussion with Lou-Lou, it was finally agreed to send her a bronze, silk cocktail dress with a silk chiffon overlay and shoe-string straps. Lou-Lou carefully wrapped the dress and packed it in a 'Mousseline de Soie Chantal' box before sending Wendi over to the model agency office for them to deliver it.

"I've been thinking, Mary. I need to increase my English

vocabulary if I'm going to be dealing with some English celebrities. I really do want to be able to express myself confidently." Lou-Lou flicked his hands out.

"You express yourself well enough for me, but sometimes Wendi tells me we speak in our own mixed language. So if you make the effort, I will with my French as well." She gave him a hug.

44

The Paris Fashion Week publicity machine was in full swing and not a day went by without some mention of the designers in the daily newspapers and weekly magazines. As a consequence, the shop turn-over had almost doubled and both Mary and Lou-Lou were working 12 hour days to cope with the manufacturing and finishing of the catwalk garments. Madame Blanche proved her worth and took over all the orders. They wouldn't have coped without her.

After attending a casting of new models, Mary and Lou-Lou chose ten diverse looking girls, including a stunning Japanese and an African. In addition to the show, they booked the models for two rehearsals. They still hadn't heard anything from Marie Helvin and Lou-Lou was far too busy to come up with any other celebrity model suggestions.

Mary left home at 7am on a perfect, warm August morning. Most of the French were away on their summer holidays, and Paris was full of tourists who didn't rise till late. So far, very few of them had come in search of 'Mousseline de Soie Chantal'. As she walked briskly from the Métro station towards the shop, she savoured the Parisian early-morning sights, sounds and fragrances. The aroma of her espresso coffee and pain-au-raisin wafted up from the take-out paper bag she clutched, stimulating her olfactory senses. She smiled to herself as that new word passed through her consciousness.

'Olfactory.' Lou-Lou had been learning one new English word a day. Yesterday's word had been associated with a 'sense of smell' as they briefly considered the possibility of developing a fragrance. She restrained herself from taking even a tiny nibble of the pastry until she reached the early morning tranquility of her home-from-home, the shop.

Ever since they opened, Mary's heart soared when her eyes rested on the sign, 'Mousseline de Soie Chantal', above the shop window and then across to the very small neat sign above the door, 'Proprietors: Mary Hampton and Lou-Lou Rock'. Being accepted for Paris Fashion Week was their biggest achievement to date and this was the day she would put the final touches to her collection.

As she unlocked the door it was the smell that hit her first. Her olfactory senses were filled with a very human-type stench. Then her attention was drawn to the heavy curtain through to the workroom. It was askew. Not as she'd left it the previous evening. She cautiously approached the work- room doorway and spotted the ankles first – thick, ugly ankles attached to darkly-stubbled legs stuffed into red stilettos.

Mary screamed. The take-out bag crashed from her grasp, coffee splattering over the pristine, white-tiled floor. Ignoring the spillage she proceeded further into the workroom. To her horror the prone-positioned person was jammed into her favourite Paris Fashion Week creation, a navy satin gown. Thick, black, under-arm hair sprouted from beneath the delicately beaded shoestring straps. Odd grunting sounds emanated from under tattered, over-lacquered, blond hair.

Fairly confident that she was in no immediate danger, Mary moved guardedly towards the grunting body. As she bent down to investigate further, the grunting sounds become more agitated, the stench grew stronger and she saw a dark, sticky stain on the posterior area of her now ripped and ruined gown.

Gingerly she rolled the body over and screamed again as, suddenly, the hair fell off revealing the back of a familiar looking balding head. Reeling with anger, she pushed the torso over so she could see the face.

"You! You arsehole!" she shrieked.

It was at that exact moment she registered the clothes rails on which had hung her once perfect collection. Some garments were still on their hangers but they were ripped to shreds. The rest were strewn over the workroom, only recognisable by the fabric.

The eyes of Santos Dubois seemed to search for her. Well, one did. The other eye didn't move. His face was grotesquely distorted and appeared to have drooped on one side. It was clear he couldn't speak and it seemed his left side was paralysed as his arm flopped on the floor beside him.

Mary stepped over him and walked towards the rails of ruined garments. Most of her work was destroyed. She fell onto a chair, clutching her face. She wanted to scream but no sound came. The anger was bile in her throat. Everything except that bitter taste was a blank to her. Then some sound, other than Santo's grunting, registered in her orbit.

"Mary, Mary, has he hurt you?" Lou-Lou was at her side. Mary stood up and Lou-Lou gently took her in his arms. Santos watched pleadingly from the floor with his one working eye.

"I guess we'd better call the police and ambulance. It's one thing the evil bastard shitting himself here, but the only way I will accept him dying here is if I kill him myself !" Lou-Lou scowled at Santos.

Mary couldn't bring herself to touch any of the ruined garments. She stood mute as Lou-Lou phoned first the police and then the ambulance service.

"Oh, my god!" Wendi stood transfixed as she looked at her ex-boss lying in his own excreta on the tiled floor. "He must have had a stroke." She stepped over him, went straight to Mary and carefully led her to a seat in the shop.

The police arrived in minutes, followed closely by an ambulance. The sirens attracted lot of attention from passers-by and neighbours and a small crowd gathered outside. The paramedics examined Santos and then lifted him, still dressed in Mary's navy blue ripped dress, onto a stretcher. They removed the red stilettos, revealing thick stubby toes complete with brightly painted square red toenails.

The police had to clear the crowd from the door to allow the paramedics through with the stretcher. At least two reporters arrived on the scene and there was a flurry of camera flashes and gasps of both intrigue and horror as the ugly man, accompanied by his wig and stilettos, was lifted into the ambulance.

Wendi locked the shop door. The reporters lingered outside. Lou-Lou made hot tea for everyone as they sat down with two detectives to give the details. From what they could gather, sometime late last night Santos managed to break in through the back entrance. He had obviously brought along his own red stilettos and wig. After squashing into Mary's dress, he had time to destroy nearly all of what was in the workroom with Mary's cutting scissors before he literally burst his boiler. He suffered a cerebral vascular accident, known commonly as a stroke.

"This is wilful damage, but first we must have him assessed at the hospital before we can charge him. Are you insured, Monsieur Rock?" the detective asked.

"We have insurance but I will have to look at the policy to see what we are covered for."

The detectives had the entire scene photographed before attempting to move the reporters and photographers away. However, as soon as the squad car left the street, the rabble returned and was banging on the door.

"You lot, piss off. Our collection is in ruins and we need some time to think. When we are ready to issue a statement, you will be the first to know." Lou- Lou took the card of the Paris Match reporter and slammed the door. Wendi locked it and placed a sign in the window 'Closed for Today'.

Mary still sat mute in the shop. She couldn't bring herself to revisit the destruction in the workroom. Lou-Lou sat down beside her with a pad and a pen.

"We are going to somehow get through this. I'm going to write down a list of what we need to do step-by-step and I need you two to help me." He reached over and touched Mary's hand. She sat up straight and took a large sip of the water that Wendi placed beside her.

"You are right. We can't let that bastard win. But I just feel stripped of everything. My insides are empty. How will I find the strength?"

Wendi cleared her throat. "I watched you deal with a terrible situation when you worked at Santos's. You were an inspiration, Mary. Don't give him the satisfaction of winning. You now have us and others to help. You can do it."

Mary stood up and willed herself through the curtained doorway. The smell of bleach replaced the stench of Santos excreta. Slowly she began to pick up each damaged gown from the floor. There were several that he had missed and they only required pressing. She hung those to one side. Then she went through each of the damaged gowns that still hung on the rails.

"There are 20 here that are either okay or I think I can repair for the catwalk."

"That means we need to replace 30 outfits." Lou-Lou quickly did an approximate calculation for fabric. "I need to call Gabriel. We don't want another of his out-bursts," he added as he continued his list. By late afternoon they had assessed the damage and been reassured their insurance policy covered them for wilful damage.

"I just have to figure out a way to make this work without having the same fabrics. We've already used every last metre." Mary's eyes welled up.

"I think we've dealt with all we can for today. Let's come in early tomorrow, leave the shop closed for another day, and look at it through fresh eyes." Lou-Lou ushered Mary into the shop and turned off the workroom lights.

"I am pleased I've caught you. Got here as soon as I could," Gabriel said as Wendi unlocked the door for him. He asked Mary if she was okay, then listened as they gave him an account of all that had happened.

"There's obviously not much I can do, but with your

approval, I will have my PR people draw up a formal press release. It could be delivered tomorrow for you to look at." He moved in just a bit too close for Mary's liking. She stepped aside.

Annabel was about to rush out to work when Mary arrived home. She relived it all over again as she retold the ghastly story.

"Look, I'll call in sick. I don't want to leave you alone, Kiwi.

"No, I'll be okay. Lou-Lou offered to be with me as well but, to be honest, I'm so tired I just want to phone Jamie and go to bed. Thanks though." Mary hugged Annabel goodbye.

Finally alone, Mary let the flood gates open. All the repressed grief for her mother, for the father she never met, and the abuse she had suffered merged together in her consciousness alongside the evil that this man had wrought upon her. She sobbed till there were no tears left.

She was struggling to make sense of why it always happened to her. Other people seemed to have normal lives but, she supposed, she was damaged and therefore attracted damaged people. The ringing of the phone interrupted her thoughts.

"Oh Jamie, I was just about to phone you," she sniffed. "What's wrong, Mary? Are you crying?" For the third time that evening, she retold the horror of her day.

He listened quietly and then said, "I'm coming over. Just give me a few days to sort my job out and I'll be with you." She mumbled a pseudo protest before he told her he loved her and hung up.

45

"I'm sorry, I hope I didn't wake you? What are you doing up? It's only 7am," Mary asked Annabel the next morning.

"I couldn't stop thinking about you all during the show last night, so I asked my supervisor for some time-off and, as from next Monday, I have two weeks' leave to help you remake and sort everything for Fashion Week."

"But how can you take time-off like that? Don't lose your job for my sake," Mary said.

"There's a new recruit learning the ropes and she's good enough to fill in. She happens to be connected to the boss so I'm making the most of the opportunity," Annabel smiled and gave Mary a hug.

"Thanks so much. I feel better today than I did last night. I just don't know what we're going to do about replacing the fabric. I have a few ideas so once I'm at work I can meet with Lou-Lou and Wendi and discuss what we can do." Mary kissed her friend on either cheek and hurried out the door.

Lou-Lou was busy unpicking buttons from the wrecked garments when Mary arrived.

"We may as well salvage everything we can as far as trims, zips and buttons go." He put down his unpicker and turned the kettle on.

"It's August 12th today and we show on September 10th. That gives us four weeks to source fabric and make 30 catwalk garments," Mary said as she stirred sugar into her coffee. "Plus, I still haven't come up with a key styling idea that will give us an edge."

"The fabric people will be in their office in the next hour so I'll see what they can do," Lou-Lou said.

"We're going to need help. Annabel is taking two weeks off so she can help cover the shop and Wendi can assist co-ordinating the model fittings. I figured I'd fit them as we make the replacement garments so we don't get bogged down with alterations. I'm worried about how we will get it all done," Mary sighed.

They both agreed they could survive on about six hours sleep a night. They would cut and sew each new garment themselves to ensure the quality and they could also make adjustments as they went along. That meant they needed to do approximately two garments a day and still give themselves the last four or five days for styling.

Wendi arrived in with the newspaper. The sabotage of their collection made front-page news. They turned on the radio and it also featured them as the lead story. The reporter speculated as to whether or not 'Mousseline de Soie Chantal' would even go ahead with showing their collection.

Lou-Lou was furious. Just as he was about to pick up the phone to call Gabriel, a courier appeared in the shop with a copy of the Press Release from Gabriel's PR company.

"Well, he's covered everything and it's clear we are going ahead regardless. I'll call Paris Match, the radio station and L'Express and read this out to them." He took the Paris Match business card out of his pocket.

The shop phone continued to ring all morning. So many people heard the news and wanted to help. Madame Blanche was the first to get through and said she would bring over what fabric remnants she had left from the wholesale order. The fabric company had five metres of Mary's special fabric on a sample roll. At Lou-Lou's request they found an inferior fabric that was almost exactly the same colour. No-one would be able to tell the difference on the catwalk once it was made up.

Mary was overwhelmed when the owner of the small haberdashery supplier they had used arrived in the shop with a box full of repeats of the tassels and trims, as close as possible to the ones Lou- Lou originally spent hours selecting.

When Wendi finally closed the shop door that evening, Lou-Lou and Mary sat down to go over things before leaving.

"Okay, so we have a critical path plan. No matter what, as soon as the fabric arrives tomorrow, Kiwi, you must start cutting. It's crucial we keep to the schedule." Lou-Lou held a two page list.

"People have been so kind. I'm beginning to think that maybe I don't always attract bad things," Mary said.

"Why would you say that? It's not your fault. You are always honest with people. Santos is twisted in the head, Mary. It's his problem, not yours. From where I'm looking, you are everything he wants to be: feminine, talented, young and beautiful." Lou-Lou put down his list and wrapped his arm around Mary's shoulders. Her eyes watered as she smiled.

"I do love you, Lou-Lou Rock. You are closer than any brother could be, more reliable than any father I've had, and I'm sure you would never break my heart like a lover might." She snuggled her mass of russet hair into his shoulder."

"That's the best thing anyone has ever said to me." They locked their shop door and walked hand-in-hand to the Métro station.

For the following five days, Mary only saw the four walls of the workroom. She cut the fabric and Lou-Lou sat beside her sewing. Then she would have a break from the cutting shears and do some hand-finishing. The shop seemed even busier than before. With all the publicity Santos's sabotage created, people were coming off the usual beaten paths to seek them out. It was only a miracle Santos hadn't taken to the current shop stock. Mary was sure if he hadn't suffered the stroke he would have finished the lot.

On Monday morning, Annabel caught the Métro to work with Mary and assumed her position on the shop floor. Midmorning she scurried into the workroom.

"Quick, let your hair down, put some lippy on and get out there. There's someone very special asking for you!" As Mary tentatively walked into the shop she overheard what she assumed to be a distinctive American drawl.

"Gee, it's a cute boutique all right, Marie! So much sexier than all that baggy stuff they're fitting us into." It was the tall Texan model, Jerry Hall. She towered over her shorter, more delicate companion.

"Hi, I am Mary Hampton." Mary extended her hand to Marie Helvin.

"I'm Marie and this is Jerry. Thanks for the stunning dress you sent me. I adore it. We heard about your misfortune and I wondered if I could help by modelling for you in your show?"

"That would be amazing. Thank you so much." Just as Mary struggled with her words, Lou-Lou walked in. His eyes nearly popped out of his head.

"This is my business partner, Lou-Lou Rock. Lou-Lou, may I introduce Jerry Hall and Marie Helvin. Marie has kindly offered to model for us." As Mary spoke she was sure that Lou-Lou was going to collapse with excitement, but he quickly pulled himself together, took the diary off the desk and agreed a time for a fitting with Marie.

Once the super models had left the shop, Mary let out a whoop. Annabel ducked as Lou-Lou took Mary by the arms and swung her around.

"The only thing is, I expected her to be taller," Mary said once she caught her breath.

"Between two giraffes like you and Jerry Hall, Kiwi, it's hardly surprising she appears short. Remember when you made me 'appear' taller," Annabel chipped in.

"Who cares? It's her celebrity we're after and, besides, she glides like a swan on the catwalk." Lou-Lou minced across the shop.

"That settles it. I'm going to see if I can do a 'bride' as my finale piece." Mary picked up her sketch pad.

"Don't you think the white bride thing has been done to death?" Lou-Lou pursed his lips.

"White is not quite what I had in mind," Mary answered just as Wendi appeared through the door with some lining they needed. Mary took Wendi to one side, gave her the cheque book and sent her back off to the fabric street in Pigalle.

They had completed half of the replacement garments and Mary had a vision brewing for her finale section. She kept it to herself as it would really put the pressure on, and she wanted to do a costing before she announced anything extra to Lou-Lou. Wendi returned from her errand and, as requested, discreetly handed Mary the fabric samples in a folder.

"I'm just popping out for an hour to see Madame Blanche," she called as she left the shop, taking advantage of Lou-Lou being distracted by a phone call.

Once she was out on the high street, Mary grabbed a cab to save time. It occurred to her that she should have called first to check the old woman hadn't gone out for some reason. However, Madame Blanche was in her office at the factory and looking nonchalant as usual. When Mary first met the old woman she actually frightened her, but now they shared a comfortable relationship with a mutual love of creating beautiful clothes. She listened carefully to Mary's idea and studied her sketches. Then she pulled the three different fabric samples out.

"Yes, I can make these up. I think I even have an old pattern somewhere. It's a very well-known Burberry style and this fabric will be okay," she said and handed Mary her chosen sample. "I'll need one and a half metres per coat and three for the bridal one." Mary felt reassured as Madame Blanche extended one of her rare smiles.

"So I take it you like the idea?" Mary doodled with the collar of the coat in her sketch.

"Yes, only you could pull this off and, like you say, if we

284

stiffen the collar so it stands up on its own, it will create the right effect."

"But are you able to complete them in time?" Mary raised her eyebrows.

"I will put my team on overtime. They will be only too happy to do anything to help. We can achieve five coats plus the bridal one, so you will only be able to have five models on the catwalk at a time. We'll make them all in size twelve so they can be cut together and they will be belted so a precise size shouldn't be too important."

"The final one for Marie will need to be customised. I'll fax her measurements over, and have the fabric delivered here directly." Mary kissed Madame gently on both cheeks.

"So, Kiwi, where have you been?" Lou-Lou asked, his hands on his hips, when she got back.

Mary put her forefinger to her lips. "It's my secret for now. I'll tell you all later, once I have the whole concept sorted. I don't want to burden any of you any more than you already are. Now, I've got dresses that need to be cut out, let's get to it!"

46

"Who the hell is that at this hour?" Mary snapped as the door buzzer shrilled. Annabel ambled up from her fully prone position on the sofa and pulled up the window.

"Gidday, my lady, it's only me," Jamie sung out.

"He wasn't meant to be here until tomorrow," Mary called out as she rushed down the stairs.

"Jez, Mary, what a way to greet your man - in a brunch coat! I thought you were a top fashion designer!" Jamie beamed as the waist tie on Mary's old dressing gown accidently dropped revealing her boobs.

"You're a day early but I'm so pleased to see you." Mary fell into his arms.

"Now, girls, I'm not here to upset the applecart, or rather the sleeping arrangements. No matter how much I lust for my bird I will be content here on the sofa, and I've brought supplies." Jamie pulled a bottle of wine and a jar of Marmite out of his backpack and placed them on the table.

Mary, Lou-Lou, Jamie, Annabel and Wendi were all assembled in the workroom with coffees and teas in hand at 9 the next morning. Lou-Lou led the meeting.

"Now, team, at great expense I have purchased this

whiteboard. You can see you each have your own column. Mousseline de Soie Chantal will literally be showcased to the world in five days time. We have only two rehearsals and neither will be on the actual catwalk - we only have access to that for 20 minutes on the afternoon of the show."

Mary moved in front of the white board. "So now it's time for me to come clean with what I'm doing for the finale. First, let me tell you the name of the collection. It is called 'Sabotage & Resurrection'. Red is for the figurative blood that has been spilled and also to stick it up Santos Dubois in his hospital bed!

"In the evening-wear finale, five of the models will come out and stand at the stage end of the catwalk, accompanied by a handsome man in a black tie. All the models will be wearing red satin trench coats over their cocktail dresses. The coat collars will be up and the waists belted. They will all wear red lipstick. Each model will provocatively un-belt and remove her coat on her first lap of the catwalk. She'll hand the coat to the man in the black tie. Then as she does a second lap showcasing the cocktail dress the next model will arrive behind her and repeat the process. The man will discreetly feed the coats to the next set of five models ready to go on stage and the routine will be repeated.

"We will alternate the four colour-ways of the dresses - navy, cream, dove grey and bronze. Once all ten models have each done their two slow laps, they will assemble on either side of the stage and the man will accompany out Marie. She will be wearing the same red satin trench coat but full length, with a matching blood-red lace bridal mantilla which will be tucked in behind her neck. Once she has taken a couple of

287

steps forward she will slowly undo and remove her coat to reveal the red silk satin gown and the mantilla will fall down to the floor from her head. She will carry a single white rose and walk to the end of the catwalk."

"Bravo!" They all clapped.

"I'm guessing you have it all sorted, but I have to ask - what about the shoes?" Lou-Lou asked.

"That's what I wanted to talk to you all about. I haven't got anything other than the standard navy courts we're using throughout," Mary replied.

"I'll get onto a few shops and see if any have red satin shoes if you like? I have all the models shoe sizes," Wendi offered.

"Great! Now Jamie, could you move boxes and clear a space of these dimensions out the back door? We can create the catwalk dimensions for the rehearsal using the workroom as the backstage area." Lou-Lou handed Jamie the piece of paper. Lou-Lou's instructions were clear and Wendi and Annabel juggled customers between running out for extra supplies and chasing up on the phone.

Wendi reported back the next morning that she had scoured Paris for the correct red shoes to no avail. Mary felt defeated.

"I so wanted a statement, something the media might pick up on. We are up against the big designers." She put her hand to her mouth. Jamie placed his arm around her.

"Hey, remember when you used to paint and staple stuff on your gumboots? I thought you were nuts but now I'm going through all this with you I sort of get it. It's really all about art!"

Mary pushed him back, but kept her hands on his elbows.

"Jamie, you are not only an inspired All Black but an inspired designer as well." She called to Lou-Lou and Wendi. "Wendi, can you please get on the phone and order eleven pairs of Wellington boots, in the models' sizes, in the lightest colour they have, please." Both Lou-Lou and Wendi looked puzzled.

"Wellington boots?" Wendi asked.

"I think they might say 'botte en caoutchouc' in French," Lou- Lou said.

"Gumboots in New Zealand," Jamie added.

"So Lou-Lou, can you sort out some red glitter and red sequins as well as navy ribbon?" Mary asked. "Once it's confirmed that we have the gumboots, we can buy some red enamel spray paint"

The following morning when the models arrived for their walk-through rehearsal at the rear of the show room, they were intrigued to see a handsome muscular Māori man spraying paint on a line of rubber wet-weather boots in the back alley.

"Shit, Mary, do you think Lew will be able to get the glitter and stuff on them in time? They are taking an age to dry." Jamie's hands were covered in red paint.

"You better scrub your hands with turps. You can't go for your fitting like that," Mary said once the rehearsal was over.

"What are you on about? What fitting?"

"Oh, didn't Lou-Lou tell you? You are the handsome chap assisting the models with their coats on stage, so you'll need to hire a suit." Mary smiled.

Once Lou-Lou had soothed Jamie down and convinced him no-one from the New Zealand press would recognise him, he eventually went off in search of a suit-hire establishment.

"Annabel, these are fantastic! They will give her at least three more inches." Annabel had persuaded the shoe maker for the Moulin Rouge to glue three sets of rubber soles and a rubber heel on the gumboots that Marie Helvin would wear.

"I'm just going to customise them a little more." Lou-Lou took the gumboots and a sharp pair of scissors and cut out the piece just above the toes. "Those girls better have followed the instructions with the red toenail polish!"

The gumboots looked stunning. Every second pair had navy ribbon criss-crossed around them like ballerina slippers.

47

It was the night prior to the biggest day of Mary Hampton's life. She lay awake listening to Annabel's gentle breathing and Jamie's not so gentle snoring out on the sofa. Susan phoned to wish her well and, although a part of her wished Susan was in Paris to see the show, she knew that at this time in Susan's life, she was better off in New Zealand. Mary wanted to believe her mother was looking down on her and wondered if she had reunited up in heaven with André, her birth father. She smiled at this silly thought as she drifted off to sleep.

The next morning Wendi, Annabel and Mary climbed into the back of the hire van. The three women firmly clutched the upright clothes rails on which hung the precious collection. She had lost it once and Mary was making sure nothing happen to it between the shop and the venue. As they pulled away from the shop, Mary was sure she caught sight of a blue sports car. A shiver shot through her body.

"Don't be daft, Mary. There are probably hundreds of blue sports cars in Paris. It's just a coincidence. Santos is well and truly stuffed - he can't even walk," Annabel assured her.

Mary was also anxious about the decision to let Lou-Lou,

who couldn't drive, navigate for Jamie as he negotiated the large van around the narrow streets of the Marais to the venue. "Shit, Lew, don't say left when you mean right! Bear in mind I don't understand much French." Lou-Lou retaliated with a tirade of swear words. Mary put one hand over the front seat and managed to pat his shoulder.

After a harrowing drive through Paris, they safely delivered everything into their designated spot back stage. There were six rails, each holding two of each models' garments and one reserved especially for Marie Helvin. Lou-Lou placed all the shoes and gumboots under the rails and Wendi laid the jewellery and accessories on the table. They would be the final touch as the models went out.

"Bonjour, are you Mary Chantal Hampton?" a short, plump man asked Mary as she shook out one of the satin coats.

"Yes, can I help you?"

"I am Jean Philippe. I can make a video of your show this evening and give it to you directly after the show if you wish. I charge 500 francs but it means you can watch it all afterwards." Mary hesitated.

Jamie took 250 francs out of his wallet. "Here, JP, half now, and I'll give you the other half after the show when you hand me the tape."

"That's a rip off," Lou-Lou said after the plump man left. "Yeah, but we're all too busy to do it and, besides, we don't have a camera, Lew."

Annabel and Wendi committed to sit with the collection until the evening. Madame Blanche was due to arrive a couple of hours before the show with some of her factory team to act as dressers for the models.

Jamie took a swig of Coca-Cola. "I'm not moving that van again until tonight. It's too bloody difficult to park anywhere."

"Well, you will both have to come back to the shop with me. We still have a few bits and bobs to bring over," Lou-Lou said, as he began to calm down.

The three friends made light of the stressful trip in the van as they sat on the Métro. They packed the last few accessories into a couple of bags along with Jamie's hired suit.

"I think we can stretch to a cab. I don't want us to be all sweaty from running up and down the Métro stairs," Lou-Lou decided as he locked the door and headed out front towards the cab rank around the corner.

It came from nowhere like a streak of blue fire. Lou-Lou registered it just a fraction too late. He ran for his life but the high powered car hit him. It happened so fast. Mary and Jamie watched as Lou-Lou flew up in the air and hit the cobbled street with a thud. As they ran to him the car momentarily stopped. The blonde haired driver looked back but, when she saw Lou-Lou' body was still, she tooted and sped off.

"Oh my god, not Lou-Lou, please let him be alive," Mary screamed as they ran to the lifeless body.

"Don't move him. His back may be broken." Jamie gently touched the pulse on Lou-Lou's neck.

"Please, call an ambulance!" Mary called to a man who stopped to see if he could help. Another shop owner brought out a rug which they gently laid over Lou-Lou while Mary sat on the ground next to him and carefully placed her rolled up sweater under his head.

"I can feel his pulse so at least he's alive," Jamie said as he sat on the other side of Lou-Lou's motionless body.

"Please Lou-Lou, be okay. Please wake up. I've lost my mother and my father. I can't lose you, too. I just can't!" Tears streamed down Mary's face as they heard the siren getting nearer. Just as the ambulance pulled up, Mary felt the blanket move and Lou-Lou turned over and opened his eyes.

"I'm sure this can't be heaven - my bloody arm hurts like hell," Lou-Lou pushed the blanket back with his one good arm, "And I'm sure angels don't cry!"

"Oh, thank you God! You are alive." Mary bent down to hold her friend.

"Easy, it hurts from my shoulder down," Lou-Lou winced as the paramedics arrived beside him. As they were examining him the police arrived and summoned Mary and Jamie away from the crowd that had gathered.

"It looked exactly like Santos Dubois's blue sports car and I'm not a hundred percent certain, but I'm fairly sure his wife was driving it," Mary said.

"She even stopped momentarily after she hit him. I'm sure she had a good view from her rear vision mirror and knew what she'd done before she drove off," Jamie added.

Lou-Lou was examined on the pavement and declared to have no obvious spine or leg injuries so they moved him out of the gaze of the gathered crowd into the ambulance.

"We are fairly confident his collarbone and arm are broken and he may possibly be suffering from concussion. We need to take him to the hospital for X-rays and to set the arm," the paramedic said, once Mary, Jamie and the police office rejoined them at the rear of the ambulance. Lou-Lou sat inside on the bed nursing his arm.

"I will have to ask you to accompany me to the station to

give a formal statement. You have witnessed a serious crime," the officer told Mary.

"That's just not possible." Mary dropped her head in her hands. Jamie put his arm around Mary and was just about to speak when Lou-Lou intervened.

"Officer, if I may explain? This is the most important day of our lives and, so far, Santos Dubois and his family have done everything they can to sabotage it. I obviously have to get to the hospital and have this arm set but please give Mary another 24 hours before she needs to make her statement?"

The policeman was thoughtful. "Well, Monsieur, the other witness is a New Zealand gentleman who doesn't speak French. That is a bit of a problem but we could call for the translator. He is normally a difficult man, but he happens to be a huge rugby fan so I'm sure he will be prompt. If Monsieur Jamie comes with us now at least we will have his statement." Mary quickly repeated it in English for Jamie who nodded in agreement.

"I'll join you as fast as I can at the venue." He kissed Mary, gave Lou-Lou a wave and went off with the police.

"Quick Mary, sit up here beside me." Lou-Lou held five fingers up at the paramedic, and Mary hopped up beside him.

"Look, I know you are in a panic, but it's all set up and you can pull it off. Just remember all the details we talked about concerning the styling. Depending how long this x-ray process takes at the hospital I may not make it tonight and, to be truthful, the pain at the moment is unbearable." He winced again as he attempted to move into a more comfortable position.

The paramedic moved Mary to one side. "Best you lay

down, Monsieur." He laid Lou-Lou flat on the bed and carefully placed the broken arm on his chest.

"I'm so sorry, Lou-Lou. I feel this is entirely my fault." Mary's eyes welled up.

"Bend down here, Kiwi." Mary put her head as close as she could to her friend in the confines of the ambulance.

"No matter what, I will be waiting at your place when you get home. Just make sure you bring that video your boyfriend saw fit to pay too much for. Then we can all watch the show together." Mary kissed him and gave him her apartment keys before she was ushered out and the ambulance took off up the street.

She suddenly felt desperately alone as she stood on the street outside her shop. She replayed the horrific scene in her mind. It was a miracle Lou-Lou wasn't killed. After a struggle with the boxes and Jamie's suit she finally found a taxi and got herself back to the venue.

Once they listened to the end of Mary's story where Lou-Lou was actually awake and giving orders, Annabel and Wendi relaxed a little. There was only half an hour to go till show time when Jamie finally arrived back stage.

"I'll just go to the men's loo and freshen up. Where's my suit?" He returned ten minutes later.

"Wow, you look amazing!" Annabel let out a wolf whistle and all the models and dressers looked over in his direction.

He walked directly over to Mary. "Will I do?" he whispered in her ear, and then kissed her lips in full view of his back stage audience. Mary was sure she caught a smile from Madame Blanche. Then she stood back and gave Jamie the once over. He wore a white shirt with a winged collar, and a white silk bow tie. The suit was black with tails and his feet were clad in shiny black patent leather shoes.

"Lou-Lou must have put these into the bag. I think they're his own as they are a tad too big, but it's not like I have to kick a rugby ball." He mimicked a Lou-Lou type move with his feet.

Annabel's experience at the Moulin Rouge was invaluable. In Mary's absence she had overseen the make-up artists and hairdressers as they made-up the models and ensured they all looked exactly as Mary and Lou-Lou had discussed. The models wore matching bronze-coloured lipstick but had instructions that, prior to the final sequence, they were to wipe it off. She had also run through the routines and model order several times in the fitting room.

It was Jamie's turn to wolf whistle when Mary appeared from behind a rail, fully made up with the front of her hair pinned up on her head. She wore a clinging, cream, sequined gown and Jamie's Tiki on her neck. Jamie beamed and mouthed 'I love you' across the room.

The stage hands hung the sign at the entry end of the catwalk. 'Mousseline de Soie Chantal' was in bold silver lettering. Next they placed the floral archway Mary had designed and had constructed by her favourite florists. It straddled the catwalk and acted as an entrance way to the audience. It was mainly covered in fresh red roses, but the florist used fake silk roses on the wire netting to make it more secure. The stage-hands looked a little panicked as some of the roses fell to the floor when they erected the archway.

"Don't worry," Mary called out in a hushed tone, "That adds to the look. Just push them around the base."

297

As the venue began to fill, the stage lights came on. Mary watched through a crack in the curtains from back stage. The Fashion Week staff ushered the media to the front rows on either side of the catwalk. The invited guests followed, rushing to get a seat as close as possible to the front. A bank of photographers gathered on ladders at the end of the runway. In the middle of them all was the plump Jean Philippe with his large video camera.

Then Mary saw a scurry of people and masses of flash bulbs going off, all pointed towards the door. Jamie squashed beside her to see what was causing the commotion. Mary's heart beat faster.

"Mick Jagger has just walked in with Jerry Hall!"

"Whoopee, Lew is going love this."

As Jamie spoke Annabel signalled, "Five minutes to go."

Mary's heart continued to pump loudly as she inspected the line of models. They looked fantastic but, without Lou-Lou, it felt like her right arm was missing. When the runway lights came on, Mary was so grateful she'd let Lou-Lou do the music. He must have guessed Mick may turn up. The room was suddenly filled with a young Mick Jagger's voice singing 'The Last Time'. That immediately set the mood of the room - upbeat. The models sashayed with a hint of rhythm along the runway in their first outfits. Marie Helvin didn't disappoint. She appeared as if gliding on butter, so smooth was her delivery.

It all happened so fast. Just as Mary was in the rhythm of it all, they were at the final sequence. It was time for a pause and for Jamie to walk on stage. Wendi held the mirror to each of the models and passed them a Chanel lipstick so they could apply their own red gloss. The lighting picked up the red glitter on the gumboots. Mary looked across at Jamie - she knew exactly what he was thinking.

"Bloody chiffon gumboots!"

As he walked out onto the stage, someone in the audience yelled, "Viva les All Blacks." The crowd erupted into a burst of applause as the tall, handsome, clearly well-known All Black escorted out the five stunning models in their red shiny satin coats. Over the sound system, Edith Piaf began to belt out the English version of the song, 'Non Regrettes.' The words said it all for Mary - No Regrets.

The audience clapped each individual evening gown. Then Marie arrived. Jamie stood behind her till she took two steps forward and slowly un-belted the full length coat. As she casually dropped it, Jamie scooped it up. Then she gently shook her jet black hair. Her curls fell to the front, and the red scallop-edged lace mantilla fell over her head and draped down either side of her gown. As she slowly paced the catwalk and the crowd got a glimpse of her high heeled red gumboots with her exposed toes, they rose to their feet and clapped frantically. The simple red silk gown, complemented by the exotic mantilla, looked magnificent.

The applause increased to a roar with people calling out 'bravo, bravo' when Jamie led Mary out. Her shimmering cream gown offered a visual contrast to the red. She stood shoulder to shoulder with Jamie in her high heels. The models parted as he led her to the end of the runway to take her bow.

Mary was practically mobbed by the media at the end of the show. They asked her to pose with Marie Helvin, with Jamie, and with Mick Jagger, but he had slipped out.

48

It was midnight by the time the three friends returned everything to the shop, parked the van in the back street and caught a cab home. The door was already unlocked and Lou-Lou was propped up on the sofa, his arm in a sling.

"Ooh, how was it?" They all bent over and kissed both his cheeks.

"Get you, Jamie, becoming very French and kissing a chap!" It was evident Lou-Lou had not lost his sense of humour. "Come on, where's the video? I had a huge fight with the ward sister when I discharged myself from the hospital so I could watch this tonight, even though I'm sedated up to the eyeballs."

Mary and Annabel kicked off their shoes. Mary flopped down on the sofa beside Lou-Lou while Annabel proceeded to open one of the bottles of champagne they'd brought home.

Jamie squatted down in front of the television with the video cassette. "Any idea how this works, Annabel?"

"No, we've only used it a couple of times. We had to read the manual. Where did you put it, Kiwi?" Annabel gave Mary's feet a playful kick.

"Hand me up that shoe box in the corner, will you please, Jamie?" Mary pointed to the battered shoe box concealed behind a pot plant.

"That's where she keeps all her secrets," Annabel laughed. "And any important household documents," Mary added as she handed Jamie the instruction manual and placed the shoe box beside her on the sofa.

As Jamie read the instructions Lou-Lou impatiently flicked through Mary's box.

"Gee, is this your Mum in this photo? She's young there." Mary glanced at the photo and nodded.

As Jamie inserted the cassette, Lou-Lou unfolded the copy of Mary's birth father's death certificate.

"Oh, Lou-Lou, let's not look at all that now. This is our 'happy moment' - we're about to watch our very own show."

She went to take the certificate from his hands but Lou-Lou held on tight to the paper. His eyes were glued to the page. Mary let go, Jamie pressed 'stop' on the video recorder, and Annabel put the bottle of champagne down. They stared at him as he clutched the paper, tears streaming down his face.

"There now, he's dead. I'm okay about it now. It must be the drugs making you weepy." Mary reached out her hand to Lou-Lou.

He struggled to speak. The three friends waited as he wiped his cheeks, then looked directly at Mary.

"No, it's not the medication. I'm in full command of my faculties. In my former life, before I became Lou-Lou

Rock, I was known as Pierre-Louis de la Rochefaucauld, son of Count André de la Rochefaucauld."

Mary smiled. "Don't be silly. Don't joke, Lou-Lou. That can't be true." But Lou-Lou didn't smile back – his eyes were riveted on the certificate again. Then he sat up as straight as he could and looked directly at Mary.

"It is true. I'm absolutely sure this is a copy of the same death certificate my mother has." Tears dropped onto his cheeks as he struggled to get his wallet out of his back pocket. After poking around in it he removed an out-of-date ID card which he handed to Mary. It showed a younger looking Lou-Lou with a much more conservative hairstyle. The name on it was 'Pierre-Louis de la Rochefaucauld'.

Mary felt waves of shock coursing through her body. She registered a sob from Annabel and a sniff from Jamie as she put her arm around Lou-Lou's good shoulder and hugged him.

Lou-Lou gazed at Mary. "I just knew I met you for a reason, Mary. I have so often thought to myself if I ever had a sister I would wish her to be just like you."

Then, in one swoop, a trio of new sensations - joy, love and a sense of belonging - engulfed Mary. The damage of her past was swept away in this tsunami of happiness. Maybe her parents were looking down on her after all. Maybe they created this coincidence to help her heal. She may have lost a father, but her search had led her to a brother, one who already loved her.

Epilogue

Jamie took a coaching position with a local French rugby team, and continued working hard at learning French. He and Mary found a flat on the second floor of the same building as Mary's existing flat, so they weren't too far from Annabel.

Lou-Lou told anyone who would listen about the amazing coincidence of his beautiful, talented half-sister.

Both French and British Vogue magazines published a two-page spread on their story. As a consequence, the profile of 'Mousseline de Soie Chantal' rocketed.

Mary still experienced moments when the scars of childhood-abuse invaded her thoughts. But she had developed the mechanisms to deal with those moments. Although the search for her birth father had been too late, she now believed it was predestined.

Her search had led her home to her Paris heritage.

Author's Comment

When I was about 22 years old I was sitting chatting with a group of six girlfriends with whom I had gone to school in New Zealand. There had been a recent article in the news stating that one in five girls under the age of fifteen will have been sexually abused by a person known to them. I mentioned this in our conversation and added it couldn't be true as it hadn't happened to any of us. After some silence two of the girls shared that they had been abused. Since then I've heard many stories of hidden abuse within so called 'respectable' families.

It was a challenge to write about this delicate subject in the first part of my book. However, once my character arrived in Paris it was so enjoyable. Paris is my second favourite city in the world.

My most favourite city is London, where I previously owned a fashion boutique with an in-house workroom. This experience and insight to the world of 'made-to-measure' and clothing manufacture helped me immensely with my story.

Also by Merryn Corcoran

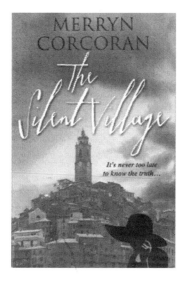

www.merryncorcoran.com
Find Merryn Corcoran on Facebook at www.facebook.
com/merryncorcoranauthor

Printed in Great Britain
by Amazon